the Earl's Lady Thief

BY
JENNIFER MONROE

The Earl's Lady Thief by Jennifer Monroe

Published by WOLF Publishing UG

Text by Jennifer Monroe
Edited by Chris Hall
Cover Art by Victoria Cooper
Paperback ISBN: 978-3-98536-197-7
Hard Cover ISBN: 9978-3-98536-198-4
Ebook ISBN: 978-3-98536-196-0

WOLF Publishing - This is us:

Two sisters, two personalities.. But only one big love!

Diving into a world of dreams..

...Romance, heartfelt emotions, lovable and witty characters, some humor, and some mystery! Because we want it all! Historical Romance at its best!

Visit our website to learn all about us, our authors and books!

Sign up to our mailing list to receive first hand information on new releases, freebies and promotions as well as exclusive giveaways and sneak-peeks!

WWW.WOLF-PUBLISHING.COM

Also by Jennifer Monroe

Lady Marigold's Matchmaking Service

When noble fathers have daughters hellbent on determining their own futures, they have only one alternative—avail themselves of Lady Marigold's Matchmaking Services. Only Lady Marigold is secretly none other than the charismatic and admired lady of the ton Violet, Countess of Whitmore!

Each book in this series is a unique story of how these strong heroines find love in some of the most unusual ways. From treasure hunts while visiting London's most famous sights to telling tales to get what they want, each book promises an adventure in love.

Get ready to cheer on your new favorite couples as you turn the pages in these swoon worthy stories that promise the Happily Ever After you adore.

#1 The Earl's Lady Thief

#2 The Lady Who Cried Wolf

#3 How the Duke was Won

The Earl's Lady Thief

Chapter One

England, May 1816

Miss Catharina Sagewick was certain of exactly two things in her life. The first was that she was not like other unmarried ladies of her class. Rather than setting her sights on the mundane existence of the wife of some ordinary nobleman, she was destined for great adventure. And it would require a rare gentleman to take her there.

He would need to be handsome, strong, and fill her heart with love. Love was the only reason for her to marry. Nothing less would be tolerated.

But above all, he had to allow Catharina to accompany him wherever he traveled. Whether it be to an exotic foreign country or even within the boundaries of her beloved England, excitement would play an integral part in her daily life.

How monotonous it would be to find oneself imprisoned by the shackles of marriage and motherhood! Days spent reviewing dinner menus with the housekeeper and meeting with the nanny to discuss how the children were behaving were not her cup of tea. Why did men get to have all the fun?

Which led to her second certainty. No matter what her father, Baron Sagewick, wished, no matter how much he threatened her or how many bribes he offered, she would do whatever it took to avoid becoming the wife of Marcius, Marquess of Langley.

The sound of laughter and whispers of gossip filled Catharina's ears as she stood amongst the guests in the crowded ballroom of Tealdon Estate. Located just outside the village of Raxford, in the northernmost part of Buckinghamshire, she could not deny that the house was impressive. And it was not Lord Langley's only home, which he was quick to point out at every available moment.

The marquess had insisted Catharina attend this party, much to her father's delight. Although she had been ready to politely decline, her father readily accepted on her behalf. As an only child, Catharina knew her father's intentions for her were of sound motive. That did not mean she had to like them.

Although Catharina had broached the subject of delaying any calls from prospective suitors, which would lead to an inevitable courtship she did not want, her father had dismissed her arguments as easily as a horse flicking away a fly. After all, what sort of father approves of a spinster daughter?

"You *will* marry within the year, Catharina, if not by the end of the summer," he had told her just last week. "Which means you'll no longer turn away any of the eligible bachelors I've already approved."

Catharina feared who was at the top of that ever-growing list of suitors. Her eyes fell on Lord Langley, a short man with a rather round build and penchant for snorting when he laughed. He may have been well-heeled and could easily provide for his wife, but that wife would not be Catharina. That was a fact.

And many of the gentlemen her father had thrown at her were not any better! Why, just last Season, she was nearly forced to marry a particular earl. That is until her father witnessed the man's penchant for overindulging. The last time he was invited to dinner, the earl consumed an entire decanter of brandy himself and fell asleep midsentence.

"An earl he may be," her father had complained the next day, "but I'd prefer my daughter marry a cobbler with a good reputation than a drunkard with a title!" Catharina doubted he truly meant it. He would never accept a tradesman as a son-in-law.

"Here we are," said Lady Olivia Burnsworth, Catharina's friend and confidante, handing Catharina a glass of wine—her second of the evening. "You will need it to endure this tedious excuse for a party."

Olivia was tall and willowy, with tawny brown hair and eyes that matched a winter sky. Her ever-wagging tongue did little to endear the young lady to Catharina's parents, but it was exactly what Catharina loved about her. Like Catharina, Olivia was opinionated and headstrong, but what Catharina appreciated most was Olivia's ability to weave the most amazing tales. So many times, Catharina wanted to be the heroine in one of her friend's stories!

Unlike Catharina, however, Olivia had her sights set on marrying a London stage actor. The two were yet unacquainted, but after reading about his exploits in *The Morning Chronicle*, Olivia had fallen madly in love with him. As much as Catharina appreciated Olivia's unconventional admiration for a man she had yet to meet, she never argued the point with her friend. After all, what gave her the right to crush another woman's dreams? Especially given that Catharina's dreams were far more unconventional.

Olivia took a sip of the murky red liquid and grimaced. "Lord Langley serves the cheapest wine, offers no musicians to entertain his guests, and I promise the food will be as bland as sand. How can a man be so stingy?"

"It's certainly a quandary," Catharina replied. "I once overheard Father speaking to a friend about Lord Langley's roof. Apparently, there were several leaks in the servants' attic rooms, and he spent three weeks searching for the least expensive roofer before having it repaired. And the rain came down by the bucketful the entire time!"

"Those poor servants," Olivia said, shaking her head.

Catharina nodded in reply. She did not believe a man had to spend his money willy-nilly, but certainly a leaky roof demanded immediate attention. Which begged the question—how would he treat Catharina if she were forced to marry him? Would he insist their children miss meals in order to reduce their living expenses?

Her attention was drawn to Luke, Lord Eastwood, a tall, handsome man who was said to be of the adventurous type. Sadly, he was now engaged and thus no longer available. Several months earlier, he had expressed an interest in Catharina, but her father had made an excuse on her behalf. Later, he explained that the man was what he deemed "too sporadic."

Yet that was what Catharina wanted in a suitor. She wanted a man who could work one day and go on some sort of adventure the next without so much as a plan of action. What sort of adventure such a man would take remained to be seen, for Catharina had never had the opportunity to partake in one.

Catharina had read of women going to far-off lands, meeting tribal people, and walking amongst ancient temples once used for human sacrifice. She shivered. The latter was far less appealing, but any other type of exploration would do her just fine. She could climb the tallest mountains or ride a camel in a desert. In India, people even rode elephants! How fun would that be?

So lost in her thoughts was she, that when her father approached, she nearly jumped out of her slippers in startlement. If she had been paying attention, she would have had the chance to ready herself for the fact that he was not alone. With him was their host, Lord Langley, and his mother. Helga, Lady Langley was a stuffy woman with a voice that carried even over the din of the crowded ballroom.

"Mother, I'm sure you remember Miss Sagewick," Lord Langley said, running a hand through his sparse hair.

Catharina had never considered the marquess a nervous man, but the way he pulled at his cravat made her reconsider that opinion.

The older lady had steel-gray hair, a great many creases in her forehead and along her jowls, and an upturned nose. Or rather, she lifted her nose as she assessed Catharina, her lips a thin line. "Of course I do," she snapped. "Does my memory ever fail me?" She turned to her son. "I approve. Now, excuse me." She fingered her necklace of shiny pink pearls. "I wish to remove my pearls. Lady Fillingsworth has mentioned them twice, and I do not wish the woman to suffer from jealousy."

"Shall I have one of the servants return them to your room?" the marquess asked, his voice filled with such fawning, Catharina was reminded of a time when she had added too much sugar to her tea.

"No, there is no need. I'll simply lock them in the desk drawer in the study. Lady Fillingsworth will not be here much longer, I'm sure. When she leaves, I will return for them, so I may wear them for the remainder of the evening."

Olivia looked as confused as Catharina felt when the marchioness marched away, her son hurrying after her.

"Papa, is there anything of which Lady Langley does approve?"

Her father smiled and took her hands in his. "Well, she approves of you, my dear. Which now leads me to some wonderful news. Lord Langley has asked for your hand in marriage. And now that his mother has given her blessing, we can move forward with the plans for the wedding. Is this not wonderful? Your mother would be so pleased."

Sadness—and anger—filled Catharina. Her mother had passed away four years earlier from a sudden illness. She had been beautiful and as self-willed as Catharina. And she certainly would not have approved of Lord Langley as a prospective husband for her daughter.

Nor did Catharina. She was not attracted to the gentleman in any way, and their brief conversations had nearly put her to sleep. Plus, he was old. He had to be what? Five and forty years of age? That was downright *ancient!*

"May I have everyone's attention?" Lord Langley called out as he returned to Catharina and her father. "I have some wonderful news to share with you, my closest friends and acquaintances."

The ballroom fell quiet, and everyone looked in their direction. Olivia reached out and gripped Catharina's hand. Catharina just wished she could wake up from this nightmare.

"What began as a wonderful gathering among friends has now become an engagement party!"

As the marquess continued his speech, Catharina considered every possible means of escape. But where would she go if she did manage to get away? And how long would she survive on her own?

Her worst fears had been realized. She would have to marry Lord Langley, and there was nothing she could do to stop it from happening.

Chapter Two

Once Lord Langley had finished with his declaration, the party resumed.

"I am so happy," her father said, his grin nearly cutting his face in two. He kissed her cheek and turned to the marquess. "I hope you'll not think me rude, but I promised to meet with someone. We'll talk more about plans for the wedding later."

"This will be a very beneficial arrangement," Lord Langley said once Catharina's father was gone. "However, I must make one request." He gave Olivia a pointed look. "I hope you will consider inviting only your father. Weddings can be costly affairs, especially given the amount of food and drink the guests will expect after the ceremony."

Lord Langley rattled off a list of demands for Catharina's new life. She was so stunned that it was not until he mentioned their future children that her usual strength returned.

"My lord," she said, mustering her sweetest tone and fanning herself with vigor, "I'm afraid that this wonderful news has been a bit overwhelming. Would you mind if I stepped away for a moment? Just so I can take in some air on the veranda." She smiled, praying it did not show any of the rage she was so carefully constraining. “I promise not to be gone long.”

The marquess chuckled and then snorted as if a bee had flown up his nose. “Of course, you may. I understand how easily excitable women can be.”

“I have no doubt you do, my lord,” Catharina said. She considered lecturing him on how little he knew about women, but she knew doing so was not worth the effort. Lord Langley had his idea of how women should behave, and nothing she said would get him to believe otherwise.

With a nod at Olivia, Catharina led her friend toward the door of the ballroom, stopping just long enough to procure two more glasses of wine. She had no intention of going out to the veranda, only to have Lord Langley get a sudden urge to follow after her. Instead, they found an alcove in the hallway, just outside the foyer.

“Oh, Olivia, what am I to do? I cannot marry that man, but what choice do I have?”

Olivia tapped her chin for several moments before lowering her voice and leaning in closer. “I can tell him you have had a string of lovers. That should upset him enough to call off the engagement.”

“You’ll say nothing of the sort,” Catharina whispered back. “Ruining my reputation like that will only make matters worse. Especially when what you plan to accuse me of is so terrible.”

“What about one man, then?”

Catharina sighed. Even one lover would have everyone believing she was a trollop. “I would prefer to find another way.”

Her friend gave a small nod, and the two stood in silent thought. Catharina tried desperately to devise some sort of plan to stop this nightmare. She could run away and find a position as a governess or a companion, but she did not know the first thing about working. And neither seemed to offer an inkling of adventure.

Lord Eastwood exited the ballroom. Perhaps Olivia’s idea was not as bad as it seemed. If she could convince the young handsome baron to meet her in a corner so she could kiss him, Lord Langley would surely be offended enough to put an end to this madness.

No, she could not do that. Doing so would be unfair to Lord Eastwood and the woman to whom he was engaged.

"I have an idea!" Olivia said in an excited whisper. "You once had an infatuation with my brother, Benedict, did you not? Do you remember the letter I delivered to him on your behalf?"

Catharina remembered that incident all too well. She was fourteen at the time and Benedict eighteen. In her letter, Catharina had confessed her love for him. Not only that, but she had also offered to marry him—if he was so inclined, of course.

When Benedict did not reply after two weeks, Catharina had confronted him, demanding that he give her answer.

"My apologies, Miss Sagewick," he had said with a kind smile. "I had thought the letter was a joke. And as deeply honored as I am, I must respectfully decline your offer of marriage."

Shaking the memory from her head, Catharina said, "I suspect that Benedict remembers me as a naive girl. Why would he think of me any differently nine years later? And surely he has a slew of young ladies doing all they can to catch his eye."

Olivia's face brightened. "That is where you are wrong, my dear friend. He's been in Paris for the past two months. I learned just yesterday that he's been spending the majority of his time making a drunken fool of himself."

"And how will that help me?"

"Oh, don't you see? He's as desperate as you are and would readily accept a proposal of marriage from someone he knows and trusts."

Catharina took a rather unladylike swallow of her wine. "Even if he were as desperate as I am—as you have so delicately put it—he is in Paris. There would not be enough time even if he did agree to help."

"Then you have no choice but to run away," Olivia said. "There are women who have survived on the spoils of thievery, you know. They are lauded as heroines."

Catharina could not make her sniff less derisive. "I know you mean the women in those scandalous plays in London. People applaud them because it's a work of fiction. The audience would not be as laudatory if those women were robbing them in the streets." She squeezed her friend's hand. "I do appreciate your help, but unless I can think of something feasible, my life is forever ruined."

As they sipped at their wine in silence, Catharina's sense of panic increased. A life with Lord Langley would be unbearable and as unadventurous as being forced into the nunnery. Well, perhaps not that boring, but there certainly would be no love.

Above all else, Catharina wished for a man to love her for who she was—a lady ready for adventure. And now that dream had burst like salt to a soap bubble.

With her third glass of wine empty, Catharina thought about Olivia's suggestion of leading a life of thievery. Perhaps it was not such a bad idea after all.

Oh, who was she fooling? She could not steal, especially from the innocent. Most people survived on a pittance, and those who were wealthy did not deserve to have their property stolen simply because they had means.

Then her gaze fell on Lady Langley, and her words from earlier came to mind.

"I wish to take my pearls and lock them in the desk in the study."

Catharina's mind began to race as she turned to her friend. "I believe I have a way to save myself," she said.

As Catharina relayed her plan, Olivia nodded slowly, her smile widening. "What a fabulous idea!" she squealed. "And I shall be your lookout."

Once they were certain the coast was clear, they slipped down the hallway, peeking through each doorway until she found what appeared to be the study.

"You wait here. I'll only be a moment."

Entering the room, the musty odor of old books that were not well cared for assailed her. A desk sat along one wall, and she hurried to open the top drawer, but it hid no jewelry of any kind. Nor did the second. The third was locked, but it did not take her long to find the key hidden beneath the inkwell.

"You are not a very clever woman, Lady Langley," she whispered, unlocking the drawer. There, she found her quarry—a simple box with the delicate string of pink pearls.

Catharina was not a thief, not in the true sense of the word. Therefore, she had no plan to take the necklace home with her. But she would be a thief in Lady Langley's eyes. And that was what she wanted.

Closing her hand around the necklace, Catharina allowed two of the pearls to dangle from her fist. That would ensure she would be caught.

When she reached the hallway, Olivia hugged her. "One day, they will write a play about your boldness. If they do, may I have the honor of playing you?"

"Let us just pray this has the desired effect," Catharina whispered. "Otherwise, the play may end with my character hanging from the gallows."

With a racing heart, Catharina extinguished the candle and returned to the ballroom. The laughter was louder than she remembered, and the whispers had turned to boisterous talk. For a brief moment, she considered returning the pearls to their place in the desk. This was pure madness!

But then a new thought entered her mind. She had always wanted adventure. Now, she was about to embark on the greatest adventure of a young lady securing her own path in life. London would likely not offer any plays to commemorate this evening, but her story would be told for years to come. Young ladies would hear of Catharina's plight and, as a result, would refuse to marry the first man their fathers pushed at them. They would recall the tale of Catharina of Adventures and how she determined her own destiny.

With renewed confidence, Catharina found Lord Langley speaking with his mother near a far table. With a nod to Olivia, she sent her friend to the other side of the room so she would not be implicated in the crime.

"My lord, I'm suddenly feeling unwell and must return home." Catharina said when she reentered the ballroom. She moved her clenched hand to her stomach, which drew the attention of Lady Langley. Just as planned.

"What is that you have there?" the marchioness demanded. Without warning, Lady Langley tugged at the protruding pearls, which

Catharina readily released. "I demand to know what you are doing with my property!"

The silence that filled the room chilled Catharina to the bone. But she did not respond.

"Well, child? Give me an answer this instant!"

Child, indeed! Catharina was so close to spinsterhood—and thus freedom to make her own decisions—she could almost taste it!

The sound of footsteps made Catharina turn to find her father hurrying over to them. "Catharina, explain yourself at once!"

"I stole her ladyship's pearls, Papa." Catharina turned to the marchioness. "And why should I not? I'll inherit them once you are gone. I thought I would take them now instead. That seems a most reasonable course of action, would you not agree?"

Her father's face was a bright red. Catharina regretted upsetting her father, but he had left her with little choice. "What has come over you? Apologize this instant! Lady Langley, I can assure you that this is some sort of prank and that my daughter meant no harm.

Catharina's heart thudded in her ears as Lady Langley wagged a finger at her. "You wish me dead, do you? Well, you have your wish. I am dead to you, for you are now out of my life. There will be no engagement and certainly no marriage. Marcius?"

Lord Langley scowled. "I'll not marry a thief. Nor a woman so willing to offend my mother in such a despicable manner!" He turned to Catharina's father. "Perhaps you and your daughter should leave, Sagewick."

"My sincerest apologies," her father said before gripping Catharina by her arm so tightly that she stifled a cry. Disapproving gazes followed them across the ballroom floor. All except one. Olivia. Her eyes were as bright as the smile on her lips.

"Of all the things I have witnessed in my life," her father roared the moment the carriage pulled away from the front of the house, "this was the last thing I expected! My daughter, a thief! I have never been so embarrassed in all my life. As soon as we are home, you are to go straight to your room. I do not wish to see hide nor hair of you for the next twenty-four hours. Do you understand?"

As her father continued his rant, Catharina gave him a sad nod and whispered her apologies. No matter what her father or anyone else said, Catharina knew the truth. She was no thief. Rather, she was a woman who had embarked on her very first adventure, one that saved her from an unhappy—and likely uneventful—marriage. Now, she could concentrate her efforts on finding a man equal to her.

But that brought about a new question.

Where would she begin her search for him?

Chapter Three

Contrary to Shakespeare's tale, Gideon, Earl of Hainsley did not believe there was honor among thieves. For the entirety of his eight and twenty years, he had considered men who took what did not belong to them as scoundrels worthy of the hangman's noose. And he still held on to that belief.

Except that this night, he would join their ranks. Which was why he had agreed to attend the party of Alister, Lord Callingswell, a man he despised. Gideon was not there to enjoy the fine food and drink the viscount offered, but he did partake. Nor was he interested in the host of eligible ladies in attendance, although he spoke with many of them.

No, his reason for attending was simple. Honor.

Fourteen months earlier, his father had confessed a secret as he lay on his deathbed. A year before Gideon was born, the former Earl of Hainsley had made several bad investments. To avoid bankruptcy, he had sold many of his possessions. Among them was a painting that his father admitted held a clue to a vast hidden treasure.

Gideon had first thought this was nothing more than the ramblings of a dying man. If what he said was true, why hadn't his father used that clue to get himself out of debt? When he asked the question outright, his father explained. At the time, he was unaware of its hidden clue. But then he came across a diary belonging to the first Earl of Hainsley. There, he had read about the treasure.

"The previous viscount," his father had told him, "agreed that if a Hainsley wished to repurchase the painting at any time, he would agree. With twenty percent interest, of course. But I failed to get that promise in writing. It took three years to refill the coffers, but by the time I returned, the old viscount was dead, and his son had resumed his position. The son refused outright, even for the offer of forty percent interest." He grabbed Gideon's arm. "Now it's up to you to get back that painting, my son. It will be well worth the trouble, I promise you."

Three months ago, Gideon had attended a dinner party hosted by the younger Callingswell. He had never liked the new viscount, but neither was he one to ignore a prospective business partner. Even a nettling gentleman could provide the right connections if the need arose.

Yet that courtesy was brought to an abrupt end when Gideon mentioned the painting.

"I remember your father begging me to resell it to him," Lord Callingswell had said with a laugh that ignited Gideon's blood. "But then he let it slip that it held the key to a hidden treasure. He even offered me ten percent of his findings, but I'm no fool. I told him no, and I'll tell you the same. Now, never mention that painting to me again, or you'll be barred from ever entering my home again. How will you look at your precious painting then?"

Gideon had not made another offer. Still, he held out hope that he could acquire the painting somehow. Perhaps Lord Callingswell had somehow deciphered the clue in the painting, but that did not make sense. He would have been the first to boast of such a thing. Which meant there was still hope.

Tonight, Gideon would secure the painting by any means necessary. And given that he had exhausted every other means, he was left with only one option. He would have to steal it.

The one problem he had been unable to solve, however, was how to escape. Sneaking out with a painting would not be easy. Therefore, he would have to abide his time, waiting for the perfect moment. And judging by Lord Callingswell's grin, that moment was fast approaching.

The viscount was a widower in his midforties—he had lost his young wife to illness several years ago, which made them both eligible bachelors. But that was where their similarities stopped. What made them different had to do with the viscount's roguish ways, which were spoken about often amongst the *ton*. He tended to lead many women to his bed, only to discard them the following day.

Gideon was not acquainted with the young lady targeted for this evening, but she had all the earmarks of what the viscount enjoyed. She was pretty, young, and naive. He considered warning her, but past experience told him that doing so would do no good. By her deep blush, she clearly wanted what Lord Callingswell was offering. Furthermore, what young lady would admit that she was about to engage in a romp between the sheets? It would only embarrass them both.

"Well, goodness me," a woman's voice said from behind him. "Lord Hainsley, I did not realize you were here."

"Lady Madeline," he said, taking her hand and kissing her knuckles, "it's a pleasure to see you again." The woman was pretty enough, with her dark-brown hair and matching eyes. Although it was rumored that she was less than virtuous, he treated her no differently than any other young lady in attendance. But neither did he accept any of her requests to accompany her on a carriage ride through Hyde Park. He refused to be one of her many conquests, no matter how he might enjoy what she had to offer.

"It appears Lord Callingswell will not be sleeping alone tonight," she said. She seemed perturbed by this. "But I suppose it matters not." She gave him a dazzling smile. "There are plenty of fine gentlemen for a lady like me. And you are one of them. I would be honored if you called on me." She lowered her voice. "Especially given how dashing you are."

Gideon was not a vain man, but he understood that he was handsome. Two years earlier, he decided it was time to begin the ardent search for a bride. But then his father took ill, which eventually led to his death. Since then, Gideon had abandoned any thoughts of marriage and focused all his efforts on getting back the painting. And replenishing his dwindling accounts.

Despite the earlier troubles his father had faced, the Hainsley coffers were not necessarily in dire straits. But neither were they exactly overflowing. The income from various investments was on a steady decline, and he dared not think what would happen if they were to disappear altogether. If they continued as they were now, he would be bankrupt by the end of next year. But if he could focus some extra funds on a mine he owned in Cornwall, he might just be able to save his estate. And his name. Which was the true reason why he needed that treasure.

It was for that reason he refused to marry. There were certain expectations for a countess, and rightly so. He had to have a way to provide for his future wife. And if he were on the hunt for a prospective bride, Lady Madeline Johanson would not be the one. Even if the rumors about her were false, she was too brash for his liking. He wanted a tame, calm wife, whose voice was like a whisper on the wind. Not one who drew the attention of everyone wherever she went.

"I'm afraid I have far too busy a schedule to call on you," he replied to the unspoken question. "But you will be the first to know when it opens up."

Her smile was polite but most definitely forced before she excused herself, allowing Gideon to refocus on the task at hand.

Spotting Lord Callingswell, Gideon frowned. Where had the woman to whom he had been speaking gone? Had she already gone to his bedchamber to await his arrival? It was a pity, really. She had been quite lovely.

Then he caught sight of her walking toward the door with whom he assumed were her parents. He applauded her decision even though it made his mission that much more difficult.

As the conversation flowed around him, Gideon growled in frustration. If the lout had only honored the former viscount's wishes and returned the painting, Gideon would not have to resort to thievery!

Lord Callingswell stood beside a large window that looked out onto a veranda, speaking to another young lady. It could be hours before he convinced her to enjoy his private company, and even then, it might not happen. And Gideon was growing impatient.

"Well, there's no time like the present." Downing the last of his brandy in one gulp, Gideon set the empty glass on the tray of a passing footman and slipped into the hallway. The butler, an older man with bushy eyebrows and a permanent scowl, had just opened the front door to a young woman and her parents.

"May I assist you with something, my lord?" the man asked.

Gideon's heartbeat quickened as guilt overtook him. Suddenly, he wanted to confess what he was about to do.

"I'm no thief but a desperate man out to honor his father and to secure his estate. May I simply borrow the painting?"

But then a new thought occurred to him. How could he possibly carry a painting past the butler? He could cut the canvas from the frame, but the idea of destroying anything that could possibly be a part of the clue kept him from even considering it.

What have I gotten myself into?

"My lord?"

"Yes, you may," Gideon replied, praying that his words did not shake as much as his legs did. "I am meeting Lord Callingswell in the parlor, and he sent me to request that a tea tray be brought to us."

A look of confusion crossed the butler's face. "Tea, my lord?"

"Is tea an uncommon beverage in this house?" Gideon asked. "Or do you doubt my word?"

The butler straightened his slim back before bowing low. "No, of course not, my lord. I'll see it done at once."

Gideon thanked the man, lowered his head, and hurried to the library. Thankfully, the room was empty. A single window looked out onto a footpath that connected the front and back gardens, and tall oak bookcases filled with leather-bound tomes lined two walls. And on the wall behind the desk hung his precious painting, where Callingswell could study it at his leisure.

It did not have an overly large frame, which was the length and width of his elbow to the tip of his fingers. A dozen knights on horseback stood in a field of green, surrounded by a variety of wildflowers.

What drew his attention, however, was the leader, who pointed off into the distance. Was he pointing out the location of the treasure? Or did the flowers have a particular meaning? Perhaps the scrawls on the knight's boots had to be deciphered.

Gideon closed his eyes and thought about his father. Tonight, he would honor his promise. With a newfound confidence, he lifted the painting from the wall. Now, all he needed was a way of escape.

With careful steps, he peeked down the hallway. All was clear. Even the butler had yet to resume his place beside the door. Therefore, he took the opportunity and made a direct line toward the front door.

"What are you doing, Hainsley?"

Gideon froze just inches from the door. The viscount, his butler, and four other prominent members of the *ton* approached.

"Oh, Callingswell... I was just..." He swallowed hard. There was no way to explain the painting in his hands. "I'm—"

"Stealing from me?" Lord Callingswell demanded.

Archibald, Lord Plaster, a well-respected elderly baron, shook his head. "Your father would be ashamed of what you've become, Hainsley."

"Times certainly have changed since I was a young man," added Timothy, Lord Standclamp, his face beet-red with rage. "What would drive a gentleman to such desperation?"

Anger bubbled inside Gideon. "This painting has been in my family for nearly a hundred years. The former Viscount Callingswell accepted it as collateral for a loan thirty years ago, promising to sell it back to any Hainsley, with interest, when we were able to do so. I'm here to see the painting returned to its rightful owner. Therefore, Callingswell, name your price."

The viscount shook his head and laughed. "Do you truly want it back that badly?"

"I do."

"Then the answer is no," the viscount said, snatching the painting from Gideon's grasp. He leaned in to whisper in Gideon's ear, "The treasure will be mine, Hainsley. Not yours."

"It belongs to my family," Gideon replied through gritted teeth. More people entered the foyer, but Gideon ignored them. "I want it back where it belongs." He leapt forward, but several men grabbed him by the arms, their voices of disapproval ringing in his ears.

"You are all witnesses. Let it be known that the Earl of Hainsley is a thief!" Lord Callingswell announced, the painting clutched beneath his arm. "He's no longer welcome in my social circle, nor in my home. And I would advise you all to declare the same, for true gentlemen do not consort with thieves."

Humiliation burned through Gideon as disapproving glares fell on him. Not only had he failed in his thievery, but he had also severely damaged his family's good name.

Filled with shame, he left the house and made his way to his waiting carriage. But as he journeyed home, the rage returned.

As he sat sipping a glass of brandy, he replayed the evening in his head. What a fool he had been thinking he could steal the painting. He was no thief. And even if he had gotten away with it, Callingswell would have known who had taken it the moment he noted its disappearance. Gideon's chances would have been better if he had invited the other attendees to follow him while he lifted the painting from the wall.

There was failure and then there was utter failure. And Gideon knew he had attained the latter.

With a sigh, he thought of his father, who had only made one request before he died. And now, Gideon had no way of seeing it fulfilled. And worse still, he was now branded a thief. And earl or not, his future was grim indeed. No one would do business with him. No woman would want him to court her. And even if they were foolish enough to allow him to call, their fathers would put a stop to it before he even arrived.

The sudden realization of what he had done came crashing around Gideon. No matter where he went in England, he had ruined his name. Which secured him a future of loneliness. The Hainsley line would die with him.

Chapter Four

Two months later...

Catharina Sagewick knew two things to be true. The first was that Lord Langley would never look her way again after her amazing display of thievery at his party. She doubted she had ever been prouder of her antics than she was that day.

Which led to the second truth. Because of her escapade, the list of suitors willing to call on her was as dry as a riverbed during a drought. Her father was the first to notice the lack of callers, and, in the way men often do when things were not going as they hoped, he panicked. For the past two months, he had tried everything possible to get someone, anyone, to call on her. To no avail.

Catharina had tried in vain to argue her points, citing this reason and that to convince her father that perhaps she was meant to become a spinster. It was not her intention to become an old maid, but at least she could put off the possibility until she found the right gentleman. Her father, however, was having none of it.

"Do not look at me as if I brought this upon you, child," he said as he sat across from her in his favorite leather wingback chair. "Women are meant to marry. History has proved that spinsters have no place in a modern society, which is why they are not treated with the same esteem as those who have married."

Dropping her gaze, Catharina simply nodded. All her arguments had fallen on deaf ears thus far, why rehash her points now?

He pointed an accusatory finger at her. "You chose to steal that necklace, and therefore, it is you who ruined your name. Why, you would have been better off being caught kissing a gentleman! Impropriety can be overlooked—eventually. But thievery?" He shook his head. "You are just lucky Lady Langley did not insist on calling the magistrates. Your lovely neck would snap in the hangman's noose as easily as that of any brigand, and that is how the courts would look at you. A lady thief is still a thief. And stealing from a marchioness, of all people! I have never been so embarrassed in all my life!"

He had said those same words in the carriage on their way home after the party at the Langley home and every day since. And each time, the anguish in his tone told her how much she had hurt him with her actions.

"I'm sorry, Papa," she repeated for what seemed the hundredth time. "I would never hurt you. Not intentionally."

Her father was not a cruel or uncaring man, but neither was he one to show his emotions, not in word or action. But she never doubted that he cared for her in his way. And when a small smile spread across his lips, she relaxed. Was he finally ready to forgive her?

"I know you are, Catharina," he said. "And I pray you will understand that what I do is for your own sake."

Catharina stared at her father. "What have you done, Papa?"

"I've secured the help of a matchmaking service in London to find you a husband." His voice was so matter of fact that Catharina's blood ran cold.

"Oh, Papa, no! Matchmakers are for wallflowers and women of unfortunate appearance."

"And for young ladies nearing spinsterhood," he added. "Which you are. If I don't do something now, you'll be too old to marry. I've exhausted all avenues in acquiring you a husband, and your stealing has forced my hand."

As much as her world had suddenly turned upside down, Catharina could not deny that he spoke the truth. Every father wanted to see his daughter married and looked after, and marriage to a gentleman of means would see that happen.

The door opened, and their butler, Collins, entered the room. Tall and thin with a large, hooked nose, he had been in the service of the Sagewick household since Catharina was a child. "My Lord, your guest has arrived."

Catharina's father stood as a stunning woman in her middle years entered the room. Her dark hair was streaked with silver, and she had wonderful taste in clothing. She wore a lovely lavender-colored satin gown with fine net sleeves trimmed with rosettes. Catharina had seen that very dress in the latest edition of *La Belle Assemblée* and had even considered having one commissioned for herself.

And the dress was not the woman's only show of wealth. Around her neck was what appeared to be a rose-colored diamond necklace, and her bracelet and earrings matched. Catharina could not help but be impressed by this woman. She knew no one who owned a single rose diamond, let alone so many! How much had her father paid for this woman's services? She had to have been making a fortune playing matchmaker!

"Lady Whitmore?" Catharina's father stammered. "What... what are you doing here?"

Then the realization of who this woman was left Catharina speechless. She had met the Countess of Whitmore the previous year, but the encounter had been brief. Lady Whitmore was perhaps the most popular lady of the *ton*. She had friends scattered throughout England and across Europe. Princes and princesses called her friend.

Yet tragedy had struck the Whitmore household several years ago when her husband, Rudolph, took ill and subsequently died. Not two months later, her only son and heir to the Whitmore earldom perished in a shipwreck.

"Did you not hire the services of Lady Marigold's Matchmaking

Services, Lord Sagewick?" Lady Whitmore asked, a small smile pulling at the corner of her lips.

Catharina's father pinched the bridge of his nose. "I did. However —and let me apologize in advance if I appear dense—what does that have to do with you?"

The countess shook her head and let out a hearty laugh. "Do you honestly believe I would use my real name in such a situation?"

The sound of approaching footsteps made Catharina turn toward the door as a young woman in her midtwenties entered the room. She had chestnut hair, a heart-shaped face, and a friendly smile, and Catharina took to her almost immediately.

"I would like to introduce Miss Lena Page," Lady Whitmore said. "She will be acting as Miss Sagewick's companion and will chaperone when the need arises. My methods may seem unconventional, but I still insist that my young ladies follow all the proprieties expected of them."

Miss Page bobbed a curtsy, and the countess walked with her to the couch and sat without waiting for an invitation. Which was likely for the best, given that Catharina's father still stared at her slack-jawed and tongue-tied.

"Now," continued Lady Whitmore, unruffled by the less than hearty welcome. "I realize that my identity comes as a surprise and that you must have questions. But if what you've told me in your correspondence is true, time is of the essence. Therefore, ask your questions so we may move on to the more important matter of finding your daughter a suitable match before she reaches spinsterhood."

Despite what this arrangement meant for her, Catharina found the entire situation intriguing. The matchmaker was not some shriveled old woman prone to conversations of days long gone. Instead, she was a vivacious countess who, while not necessarily young, at least was not ancient. And her companion was close to Catharina's age. Perhaps the two of them would become close friends. The idea of leaving for London now looked less bleak than it had.

"I hate to seem rude," Catharina's father said as he stumbled to his chair, "but how is it that you, of all people, run a matchmaking service?"

The countess sighed, seemingly unsurprised by his question. "I'm afraid the story is a long one, my lord. It would take me several hours to tell it, but if you wish to waste time on what will do nothing to find your daughter a husband, I'm happy to share it with you." To Catharina's surprise, the lady winked at her!

"No, no, there will be no need," Catharina's father said.

Lady Whitmore slapped her hands on her thighs. "Good. Then allow me to explain what will happen to Miss Sagewick. She will stay with me as a favored guest, which will immediately improve her standing in society." She turned to Catharina. "You may believe you have made it impossible to find a husband, but I assure you, that is not the case. So, there is no need to worry."

Catharina had not been worried, not about what she had done, so she said nothing. She had embarrassed her father enough.

"She will receive gentlemen callers in my Mayfair home," Lady Whitmore continued, "and will have her needs met in the manner to which she is accustomed."

As her father and the countess continued their conversation, a thought occurred to Catharina. London was full of people. Perhaps she would find a gentleman of adventure there.

After Catharina's father had exhausted all his questions, Lady Whitmore stood, Miss Page following suit. But her father had one last question.

"How is it your identity remains a secret? You and I both know the *ton* is rife with rumors. Even a lady such as yourself cannot avoid its wrath."

The countess smiled, adjusting one of the gem-studded rings on her finger. "It's quite simple if you give it the right amount of thought. No father wants his peers to know that he had to hire my services because he failed to find his daughter a husband." She turned to Catharina. "And no daughter shares my secret because she knows I can have her married off to the most despicable of men." She narrowed her eyes. "A holiday in Hades would be preferable to a life with the man I choose for her if she so much as whispers my name and that of Lady Marigold in the same sentence. Do I make myself clear?"

Catharina's heart leapt into her throat. The countess would not dare pair her with a man worse than Lord Langley, would she? She had not been in the least fearful in this woman's company thus far, but now she was terrified of her!

"Yes, Lady Whitmore," she managed to squeak.

The scornful look disappeared, and the countess smiled as if nothing untoward had happened. "Excellent. The moment we leave this house, the matchmaking service—and Lady Marigold—is never mentioned again. From now on, we are merely friends, and you are my guest. Agreed?"

Catharina and her father nodded in unison. Lady Whitmore was beautiful, intelligent, and confident, all characteristics that fascinated Catharina. Perhaps she could learn a thing or two from her.

"Excellent. Then, I believe it is best we leave at once."

Catharina's jaw fell open. "We are to leave today?" She turned to her father. "I had hoped to see Olivia first. Perhaps have tea with—"

Her father raised his hand. "As Lady Whitmore said, the sooner you leave, the sooner you will find a husband. Now, no more arguments. This *will* happen, whether you like it or not."

Seeing his pained expression, Catharina felt a twinge of guilt. "I know I disappointed you, Papa," she whispered as she hugged her father. "I truly am sorry for that. But I promise I'll not do so again."

"I'm pleased to hear that," her father replied. "For it would hurt me deeply if you did so. Now, I had your things packed, and the trunks should already be loaded onto Lady Mari... Lady Whitmore's carriage. Follow her instructions and do your duty. I cannot imagine my only daughter left alone once I'm gone.

"Don't say such things! You have many years ahead of you, Papa."

He chuckled. "We all leave this world eventually, Catharina. I'm not saying it will be tomorrow or even in the next ten years. But it will happen. And I'll be happier knowing that you are cared for."

Once Catharina was settled in the carriage beside Miss Page, the countess said, "Your father informed me of the theft of Lady Langley's pearls."

Catharina's heart quickened. "I'm no thief, my lady. And I made certain I was caught. Lord Langley is so dull. He shows no curiosity about the world or the people in it."

The countess smiled but said nothing, so Catharina continued. For some reason she could not explain, she had to convince this woman that what she'd done was not as bad as it seemed.

"He's also well-known for his stinginess. And have you seen how he gives into his mother's every whim? But above all, he is no man of adventure, which is why I took the necklace. I could never love such a man, no matter how wealthy he is, for that I am certain."

Lady Whitmore smiled. "Heroes from stories are as likely to be found in real life as a kitten being raised by a dog. It happens, but it is rare. Unless you lower your expectations somewhat, you will only be disappointed."

Despite the fact that she disagreed, Catharina nodded. Even fiction was based on a mustard seed of fact. She would not accept defeat. A man existed out there who was her perfect match.

As the journey continued, Lady Whitmore laid out the basic rules any young lady of means should already know. She was to use decorum at all times and keep out of trouble.

"As I mentioned to your father, Lena will take on the role of chaperone. Whatever you need, she will be there to help. Our duty is to ensure that you are comfortable. And to find you a suitable husband, of course."

Although Miss Page had hardly said a word, that feeling of companionship Catharina had felt upon meeting her had not waned. She was a quiet woman, but there was an air of kindness about her.

Two hours later, they arrived in London. Catharina had been to several parties in the Mayfair district, so she was unsurprised when the carriage stopped before a five-story white house with an iron fence around a tiny front garden. Three white pillars held up the elongated portico, and a small path led from the ornate gate to the front door of Ivywood Manor.

Before they reached the door, it opened and a stately man of perhaps sixty with a mop of silver hair and a slightly pudgy build bowed. "Welcome home, my lady."

"This is Hornsby," Lady Whitmore said. "If you need anything, all you need to do is ask. Hornsby, this is Miss Catharina Sagewick. She will be staying with us for a while. See that she is treated with the same respect as I am."

"Yes, my lady," the butler replied, giving the countess another deep bow.

The foyer was opulent with marble flooring and polished wood trim. Exquisite vases held carefully arranged flowers, and a sizable chandelier made up of hundreds of crystals spoke of the countess's wealth.

One painting hanging at the bottom of the staircase against the right wall caught Catharina's attention. It was the portrait of a strikingly handsome man with dark brown hair and a strong chin.

"My son, Anthony," the countess said as she joined Catharina. "Three years he's been gone from this world."

"My deepest condolences," Catharina said. "I lost my mother, so I understand your grief somewhat."

Lady Whitmore drew in a deep, calming breath. "My housekeeper will assign a maid to unpack your things and to see to your needs. Come, I'll give you a tour of the house."

Catharina was shown every room. On the ground floor was a light-blue sitting room and the dining room. The second floor housed a parlor of a pleasant yellow, and a library filled with books. Bedrooms were located on the third and fourth floors, and the servants' quarters were on the top floor. The kitchens were below ground level.

When they were done, they returned to the foyer. "Dinner will be ready in two hours," Lady Whitmore said. "But before you go to your room to change, I must again stress the importance of secrecy. If you reveal to anyone what I do, it will not bode well for you." She placed a gentle hand on Catharina's arm. "I do not foresee that happening, mind you. But I cannot do what I do if the entire world knows about it. Do you understand? And I have yet to make a match that both parties have not enjoyed."

Once Catharina assured her hostess that she would say nothing, she went to her room, which was located on the third floor. Miss Page was already there, supervising as a young maid laid out Catharina's dresses on the bed.

"I'm nearly finished, miss," the maid said, smiling. She had a round face and blond strands of hair peeking out from beneath her mob cap.

"And what is your name?" Catharina asked.

The young woman blushed. "Stella, miss."

"Well, thank you, Stella," she said.

Once Stella finished her work, she left the room. Catharina turned to Miss Page. She had a thousand questions, but only one was important to ask at that moment. "You heard me confess to Lady Whitmore that I want a gentleman of adventure. Do you believe it's possible she can find me one?"

Miss Page tilted her head as if deep in thought. "I know her ladyship can do anything she puts her mind to. So yes, it's possible."

Catharina smiled. "What a relief. I want you to know that I'm not truly a thief. Not really. And I'll never take anything that does not belong to me again. I want my name restored, and I'll do nothing to jeopardize that."

"Of course, miss."

Catharina sat on the edge of the bed. "If we're to become close friends, let us dispense with the formalities. I'm Catharina. Do you mind if I call you Lena? All this 'Miss Whoever' tends to become tedious."

Lena smiled. "I would like that."

"And I meant it when I said I'll not steal again. Even if the most handsome man in the world requested it of me, I would refuse. I have seen the harm such actions cause others." Why she felt the need to justify herself to a companion was beyond her, but if Lena also acted as Lady Whitmore's ears, Catharina wanted her to have only positive things to say.

"That's good to hear, miss," Lena said.

As Catherina finished putting away her personal items, they spoke on a variety of subjects. Lena proved to be not only pleasant, but she was also intelligent and better educated than Catharina had expected, which Catharina relayed.

"I suppose it's my love of reading," Lena said. "And when her ladyship has her guests here, I later practice what I've seen. There's much that can be learned through observation."

Catharina was impressed. "Are you not married? Or do you have a young man pining for you?"

"No," Lena replied rather quickly. "Now, we should get you changed for dinner. And I was asked to relay to you that you'll be attending a party on Friday at the home of an earl. Which dress do you think you would like to wear? I want to be sure it's pressed and ready for you."

Selecting a blue gown with silver threading, Catharina asked questions about the party and the earl who would be hosting it. To her frustration, Lena replied the same to every question: "I wouldn't know, miss."

Well, whoever this earl was, Catharina did not care. If he did not meet her standards, she would do whatever it took to push him away.

Besides stealing, of course. She would never resort to that again.

Chapter Five

Gideon, Lord Hainsley's name was ruined, and the signs of that ruination were everywhere. He had not received a single invitation to a party or dinner in two months. Ladies who would have fawned over him wanted nothing to do with him, some going so far as to cross the street when they saw him coming. Rumors abounded amongst the nobility when one of their own made the smallest blunder, but even the butcher looked at him cross-eyed.

He had expected repercussions after being caught attempting to steal the painting from Lord Callingswell's house. But as Gideon looked around the scant number of attendees at his party, he knew he was finished. He had gone out of his way to invite anyone and everyone he had ever met, promising them all the finest music, drink, and food. He had expected a crowd, yet the results of his efforts were less than stellar.

Of the over two hundred and fifty invitations he had sent out, only twenty people came. Many were members of the gentry rather than nobility, and most were over the age of sixty. Even Lady Madeline had been extended an invitation, with permission to invite any friends she wished. She had responded with a polite, yet firm, refusal.

The party began an hour earlier, and even Countess of Whitmore had yet to arrive. And Lady Whitmore was never late. Her absence would be the proverbial nail in his coffin. Once word got out that even she refused to attend his party—and she made a point to visit as many parties and gatherings as she possibly could—any hope he still held would be gone.

Lady Whitmore had been a friend of his parents, just as she was to many affluent families. Gideon appreciated her sharp mind and her ready ear when he needed advice. She was one of the few people he trusted in this world. When he had confessed the truth about why he had tried to steal the painting, she had been sympathetic to his plight.

Sighing, he took a sip of his wine—his finest and most expensive vintage—and tried to focus his attention on the man approaching.

"A wonderful gathering, Hainsley." Moses, Baron Walker was at least eighty, with a voice that quivered as much as his hand. He was nearly deaf and yelled everything he said. "As much as I have enjoyed myself, however, I must take my leave. The hour is late, and I do not wish anyone to mistake me for a brigand."

Gideon understood. It was barely past seven, but at the baron's age, it must have felt like midnight.

"I heard about you stealing from Callingswell," Lord Walker continued, drawing several glances. "But do not worry, my boy. I've told no one." He chuckled. "Well, no one except a cousin I encountered outside the butcher's shop last week."

Embarrassment burned in Gideon's cheeks. If he had been uncertain only moments ago how many people knew about his desperate situation, he now suspected that the entire East End of London knew about his actions.

With a final farewell, the baron left.

Gideon sighed heavily. He had made two attempts, both in writing since he was no longer welcome at the man's home, to contact Lord Callingswell to apologize, but there had been no reply. Despite the trouble he had put himself in, however, Gideon could not take his mind off that painting. If anything, he wanted it even more now that it was forbidden to him.

He had considered, and discarded, the idea of hiring an experienced thief to steal it for him. His main reason? He could not trust such a person.

There simply had to be a way.

"Forgive my tardiness."

Gideon pushed the thoughts from his mind and turned his attention to the woman who had approached him. "Lady Whitmore," he said, taking the hands of his good friend, the Countess of Whitmore, "I'm so pleased you came. I'll admit, I was worried you would not."

The countess clicked her tongue. "Don't be silly. Of course, I would. You should know better than to think I'd allow anything to keep me away."

Gideon agreed. He should have known better.

"Allow me to introduce you to Miss Catharina Sagewick," Lady Whitmore continued. "She is the daughter of a very dear friend, Lord Sagewick. I'm sure you've met him or at least have heard of him."

"Only in passing," Gideon replied.

Lady Whitmore smiled. "Well, she is staying with me for a while. I hope you do not mind that I brought her as my guest."

When the countess took a step back, Gideon's breath caught, and his head felt as if it would float away. Miss Sagewick could only be described as exquisite. Her dark hair was piled high on her head and hung in ringlets that touched the nape of her neck. She had a heart-shaped face, well-formed lips, and high cheekbones. And Gideon doubted he had ever seen a more remarkable beauty in his life.

She was not a debutante, but neither was she a spinster. He was more than certain they had never met—he would have remembered being introduced to such a beauty—but her name had a familiar ring to it. He just could not place a finger on where he had heard it before.

"It's an honor to make your acquaintance, Miss Sagewick," he said with a bow. "Please, have a seat." He indicated a nearby sofa and chairs that had been set up in the corner of the ballroom for his guests' comfort. Perhaps he had known how few people would attend after all. And their subsequent ages.

"Thank you, my lord. I shall."

A fire erupted in Gideon. Her voice was a contraction, for it was soft like a caress but had an underlying strength to it. A feather lying upon a stone was the only image that came to mind. But what excited him most was the twinkle of mischievousness in her deep-blue eyes. This woman had a story to tell.

The ladies sat on the gold and white flowered sofa, and Gideon took the armchair across from them. "So, you are staying with Lady Whitmore," he said. "How did that arrangement come about?"

The countess smiled. "Her father is away on business, and I thought it would be nice for her to have a reprieve from her country home. London is a much livelier place for the young." She turned a smile to Miss Sagewick. "Plus, I enjoy her company. And with no young gentlemen to call on her in the tiny village in which she lives, it seems reasonable to have her with me."

Gideon nodded. The countess seemed to always have the daughter of a friend visiting her at any given moment. He suspected that having the younger ladies with her made her feel young again. And after the loss of her husband and her only child, it was no wonder. She would be lonely otherwise.

Without warning, Lady Whitmore stood, and her companion followed suit. "Well, I shan't keep you. I wish to introduce Miss Sagewick to some of my friends. I see one now, there by the fireplace, and I've not seen him for ages. If you'll excuse us."

Watching the pair walk away, Gideon was mystified that the young lady had not yet been spoken for. Men should have been beating down her door for the chance to spend time with her. Why hadn't they? Still, their loss could become his gain. The idea of sharing a luncheon with such a beauty appealed to him.

But no. That could never happen. Once Miss Sagewick learned what he had done, she would laugh at any attempt at romance. Would Lady Whitmore allow him to call on the young lady? Perhaps. After all, they were on friendly enough terms, and she knew he was a good man beneath the terrible decision he had made with the painting.

Well, there was nothing to do about it now. He might not have a hundred guests, but that did not mean he should ignore the few who had taken time out of their likely not-so-busy schedules to attend his party. But his gaze kept returning to Miss Sagewick.

An hour later, he found Lady Whitmore gazing out one of the ballroom windows. "It appears your young friend does well in societal circles." He grimaced inwardly. She was the daughter of a baron. Of course, she would have received proper training in how to conduct herself. "Every guest who has conversed with her smiles."

"She is quite the gem," Lady Whitmore replied with a smile of her own. "Like you, she is steeped in controversy. But also like you, she will emerge better than she was."

The realization dawned on Gideon. "The thief. Is she not the woman who stole from Lady Langley? Jewelry of some sort if I recall."

Apparently, two months earlier, a drunken lady was caught stealing from the home of the Marquess of Langley. Initially, he had pictured a woman of the lower nobility of such a heinous crime but to think the culprit had been the beauty in Lady Whitmore's company tonight was unthinkable. How could a woman as lovely as she be a thief?

Lady Whitmore shook her head sadly. "It is quite a horrible tale. One must wonder how a woman as beautiful and intelligent as Miss Sagewick had come to possess skills in thievery that rank among the best highwaymen."

So, his impressions of Miss Sagewick had been incorrect. She was no naive beauty but rather a master thief. At least according to Lady Whitmore. This story explained that look of mischievousness he had seen in her eyes.

It was a pity, really. He would have considered calling on her while she was in London, perhaps even inviting her on a carriage ride through Regent's Park or for a walk along New Bond Street to see the latest shop displays. But now that was out of the question. How could two known thieves have any chance at a life together? They would be judged doubly so.

"Of course," Lady Whitmore continued, "please do not repeat what I just told you. Miss Sagewick has changed her ways, and I would prefer not to embarrass her by bringing up her past."

"Never," Gideon replied. He knew the burning shame such talk would cause.

Not two breaths later, the lady in question joined them. "This is a splendid affair, my lord. Thank you for allowing me to attend." Was it his imagination, or was she blushing?

He eyed the nearly empty glass in her hand and realized why. Many young ladies complained about the heat after more than a single glass of wine. They tended to have a more genteel nature than men when it came to drinking.

But when she brought the rim of the glass to her full lips, his cravat tried to strangle him.

"This is a wonderful vintage of *hock*, my lord," she said.

He forced his hands at his side to keep from tugging on the noose around his neck. "I'm impressed. Most ladies prefer claret to white wine. But it's one of my favorites. I had it shipped in from Germany last year. Would you like to take a glass with me?"

"I would love to, my lord," Miss Sagewick replied with a sweet smile. "Especially now that I've found my own favorite wine."

She was no mouse. Which strangely only made her more attractive. Thief or not.

Their continued discussions covered a range of polite topics—weather, acquaintances to see how many they shared, favorite places to see in the Town, the usual conversational pieces people shared. And although he found their conversation enjoyable, a thought occurred to him that made him feel nearly giddy.

How had he missed the obvious? He needed a particular painting, and this woman was a master thief in truth. And beautiful, at that. Could she not use her skills, and her stunning good looks, to procure it for him? She could likely walk right up to the home of Lord Callingswell and take the painting, and no one would think twice about it.

Yet, he could not ask her outright. Not here and not now. Lady Whitmore had said Miss Sagewick had given up that life, but perhaps he could persuade her to perform one last job. He believed that was the term used by those of that particular profession.

Plus, all women, thieves or otherwise, needed to feel appreciated before a gentleman could make requests of this degree. And a luncheon would do just that.

"I hope you do not think me too forward, Miss Sagewick, but would you accompany me on a picnic Monday next?" He turned to the countess. "That is, if Lady Whitmore agrees, of course."

"My dear friend," Lady Whitmore said with a strangely wide grin on her face, "I believe that would be a marvelous idea. Would you not agree, Miss Sagewick?"

Miss Sagewick nodded, her cheeks so red, they appeared overly rouged. "I would like nothing more, my lord."

Hope returned to Gideon for the first time since Lord Callingswell's party and Gideon's subsequent ruination. He would have the painting returned to its rightful owner and thus fulfill his father's dying wish. Then he would find the treasure and restore his estate and thus his name. And all it would take was a luncheon or two with a comely young lady, which was a premium added to the rest of the rewards.

How easy it all would be!

Chapter Six

For the last three days, only one thing was on Catharina's mind. Or rather one person. Lord Hainsley. The last time they were together, her legs had nearly given out, but she managed to stay upright with great effort. Not one thing was wrong with him. And so much was right. He was tall, broad, and devilishly handsome. She could make out the outline of large arm muscles beneath the sleeve of his well-tailored coat each time he lifted his glass to take a drink. His hair was light and wavy, and thick enough to run her hand through. Never had her heart beat so fiercely as it did in his presence.

Yet that one burning question remained. She had met handsome men before, but was he a man of adventure? Surely his muscular form and strong arms could easily carry her through a jungle when she grew weak with fatigue. Or he would stand up against highwaymen—or another gentleman showing interest in her. What if a roguish lord attempted to steal a kiss? Would Lord Hainsley challenge him to a bout of fisticuffs? Or perhaps a duel!

Thank heavens no one could hear or see her thoughts, for she imagined him removing his coat and shirt so they would not get soiled while he fought for her honor...

What was wrong with her? She had never had such impure

thoughts about any man before. Even when she thought of Lord Eastwood. As handsome as she believed him to be, her mind never tried to undress him!

With Stella's help, Catharina finished dressing for her outing. She donned a lilac walking dress with white rosettes along the bottom hem. Her hat was also lilac, trimmed with a deep-purple ribbon and white and purple feathers. It was one of her favorites.

"I do hope he does not lead a boring life," Catharina confided in Lena as she admired her reflection. "It would be a shame if he does."

Lena smiled as she adjusted the sleeve on Catharina's dress. "I don't think he'll be boring, miss. By all accounts, he's a lively gentleman."

Catharina was not as sure as Lena was, but she agreed, nonetheless. She had watched the earl from across the ballroom during his party. He had neglected his guests for inappropriate periods of time. A host should interact with his guests.

Which led to the next concern. Why were the majority of those in attendance elderly? The Season might be several months away yet, but not all noblemen went to the country. Even a handful of younger guests would have made her less suspicious.

But worst of all, where were the young ladies? A handsome man of marrying age should have a host of prospects, all beautiful, of course—in attendance at a party he was throwing. Surely, she was not the only one left in London?

Perhaps the situation will work out well for me, she thought wryly. She could not deny her attraction to him, and the fact he was an earl would please her father. At least she would not have to compete for his attention.

Giving herself one final look over, she led Lena downstairs where the countess waited for them.

"My dear, you look lovely," Lady Whitmore said. "And I do hope you enjoy your outing. I have business I must attend to, or I would accompany you. I shan't be returning to the house until much later, but Lena will be with you all afternoon. Or later if need be." She winked. "Oh, I nearly forgot." She walked over to a side table and picked up an ornate envelope. "You've been invited to a party hosted by Alister, Lord Callingswell. He's a viscount."

Catharina smiled. Another party would be entertaining. And perhaps Lord Hainsley would attend as well. Hopefully, Lord Callingswell would offer dancing.

Two white carriages waited outside. The vehicles were finely decorated with gold trim and plush benches. The countess's carriage left first, followed immediately after by the carriage in which Catharina and Lena sat.

"I'm curious," Catharina told her chaperone. "Why does Lady Whitmore operate a matchmaking service? I mean, she appears to have a great deal of money. Would it not be more entertaining to go on holiday or tour the continent? Much more exciting than playing matchmaker."

Lena smiled. "I think she gets satisfaction in helping young ladies find compatible suitors who can eventually become their husbands. Is that not enough?" Catharina considered her words. If what the countess did brought her joy, perhaps it was enough.

"What about you, Lena? Do you not want to one day fall in love and marry?"

"I loved once," Lena said, her gaze dropping. "But he died before we could speak our vows. Now, I busy myself with my work."

Catharina's heart clenched at this. The poor woman! Here Catharina was with a man showing her a great deal of interest, yet her companion still clearly pined for the man she lost. How very sad for her. Catharina had a hundred more questions, but she asked none. Even servants had the right to their private lives.

When they arrived at the home of Lord Hainsley, he himself greeted them at the door.

He's even more handsome than I remembered, Catharina thought. *And taller, too.*

"Miss Sagewick, it is so wonderful to see you again."

Her heart skipped a beat. "Thank you, my lord. I'm very pleased to see you again as well."

"We'll go straight to the back gardens," the earl said. "Collins has everything all ready for us."

Indeed, the butler had set up two marquees. Beneath one was a long table filled with covered dishes and a smaller table with a single chair. The other housed a square table and two chairs. An old butler stood hunched over the smaller table, setting what appeared to be the last of the eating utensils.

"I was unsure if your chaperone would be eating with us or if you preferred that she sit alone. The expectations can be so different from family to family."

Before Catharina could respond, Lena said, "Oh, I don't mind eating alone, my lord. In fact, I prefer it. I'm still within sight to do what's required of me, but it also allows for a small amount of privacy for the two of you."

Lord Hainsley nodded. "Very well, then." As Lena went to the smaller table, the earl pulled out a chair for Catharina, then sat across from her. The butler filled their wine glasses.

Catharina found Lord Hainsley looking at her.

"How are you finding London thus far?" he asked.

"It's quite delightful," Catharina replied. "But I've not had the opportunity to explore it as of yet." She glanced at Lena. "Not properly, that is."

This was only a half-truth. She had been all over London during her debut Season but that was always when it was too cold to enjoy all London had to offer.

Then her mother died. The following year, her family was in mourning and therefore had remained in Raxford. Any desire to attend the extravagant gatherings and to be around all those people had dried up like a depleted well, and Catharina managed to convince her father to remain home for the Seasons that followed.

Not that she would share all that with Lord Hainsley. Or anyone else, for that matter. She had every right to keep to herself her innermost thoughts. Her hope now was that he would take her words as a hint that she would welcome an invitation for a tour, with him as her guide.

And to her pleasure, he offered it. "Then I must be a good host and show you what this wonderful Town has to offer."

Catharina took a polite sip of her wine to keep herself from clasping her hands together like an excited child. Their conversation turned to various topics, and soon, a selection of various breads, meats, and cheese adorned the table.

"Because of work and other matters," Lord Hainsley was saying, "I've not had the time to enjoy the company of young ladies such as yourself. But I have a feeling that will change very soon."

With warmed cheeks, Catharina nibbled at a morsel of cheese. She found the earl's forthrightness refreshing. Too many of the gentlemen who had called on her before the "incident"—that was how her father now called what she had done at the Langley house—presented themselves as someone other than who they truly were. Many were overindulgent in their compliments, but Lord Hainsley used just the right number.

"Is that so?" she asked, flashing him a smile. "I sense that a lady such as myself would feel quite safe in your company."

She glanced at the sleeve of his coat, imagining again the muscles that lay beneath it. His eyes sparkled, and his smile was confident, which only made her heart race faster.

"What do you do in your free time?" she asked.

Lord Hainsley sat back in his chair. "Let's see. I enjoy reading. I don't play chess as much as I once did. The theater is a marvelous way to spend an evening. Oh, and I do enjoy visiting museums from time to time. History is quite fascinating, both in written form and in what is displayed at museums."

Catharina stifled a frown. Theater? Chess? Where were his exploits of playing dangerous games of chance at some gaming hell? Or engaging in fisticuffs with bands of highwaymen?

"Miss Sagewick," he said. "You appear saddened. Is everything well?"

"Oh yes, my lord," she replied, perhaps a bit too quickly. "I was considering what you said. Your life sounds... intriguing. I was wondering if you've found excitement in... other areas."

The silence that followed set Catharina's teeth on edge, and she took a rather large swallow of her wine. Here she was so certain he would be the right man for her, and now she had learned it was nowhere near the case.

"May I confess something?" he asked, leaning in and lowering his voice conspiratorially. She nodded, and he continued. "I've been under the scrutiny of the *ton* since I was..." He paused and looked around. "Since I was caught stealing."

Catharina could not stop herself. She gaped at him. Was he telling the truth? But why would he lie about such a serious matter? More importantly, why was he telling her?

As she listened to his tale of attempting to steal a painting and his subsequent apprehension, she became intrigued. Why would he want to steal a painting? No, his reasons did not matter. This was exactly what she had hoped to hear! The boldness of this man was unprecedented!

When he completed the story, he crossed an ankle over his knee. "Now you must think me a horrible cad. And how could you not?" He shook his head. "But you would never understand."

"But I do, my lord," Catharina said. "I understand more than you can imagine."

He frowned. "But why?"

She leaned in closer and lowered her voice. Even servants gossiped. "I, too, have been caught stealing."

The earl's eyes went wide. "You, a thief? No, I cannot believe it. I won't believe it!"

Catharina glanced at Lena, who was looking off toward the back of the garden, deep in thought. "It's true, my lord," she whispered. "I stole a lady's pearls. But it was for good reason." Now it was time for her to tell her story, and as she did, Lord Hainsley's smile grew. By the time she had finished, he appeared almost joyous.

"Are you saying that you orchestrated this farce to be caught on purpose?" He shook his head in wonderment. "What a brilliant plan! I'm astounded by your cleverness."

Catharina's head began to spin. He did not ridicule or scoff at her. Instead, he lauded her ingenuity.

Then a thought came to mind. "When you explained the activities you enjoy, you presented some of the most boring pastimes. And I can understand why. Ladies must only spend their time learning needlework or practicing the pianoforte. But I have a feeling that you were not being completely truthful with me."

"Boring?" He sounded offended. But then he cleared his throat and chuckled. "I suppose you got my lie. Like you, I also enjoy stealing for amusement."

She stared at him. He thought she enjoyed stealing Lady Langley's property? Had he not listened when she explained the reason for taking the pearls? No, of course, he did not. He was a man, and men tended to listen only to what they wanted to hear. The rest was left to the wind.

Still, if thievery brought him enjoyment—and clearly, he believed it did—then she would play along. Great adventures had to begin somewhere.

"There is no greater thrill than taking an item one wants," she said offhandedly. "And the more difficult it is to get an item, the more exciting it is. And it does not matter what is being taken—jewelry, horses, coins, if I want it, I shall have it. My life has been one grand adventure after another. And it will never end if I have anything to say about it."

Lady Olivia would have been impressed by Catharina's tale, but Catharina was more ashamed than proud. Yet when the earl reached across the table and touched his fingertips to her wrist, whatever shame she had been feeling vanished. Heat transferred from his body into hers like a wild river. Her breath caught and the images of him standing shirtless and carrying her through a forest while being chased by a hundred highwaymen flashed in her mind.

"Miss Sagewick, you spoke of wanting adventure. Then allow me to tell you the truth. My life has been a series of adventures."

For the first time in her life, Catharina was going to faint! What were the odds that she would encounter the very man for whom she had been searching within a week of her father hiring Lady Marigold? No, not Lady Marigold. Lady Whitmore. A countess. If she could have bet money, she would have earned a lifetime worth of income with the winnings, the odds were so high!

"But what about your days of reading and museums?" she asked, wondering where she had found the breath to speak the word. "Was all that truly lies?"

He chuckled. "Not lies but rather a story I tell others so as not to arouse their suspicion. I cannot have the wrong people learning of my... pastime." He winked at her. "I'll tell you more about my adventures soon, but I have a request of you before I do."

Catharina sat up straighter, ready to accept his offer of marriage. "Yes, my lord? Whatever you wish, you only need to ask."

Please let it be a kiss!

"I would like to avail of your services."

For a moment, Catharina did not understand. "My... my services, my lord?"

"Indeed. You see, I desperately must have the painting back that I attempted to steal."

Chapter Seven

Gideon had never met anyone like Miss Sagewick before. Oh, he had met beautiful women in the past, but never one with her level of intelligence and charm. And few were as forthright in their opinions.

It was because of these wonderful traits that her tales of thievery confounded him. Horses and jewelry? How could she even consider using stealth to take items that did not belong to her? Such actions, especially by a woman, were reprehensible. Yet hearing Miss Sagewick tell of it was somehow... alluring. And that baffled him all the more. She was more a highwayman—or in her case, a highwaywoman—than the daughter of noble breeding. Such heroines existed only in novels. Or were part of elaborate tales shared among drunkards in the local tavern.

As interesting as her sordid life was, however, her referring to his as "boring" annoyed him. How dare she decide so quickly that he did not enjoy the occasional distraction! Why, just last month, his carriage nearly collided with another. Lobbs, his driver, had been forced to swerve out of the other driver's way, sending Gideon flying across the carriage. Luckily for him, the door remained closed, or he would have been thrown from the vehicle. He had received such a fright that his heart was close to bursting from his chest.

Perhaps that was not a proper example. He had not enjoyed that incident in the least.

He sighed. How would she have known about that? He should not have snapped at her, but at least he had corrected himself.

And worse still, he should not have touched her exposed skin. Not only for propriety's sake but for the sake of his own sanity. Never before had he experienced such desire for any woman. He was no monk with no experience with women, but they had been nothing but diversions until the time he married. It took all his willpower not to place the back of his hand to her face and learn how smooth her skin truly was. To pull her into his arms and deeply kiss her.

Yet he had remained a gentleman. At least if one were to ignore the conversation in which they were engaged. After all, he had lied and said he was engaged in the same type of illegal activity as she. After all, he needed the services of a master thief.

"The painting I mentioned earlier?" he said, leaning closer so the chaperone would not overhear. "I must have it. But its location is such that I'm unable to take it myself."

"How so?" she asked.

"Unfortunately, I'm well-known to the owner. We had a falling out of sorts, and he has forbidden me from returning to his home, which makes taking the painting a practical impossibility. Oh, I could break into the house and take it myself by stealth, but I've been in the house enough that even the servants might recognize me. I could also wait for our disagreement to be forgotten, but I'm not sure I can wait that long. Lord Callingswell has a long memory."

Miss Sagewick smiled, and her eyes twinkled. "Our meeting must be an act of fate! Just this morning, I received an invitation to a party at the home of Lord Callingswell this Friday. I can take the painting for you, then."

Now he wanted to kiss her even more than before, but the time was not right. Not with her chaperone so nearby. But once the painting was secured, he would collect a kiss and then send Miss Sagewick on her way. Lovely she may be, but he could not marry a woman with a reputation as dappled as his was.

"You have no idea how much this means to me. Now, we must plan how you will remove the artwork from the home." He went on to explain its location within the house and answered various questions Miss Sagewick asked.

"Well, given I'm the better thief," Miss Sagewick replied, "and the one doing the stealing, I believe I must be the one to devise the plan. Wouldn't you agree?"

Gideon stifled a snort. He had to play along if he was to keep her confidence. Women could turn on someone as quickly as a dog protecting her pups. "Most likely." The fact he agreed did not stop his hackles from rising. Admitting someone was better than him at something was not an easy task. "But you must be able to remove it without raising anyone's suspicion."

"That is the constant in every situation such as this," Miss Sagewick said with a sniff. "From what you have told me, only one plan will see success. You mentioned that the library has a window. I'll take the painting out through there."

"Should I wait outside, so you can hand it off to me?"

With a sly smile, Miss Sagewick lifted her glass. "I'm sure you heard about the Vanderburgh painting that was stolen last year."

Gideon nodded. "Anyone and everyone knows about that. It was skied above even the portrait of the Prince Regent himself. Skied being the term used for placing the most important paintings where they can receive the best lighting."

Miss Sagewick gave him a flat stare. "I'm aware what 'skied' means, my lord. I'm not an uneducated oaf. In any case, it was I who stole it. And I did not have to sneak into the place. I strolled right in and walked it right back out. All it required was the admiring eyes of the guardsmen. Now, do you accept my plan? Or do you happen to have a better one?"

Gideon was amazed. Truly this lady was a master thief! And her tongue was as sharp as a Knight Templar's sword. Both would serve one another well. His mind conjured images of this lady entering the gallery in question and using her feminine wiles to hoodwink the guards. Nothing but the lore of its disappearance left in its place forever.

"I agree," he said. How could he not? Her plan was elementary, granted, but perhaps it had an air of brilliance to it, after all. Plus, how could he argue with the very thief who stole a Vanderburgh from right under the noses of those who were meant to keep it safe?

"I do have a question," Miss Sagewick said. "Why is this painting so important to you? And this man who has it, will the loss hurt him in any way?"

This last confused him. Why would a thief be concerned with the impact her thievery would have on the one from whom she would be stealing? Still, he had told enough lies today. It was time to add in a bit of truth.

"It has to do with my father dying and a family journal." He went on to tell her about his father's request and his reasons for needing the painting. "You see, it contains a clue of some sort. Unfortunately, I have not had the chance to study it closely enough to puzzle out what that clue is. All I know is that it eventually leads to a vast treasure."

Miss Sagewick's wide eyes sparkled. "Treasure, you say? What sort of treasure?"

Could a man be hypnotized by simply gazing at a woman? It had to be so, for he was lost in her blue eyes. "I've no idea. It could be gold or jewels. Perhaps both. Perhaps more. But my father was insistent that the treasure was of great value."

He glanced at the chaperone and was pleased to find her attention on something on the other side of the garden. A sudden rush of courage came over him as her small hand disappeared in his. "I cannot do this without you." He released her hand, reluctantly. Tempting fate could compromise what they had to do.

"Worry not, my lord. We shall have what is rightfully yours returned to you. Once it is in your possession, we can decipher the clue together." She clasped her hands against her breast. "Oh, what an adventure this will be!"

Gideon's initial reaction was to tell her that no, he did not need her help. After all, the painting—and by extension the treasure—belonged to him. But that hope of receiving at least a kiss from her was far too tempting to say it aloud. "Then I'll send you a card with the time and place to meet. We should also schedule another luncheon where we can study the painting. Together."

"Are you saying that you believe you can figure out the clue? Are you good with riddles?"

After two drinks, Gideon struggled to work a key into a lock let alone decipher clues. But if Miss Sagewick saw him as anything other than a man with a love for adventure, he would never get that kiss from her.

"I'm quite good," he said, his mind searching for a story to tell that would corroborate that statement. "Why, just last year, I was on an expedition in the Highlands of Scotland where I was summoned to work out a puzzle found in a cave."

From where did these lies come? They flowed from his tongue like a waterfall over a cliff, as he told the story of a map that only he could interpret, a cave, and the hidden treasure that he had found. When he was finished, Miss Sagewick was studying him. He held his breath. Could she sense that he was not being truthful?

"This is the sort of life I wish to lead," she said breathlessly. "I do not want a husband interested in attending boring parties every other weekend. Or one who plays chess or attends the theater as forms of entertainment." She said the last with a wink. "I want a man who is daring. A man... like you." Her cheeks turned a deep crimson. "Not that I'm asking you to propose to me, my lord," she added quickly. "Or to even call on me. Though, I would not refuse you if you wished to do so."

Gideon's thoughts went off on a tangent. He imagined himself holding a candle in a dark abandoned castle, Miss Sagewick at his side as they explored the wonders hidden within. She would be frightened, but his kiss would calm her. After all, she was now his wife.

His throat suddenly became dry, and he gulped down his wine. What was he thinking? The lady had put him under a spell of some sort. He could not marry her. Her soiled reputation would only make his worse than it already was. Or the other way around.

But what harm would there be if he enjoyed her company for the time being?

When he caught the chaperone with her eyes fixed on them, he abruptly pulled back his hand. Perhaps it was time to bring this luncheon to an end. For if he did not do so now, he would likely blurt out a proposal.

As he stood ready to hand her into her carriage, Gideon smiled at Miss Sagewick. She really was a lovely woman.

The chaperone stepped into the vehicle, and Miss Sagewick leaned in and whispered, "I shall see you Friday at exactly ten. And do not worry, my lord. I'll not fail you."

Was it the heat of the sun, or did she bat her eyelashes at him? Regardless, Gideon tugged at his too-tight cravat and somehow found enough air to utter a quick "Thank you. I shall be there." He bowed. "Until then, Miss Sagewick."

Taking a step back, Gideon watched the carriage trundle away and disappear around a bend in the street. A week ago, he was certain the painting he so needed was forever out of his reach. Now, however, he knew differently. Everything would be well. All thanks to a lady thief by the name of Catharina.

Chapter Eight

Every time Catharina visited Regent Street, she was in awe. It was a bustling area where ladies and gentlemen in their finest strolled along the footpaths, stopping to look at window displays or to chat with friends they encountered. Liveried servants hurried past them, delivering packages to customers. Carriages ambled along the street, their drivers shouting whenever pedestrians did not move quickly enough to allow them to pass. Shopkeepers greeting their guests. Hawkers selling their wares. It was all so exciting for a young lady who experienced this type of life no more than a few months a year.

Lady Whitmore had invited Catharina to accompany her on a day of shopping. Thus far, Catharina had enjoyed her day immensely. They had taken tea in a teahouse, ordered Catharina a new dress, and met a plethora of people with whom the countess was acquainted. The fact that none referred to her as Lady Marigold did not come as a surprise to Catharina. Lady Whitmore had been quite insistent about what would happen if Catharina mentioned that part of the countess's life. The lady would have made the same promises to others.

Although she was comfortable at Ivywood Manor, one thing continued to bother Catharina. Lena's explanation of why Lady Whitmore ran a secret matchmaking service was plausible, but it also had been vague. Catharina could not shake the feeling that such an occupation was odd for a member of the nobility. Granted, many elderly ladies enjoyed pairing couples but not as an occupation.

"What do you think of these, my lady?" the blonde shopkeeper asked as she handed Lady Whitmore a pair of white satin gloves trimmed with lace. They were on the hunt for a pair of gloves for Catharina to wear to the viscount's party, and Lady Whitmore had insisted this shop carried the finest.

"Indeed, these are lovely, Miss Millons." The countess handed them to Catharina. "What do you think?"

Catharina nodded. "They will go nicely with my gown. I'll take them."

As Miss Millons wrapped the gloves, Catharina thought about tomorrow evening. The idea of stealing again rankled her, but her reason was more than justified. After all, the Callingswell family had refused to honor a promise they had made, which meant that they were in the wrong.

Yes, that was the reason she would do what she had sworn never to do again—she was righting a terrible wrong.

Yet it was more than that. The look Lord Hainsley wore as they finalized their plans, the way he spoke of what he was willing to do to honor his father's wishes, it had all tugged at her heartstrings. Any man willing to go to such lengths for someone for whom he cared had to be admired. This adventure gave her a way to impress him, for she found that she admired him greatly.

Just thinking about him warmed her cheeks. He was handsome, brilliant, and a master adventurer. What more could she want in a man? His tale of the caves in Scotland had captured her imagination. She had pictured herself joining him on his explorations where they would stumble upon troves of gold, precious gems, and fine art stolen from the most prestigious galleries. If Lord Hainsley asked her to do anything, Catharina would oblige. Even kiss him.

Yet it was during that flurry of imaginings that she had let slip her willingness to marry him if he asked. And worse, he became nervous, as if he was ready to consider doing just that!

How could she have been so careless? She knew nothing about him beyond his boldness. What sort of business ventures was he involved in? What was his family like? Did he have family? Should a lady not know these things before blurting out that she found him interesting enough to consider marriage?

"Shall we?" Lady Whitmore asked, making Catharina start.

"Yes," she replied. How long had she been inside her own mind?

They exited the shop back onto the busy street where they made their way to the waiting carriage. Once inside, the countess said, "You seemed to be deep in thought, my dear. Is anything troubling you?"

Catharina shook her head. "No, nothing at all. In fact, I would say that things have never been better."

And that was the truth, for the worries about her past were now gone. Her father would be terribly pleased when he learned an earl intended to marry her. After a decent courtship, of course. Granted, her father would jump at the chance to have her married the moment the banns were read, given his frustration with her lack of suitors. But Catharina had to be sure the union was right. The days of marriages of convenience were going out of style. Now couples married for love.

Before they could court, of course, she would have to steal a painting. And she would not fail in that endeavor.

Lady Whitmore smiled, and Catharina thought she saw a twinkle in the older lady's eye. "Are you looking forward to the viscount's party?"

Catharina nodded. "I am."

"But it is nothing more than another party," the countess said. She seemed to study Catharina as if she, Catharina, were a painting. "What makes this particular gathering so exciting?"

Catharina's breath caught. Did Lady Whitmore know about their plans? No, of course not. How could she? Still an uneasiness crept over Catharina. "I've never been to the home of Lord Callingswell, which means I'll be meeting new people. There is potential for new friendships."

"I see. That is a shame. I thought you might have an interest in Lord Hainsley."

"Oh, but I do!" Catharina blurted out before she could stop herself.

She smoothed her skirts and added, "That is, I've already explained that he invited me to his house for another luncheon on Monday, after I..." Her words trailed off as the countess arched a single eyebrow. "After I make sure I get plenty of rest on Sunday."

Lady Whitmore chuckled lightly and turned her attention to the window. "The earl's a good man. Honorable and trustworthy. I'm grateful that he has been willing to advise me on matters of business."

"Do you know him well?" Catharina asked.

"Do I not know everyone well?" the countess asked with a laugh. "But yes, we are well acquainted. I have been friends with the Hainsley family for many years and have known him since he was a child."

Catharina frowned. If Lady Whitmore knew the earl well, she also had to know about this painting he so desperately wanted returned to him. Or at least his attempt to steal it. But a lady did not come right out with such accusations. Even if they were true.

"Have you heard the rumors concerning him?" Catharina gently prodded.

"Do you mean about the theft of a painting? Yes, of course I have heard. He was well into his cups that night, quite drunk if what I have heard is true. I'm sure he meant no harm. Lord Hainsley is an upstanding gentleman of high morals. He is certainly no thief."

Oh, if she only knew, Catharina thought, stifling a giggle. This was the first time she had ever encountered a man with a dual existence. A reputable man of the *ton* one moment—or at least a semblance of one—and a risk-taker the next. Still, it was not her duty to expose his secrets to the countess. Nor anyone else, for that matter. A man living such a dangerous life chose those in whom he would confide. And Catharina had been one of them.

"What of Lord Pearson? What would you say if I invited him to tea again? Or perhaps Lord Dremp was more to your liking."

As was her duty, Lady Whitmore had secured invitations for Catharina from other potential suitors. Although she had tolerated Lord Pearson's company, that of Lord Dremp was less so.

"I understand men tend to boast," she said. "Though with Lord Dremp, he spent the entire time crowing. About everything! Whatever I offered in conversation, he had to trump it with wilder tales."

She shook her head at the memory. When she mentioned her dear friend Lady Olivia Burnsworth and her love of the theater, Lord Dremp claimed he owned a theater. Speaking of her father's love for playing cards with his friends, Lord Dremp quickly interjected that he would easily best him at any card game. A gentleman who thought he could impress a lady by insulting her father was ludicrous.

"Lord Dremp is a fine gentleman," Lady Whitmore said in a stern voice. "He's humble and kind, a saint among sinners."

Catharina's heart thumped against her breast. She had not intended to offend the countess, but being truthful about such things was a must. Otherwise, she would end up being forced to spend more time with such men.

Lady Whitmore laughed. "My dear, I am teasing. He can be a bit brash and insulting, but I had thought that maybe you could be the one to bring him down a peg. But if you're not up for the task, I shan't ask you to endure his company again. For now, however, I shall hold off any more requests to call. After all, it appears you have found an interest in another gentleman. And it's quite clear he returns that interest."

Catharina smiled, knowing she spoke of Lord Hainsley. Yes, she would not be disappointed if no other suitor called on her ever again, save him.

The conversation turned to other matters, and then the countess laid out their plans for the following week. "We've been invited to tea with a friend of mine. If there is time, we'll call on another friend."

So many friends! Catharina thought. How did the countess keep up with such a busy schedule?

"May I ask a question?"

Lady Whitmore smiled. "Yes, of course."

"Why do you enjoy minding girls such as me?"

The countess tilted her head and furrowed her brow. "Minding girls like you? And what type of girl is that?"

Catharina flushed and looked down as she brushed away invisible dirt from her skirts. "Ones who create problems for themselves, so no man will ever wish to court them."

"Oh, I think you are far more than your mistakes, Catharina. But in answer to your question, I enjoy bringing together couples I know will be compatible."

"It's not that I doubt your answer," Catharina said, nibbling at her lip. "But why? There must be more to it than that."

Lady Whitmore laughed. "Oh, my dear Catharina, you are a stubborn one."

Catharina sighed. "Father has said as much. And others. But I would not say I'm stubborn as much as fixed in my opinions. That is not such a bad thing, is it?"

The countess patted her hand. "I would say it is a great quality to have. And in answer to your question, you are aware that my husband died a few years ago, are you not? And soon after, my son."

"Yes. And you have my deepest condolences."

"Thank you," Lady Whitmore said. "The truth is, I loved my husband dearly. His death took a terrible toll on me. But when my son was lost at sea, I thought my life had ended." Although sadness filled her eyes, a small smile played on her lips. "But rather than wallow in my sorrow, I began to recognize in others the chance that they, too, could have the same love my husband and I shared. And that my son, Anthony, had for his fiancée. So, I began my matchmaking services. To bring together those I know will find love with each other."

Catharina found the countess's reasoning more beautiful than a glorious sunset and said as much. "Thank you for explaining. And I'll keep my promise to never reveal what you do to anyone. Not even to Lord Hainsley." She frowned. "He's not aware of what you do, is he?"

"No. There are some things I share with no one, no matter how close they are to me. Well, except for Lena. With her I share everything."

Catharina understood why. Lena had proved to be a good listener.

When they returned to Ivywood Manor, Catharina dressed for dinner, and Catharina told Lena all about her day out with the countess. Soon, the conversation turned to Lady Whitmore's explanation as to why she did what she did.

"She's a remarkable woman," Catharina said. "Truly one of integrity. I can only hope that my name is as good as hers one day."

"Oh, I've no doubt it will be. As long as you continue down a path that's true, it will happen. Deviate in any way, and one may just find her name ruined forever."

Catharina swallowed hard. She had been so caught up in having an adventure that she had not considered the consequences if she were caught stealing the painting tomorrow night. Her name would be doubly ruined, and no one, not even the countess, could save her.

And as much as she wanted to earn the earl's admiration, she could not help but wonder if the cost might not be worth the reward.

Chapter Nine

The Noble Giant was a gentleman's club located just off Regent Street. With fine leather chairs and gold tapestries, it was where Gideon could chat about the latest goings on of the *ton* without the pomp and circumstance one might find at White's. Or the exorbitant prices one was expected to pay there.

Most of his peers now shunned him because of his misstep at the home of Lord Callingswell. Yet those of the gentry, like Mr. Thomas Harwell who sat across from him now, did not listen to rumors. Or at least did not allow rumors to stop them from speaking to him. Likely because they would take any opportunity to get their foot in the door, even if it meant getting their toe cut off in the process.

Unfortunately for Gideon, the current conversation was about the man's wife.

"I swear, Hainsley," Mr. Harwell was saying, "every time her sister visits, the pair begin to plot against me. If I suddenly disappear, have them investigated for my possible murder." He leaned in closer and pointed a drunken finger at Gideon. "And I still think she has eyes for that butcher."

Gideon gave him a friendly nod, although it took all his willpower not to groan. He and Mr. Harwell had been acquainted for a number of years, but the man's paranoia about his wife had grown exponentially over the last year. Mrs. Emma Harwell was a striking woman, and her husband was jealous of any man who even looked in her direction.

Finally, to Gideon's relief, Mr. Harwell said, "But enough about me. Has the *ton* welcomed you back into their inner circle?"

"Unfortunately, not," Gideon replied as a barmaid placed two brandies on the table. He pulled out his purse, intending to pay, but Mr. Harwell waved him away.

"I believe it's my turn."

Gideon returned his purse to his pocket and continued with the conversation. "It shouldn't be much longer before I'm invited to various functions again. At least, I hope it is not."

As Mr. Harwell prattled on about various rumors he had heard, Gideon's mind turned to Miss Sagewick. What she planned to do tonight was bold. And as much as he appreciated her services, it was a shame how willing she was to resort to her criminal ways. He had considered warning Lady Whitmore but had decided against it. Lady Whitmore could take care of herself. Of that, he had no doubt. Plus, the thought of shaming Miss Sagewick did not sit well with him. Which in itself was odd. After all, he barely knew her.

After what felt like years, Mr. Harwell sighed. "Such is life. Up one moment, down the next." He snapped his fingers at the barmaid. "Let's have another drink, shall we?"

Gideon waved his hand. "I'm feeling a bit drunk already, and I have a meeting with a friend at ten."

"Ten?" Mr. Harwell asked, frowning. "Then you'd best be on your way. It's nearly ten now."

Gideon pulled out his watch and gaped. He was supposed to meet Miss Sagewick in fifteen minutes! It would take at least twenty to make it to Lord Callingswell's house.

With a quick farewell, he stood, stopping to steady his legs, and hurried out the door. Shouting at Lobbs to forgo the steps, he barked the address and leapt into the carriage. The journey was slow at first, not because his driver was inept but rather because of an ambling carriage in front of them.

"Just my luck," Gideon growled.

After leaving London, and a short journey through the countryside, they arrived. Gideon exited the vehicle down the street and instructed Lobbs to wait there for him.

"I won't be long. Once I return, you are to drive me straight home. We will stop for no one."

"Yes, my lord."

Walking down the country lane, Gideon drew closer to the home of Lord Callingswell with each passing step. Numerous carriages lined the drive, and he kept to their shadows as he made his way to the house. He could hear the muted yet lively laughter coming from within.

Pressing his back against the wall, he peeked around the corner. As expected, no one was lurking in the darkness. He approached the library window and groaned. By the glow of the light from the window, he could just make out a cluster of rose bushes. No, not a cluster, but an entire row that ran the length of the house.

He eased between two bushes, the numerous thorns tearing at his breeches and coat. Several even scraped his thigh. When he reached the window, he stood on the tips of his toes to peer inside.

Where was she?

According to his pocket watch, it was a quarter past ten. Had the girl not had enough patience to wait for him? Did she not realize that men were sometimes delayed because of important duties? Not that drinking was all that important, but she would not know what had caused his tardiness.

Crouching lest someone enter the room and catch him peeking inside, he cursed as the scratches on his thighs began to burn. It was amazing how much braver a man could be after several glasses of brandy. Miss Sagewick was not there. Perhaps he should go in search of her.

Thorns tore at his clothing once more as he wiggled his way through the bushes. She would get an earful later! If she had been where she was supposed to be, he would not be ruining a perfectly good suit of clothing!

Gideon skirted the house to where laughter and music floated out the open doors and windows of the ballroom. A row of hedges that ran along either side of the veranda provided perfect concealment, so he could spy on the party.

He recognized a number of faces, including that of Lady Whitmore. But his fists clenched when he caught sight of Miss Sagewick walking toward him. In the company of Lord Callingswell, no less.

"I heard a terrible rumor about you, Miss Sagewick," Lord Callingswell was saying as they came to a stop just above the window where Gideon was hiding. The viscount used a teasing tone that rankled more than it should have. "Is it true you had a luncheon with Lord Hainsley?"

"It is," Miss Sagewick replied. "And I had an enjoyable time."

Lord Callingswell laughed. "You cannot seriously say that Hainsley provides intelligent conversation."

To Gideon's horror, not only did Miss Sagewick laugh, but she also placed a hand on the viscount's arm.

"Well, the food was fantastic," she replied. "But if I'm perfectly honest, his conversational skills are lacking. He talks entirely too much about nothing of consequence. I found studying the grass was much more interesting."

Gideon's fingernails dug into his palms. She was supposed to steal the painting, not throw herself at Lord Callingswell! And why was she touching him so intimately? If he had never met her, he would have said she was flirting with the man! He would not allow Callingswell to steal his painting as well as his woman.

He paused. His woman? Where did such thoughts come from? It had to be the drink that was causing a surge of jealousy. It had to be.

Frustrated, he stepped back. A thorn dug into the back of his thigh, and he covered his mouth to keep a groan from escaping. He ducked his head, fearing he had drawn the viscount's attention.

A few moments later, and to his relief, the two walked away, each heading in a different direction.

When he returned to his place beneath the library window, he stifled a yelp as another thorn dug into his leg. Fuming, he squatted, preparing to receive his painting.

Chapter Ten

Catharina had gone to the library at precisely ten, but the earl was not there. She waited five minutes, just in case he was running late. Any longer, and she would have roused the suspicion of her host. Which was why she found herself now speaking with Lord Callingswell beside the ballroom window. She was by no means attracted to the viscount, but he did not seem as cruel as Lord Hainsley had made him out to be. What she saw was a kind and attentive gentleman. Only he was not as kind and attentive as Lord Hainsley.

Her description of the earl as a boring companion was meant to gain Lord Callingswell's trust. She had thoroughly enjoyed her time with Lord Hainsley and looked forward to their next luncheon. If she had her way, he would be the only gentleman with whom she spent her meals.

The viscount clearly thought little of Lord Hainsley, so she used that distrust as a way to gain his trust. The lie burned her tongue as she spoke it, but she had to put as much distance between her and the earl as possible. She had to make certain that she did not become a suspect when the viscount realized the painting was missing. And Lord Hainsley could not be implicated, either. And given her poor decision with Lady Langley's pearls, Lord Callingswell would easily make the connection.

"I must admit," Lord Callingswell said, "being in the company of a strikingly beautiful lady such as yourself is most welcome. Perhaps I can show you how a proper luncheon is done."

"Oh?" Catharina asked with raised eyebrows. "And how is that, my lord?"

The viscount grinned. "Why, I'd see the best lady received the best wine."

Catharina smiled. She recognized his open flirting. She was doing the same, but she suspected it was not for the same reason. She had no romantic interest in the viscount. However, if she was to be the last on his list of suspects in the hunt for the missing painting, she had to play this game.

"I have yet to meet the best man in London, my lord," she said, touching his arm once more. "Perhaps you will prove to be that man. If you send a card, I just may reply."

She paused. Had she heard a groan? Or had the viscount's stomach growled? Whatever the noise, Catharina found it odd as she and Lord Callingswell walked away from the window.

After mingling with several of the guests, and stopping to converse with Lady Whitmore, Catharina decided to try the library once more. To her relief, she caught sight of a head just outside the window.

"You're late!" she said in a harsh whisper as she pulled up the sash. "Whatever were you doing?"

Lord Hainsley laughed. "I should ask you the same thing. You have but one task to do, and instead I catch you flirting with Callingswell!"

Catharina clutched her skirts. "Flirting? You were spying on me?"

"No, I was looking for you. Regardless, it is insulting that you mention marriage to me and then throw yourself at *that cad*!"

A sly smile crept onto Catharina's lips. Ah, the earl was indeed jealous, a fact she now found rather intriguing. She could have fun with that tidbit of information.

"He seems like a very nice man," she said, twirling a strand of hair around her finger. "He invited me to luncheon, you know." Feeling a bit mischievous, she decided to stretch the truth. "And a special carriage ride as well."

"What do you mean special?"

The harsh whisper he used as he said the words was adorable! "A carriage ride through Hyde Park, of course. I thought it rather kind of him to make such an offer."

The earl's face darkened as he rubbed his temples. "Are you that naive? That is where lovers go! Surely you would not even accompany him on such an excursion! What will others say?"

Catharina pushed out her bottom lip. "I don't know. I think I would be safe with him. And honestly, who cares about the opinions of others? I certainly do not."

If Lord Hainsley's face was dark before, it was a thundercloud now. "I forbid you to go!"

It took all Catharina's willpower not to burst out laughing. This was proving to be much more entertaining than she had anticipated. She smiled at him. "You are handsome at any given moment but more so when you're jealous. It's rather adorable."

He gripped the window frame, and Catharina wondered if he would try to climb inside. "I am not jealous," he said. "And certainly not of a young lady willing to flirt in an open ballroom."

She placed her hands on her hips. "Very well. It seems you are no longer in need of my services. Good evening to you." With that, she turned on her heel.

"Wait!" he called in a harsh whisper. "I'm a tad drunk."

She lowered herself to where their noses nearly touched. "A tad? I believe the stench of brandy on your breath is enough to inebriate me."

Lord Hainsley grinned. "Fine. I'm quite drunk." He stared at her for several moments before adding, "Have you any idea how beautiful and charming I think you are? So much so that I have been wanting to kiss you."

Heat filled Catharina. She was surprised, and pleased, by this declaration. "That is a bold thing to admit, my lord."

"As bold as you to steal a painting, I'd say," he countered, his grin turning mischievous. "Tell me, Miss Sagewick, what do you think of my admission?"

The truth was, she found his declaration exciting and bold. She wanted to return his admiring words, but the banter was far too enjoyable to ignore. Even for a kiss.

"I believe that such forward speaking is roguish at best. Yet why should I be surprised, given your duplicitous life? Now, apologize, or I shall leave."

"Apologize?" he asked with a laugh. "I'm a gentleman, for goodness' sake. I'm never required to apologize, especially to a woman."

With a derisive sniff, she went to stand but caught the whisper of an apology. "I beg your pardon, my lord. What did you say?"

"Come closer, so you may hear me properly," he whispered, and Catharina did. "Now, as I was saying..."

Time stood still as Lord Hainsley placed his hands on either side of her face. His touch was gentle. Yet his kiss was anything but.

His lips were powerful, possessive, and instantly consumed her. She had never been kissed before, but she knew in that moment that she would never want another man to kiss her. Her body ignited with a fire from within, and she found herself returning the kiss with as much fervor as he gave.

When it came to an end, she managed to squeak, "Apology accepted, my lord. Now, let me get your property." When she stood, she nearly screamed upon seeing Lord Callingswell standing in the doorway.

"Miss Sagewick?" he asked, stepping into the room. "What are you doing kneeling by the window? And with whom were you speaking?"

She released the breath she had been holding. He had not seen Lord Hainsley, thank heaven. She said a silent prayer of forgiveness for the lie she was about to tell.

"I needed fresh air and a quiet place to pray." He tilted his head and gave her a look of suspicion. She had to be more convincing. "I... I've had improper thoughts about you, my lord."

The viscount's grin could only be described as triumphant. "Is that so?"

She nodded. Her heart thudded against her chest as he took her hand and kissed her knuckles.

"You are not the first to think of me in that way, Miss Sagewick.

Many women have found confessing their innermost secrets to me comforting. Such conversations tend to lead to far better things. Tell me, Miss Sagewick, shall we talk about these thoughts you have had about me?"

Catharina swallowed hard. "Yes, my lord. I would like nothing more."

"Then why wait? Lady Whitmore is in a deep conversation with Lord and Lady Kittler, so she will not miss the fact that you're not in attendance. You must be a wonderful trickster to slip away so boldly from your chaperone. Quite convenient for us both, would you not say?"

He pulled her toward him, but she put her hands against his chest to keep him from doing something he would regret. And regret it he would. A well-placed knee could have any man see the error of his ways quicker than a tongue lashing.

"May I have a few more minutes of quiet contemplation, my lord? I've not completed my prayers."

He chuckled. "I see no reason why not. We have the rest of the night."

When he was gone, Catharina sighed. Now to do what she was meant to do. Pulling the chair from behind the desk, Catharina used it to reach the painting. Once it was removed from the wall, she hurried to the window and handed it to Lord Hainsley. "The things I'm willing to do for you," she said with mock exasperation.

"Such as?" he asked, grinning.

"Stealing, lying, and openly flirting with gentlemen in whom I have no interest, just to name a few!"

"And I very much appreciate your efforts," the earl said with a wink. "But congratulations on not kissing him as you did me."

Catharina gasped. "I was not the one who did the kissing. You are the rogue, my lord, not I."

"That remains to be seen," he said with a grin. "Still, because of what you did for me tonight, I am in your debt and eternally grateful." Catharina smiled. His words were sincere. He might be as stubborn as any other man, but there was no doubt he was thankful for what she had done. "And I will see you again on Monday."

Once he was gone, Catharina wasted no time replacing the chair to its spot and returning to the party. She made a point of chatting with several women before even glancing at Lord Callingswell. And when she did, she was not surprised to find him staring at her.

What she had done tonight was despicable. Stealing was not right, nor were the lies she had told. And nearly being caught by Lord Callingswell had been terrifying.

But Lord Hainsley's kiss had made it all worth it. Never had she imagined her first kiss to be so powerful. Nor as furtive. Wait until she told Lady Olivia about what had happened! She would be green with envy.

As the party progressed, Catharina was thankful that Lord Callingswell was kept occupied with other guests. She soon found herself back in the company of Lady Whitmore.

"I know you must be enjoying yourself," the countess said, covering her yawn with the back of her hand, "but I'm growing tired. Would you mind too much if we left soon?"

A wave of relief washed over Catharina. "Not at all. I hadn't wanted to say anything for fear you were enjoying yourself, but I'm quite tired myself."

Twenty minutes later, they were back in the carriage and returning to Mayfair. And although she and the countess talked about the party, Catharina's thoughts continued to wander back to the enigmatic Lord Hainsley. On Monday, she would learn what progress he had made with the painting. And with some playful flirting, he just might kiss her again.

Chapter Eleven

Certain things in life can drive a man to desperation—an unfaithful wife, a dubious business partner. Or a painting bearing an indecipherable clue.

Since the night the painting was returned to him, Gideon had dedicated countless hours to staring at it, the family journal opened to a particular page. He had even examined every inch of the image through a quizzing glass, hoping to uncover any anomalies that might conceal a secret, but his efforts yielded nothing.

He had spent three hours this Monday morning staring at it, and his patience was wearing thin. No, he had moved well beyond irritation. He was downright frustrated.

The painting was displayed on an easel, as Gideon rested an elbow on the arm of one of the drawing-room chairs. Wait, was that knight beside the blue forget-me-nots distracted? Perhaps he was staring at a clue Gideon had missed. But no, he was looking at one of his comrades. He sat up straighter. And what of the daisy that brushed against the tip of the shorter knight's boots? Was there any significance to that? Yet, upon closer inspection, that daisy resembled the three others strewn across the field.

He sighed heavily. His irritation at being unable to unmask the riddle did not come only from his desire to find the much-needed treasure. What would Miss Sagewick think of him if he was unsuccessful in this endeavor? Although her flirtatious behavior with Lord Callingswell had bothered him more than it should have, he still wished to impress her. Which was strange, given that it had been a very long time since any woman had captivated him like this.

She was due for luncheon in an hour, and Gideon had hoped to have this clue found and whatever riddle it gave him solved before she arrived. He imagined her so overcome with passion that she would readily request another kiss. Being so bold as to confess his desire to kiss a woman was not characteristic of him. Propriety had its place for a reason, and he, for one, preferred to adhere to those standards.

Yet his daring nature of the kiss they had shared had consumed him all weekend. Miss Sagewick's lips were tantalizingly plump and as smooth as silk. When he was not engrossed with the painting, his thoughts were consumed by her. But what could she possibly see in him? She was searching for a man of adventure, not some spineless *poltroon* who clung to safety.

"My lord," Collins said from the doorway, "they are here as per your request."

Gideon turned to find the entire household staff huddled in the hallway. Every one of them, from chambermaids to Mrs. Plotts, the housekeeper, wore a worried expression. Typically, such a gathering meant bad news, such as staff being dismissed or reprimands for poor work performance.

Yet neither of those was the motive behind his gathering them here today. No, the more minds the better. Gideon meant to ask them for their help. In a way that did not garner too much suspicion, that is.

Was he that desperate to call on his staff for help? Yes, quite clearly, he was.

Gideon stood, smiling. "Please, do not worry. No one is in trouble, and your positions are safe. For the time being." He let out a chuckle, although it faded when no one joined in. He did, however, catch Mrs. Laughlin, the cook, murmuring a prayer of thanks under her breath. "I've asked you here today to show you my latest acquisition." He stepped aside and motioned to the painting. "Please, take a moment to study it. And feel free to express your thoughts aloud."

A fair-haired footman with a prominent nose and a freckled face in his twenties by the name of Felix Bones glanced at another footman, eighteen and dark-haired with a pointed chin. They shrugged and pushed past the butler into the drawing room.

They stood, backs bent and their hands behind their backs as if this was an everyday occurrence. When they did not speak for several moments, Gideon said, "Studying art displays logical thinking but to speak of it aloud is a sign of intelligence. All art contains a message, and I would be delighted to hear what you believe the artist of this painting is trying to tell us. Here," he picked up the ancestral journal, "allow me to read a clue of sorts. 'Two by two, whether sitting room or parlor, both remain together forever.'"

Returning the journal to the table, he turned to the staff once more. "So, what do you make of it? Anyone?"

A hand timidly rose in the air—belonging to a young chambermaid no older than fourteen. "Um... I think the man up front's pointin' to the way home. And the one behind him, he's smilin' so he's the second one? I reckon it's 'bout friendships."

"Very good," Gideon said, quite impressed by the young girl's insight. Even if it was unlikely the clue for which he was searching. "Please, everyone, don't be shy. Speak up. Art is open to interpretation. There is no wrong way to look at it."

Donald Halliway, Gideon's balding valet, stepped forward. "May I examine the painting up close, my lord?" Gideon nodded, and the portly man walked up to the easel. "Notice the flowers surrounding the men? Now notice that on their shields is a single rose. Clearly, they are knights, in service to the Crown, embarking on a quest to procure a rose for their queen."

One by one, each servant gave his or her interpretation, yet none provided any valuable insight. Gideon stifled a sigh. Their speculations ranged from the men being lost to embarking on a war, leaving him more bewildered than when they began. Their observations had proven unhelpful for his purposes and only deepened his confusion.

He had been so certain that once he had the painting in his possession, the clues would all fall into place. Now, however, he was unsure if he would ever find the treasure.

With a final word of gratitude, he released the staff from their gathering, leaving him and the painting alone again. He was unsure how long he stood there, but the voice of the butler startled him out of his trance.

"Miss Sagewick, my lord."

Miss Sagewick wore a white muslin dress trimmed in white lace. Tiny white daisies dotted her dark hair, silver earrings hung from her ears, and a choker necklace made from white ribbon adorned her neck. He doubted she had ever looked lovelier.

"It is a pleasure to see you again, Miss Sagewick," Gideon said. "Miss Page," he added in an afterthought, acknowledging the chaperone beside her.

"And you as well, my lord." Miss Sagewick's smile took his breath away. "So, have you managed to decipher your riddle yet?"

Rather than admitting defeat, he called for tea and gestured for the ladies to take their seats.

"I hope you don't mind if I see to some sewing while you chat," Miss Page said in her quiet voice.

"Not at all," Gideon replied, silently pleased that they would have some modicum of privacy. Taking a nearby chair so he could be as close as possible to Miss Sagewick without sitting beside her on the sofa—decorum and all that—he turned to his guest. "If you have no objections, of course."

Miss Sagewick's laugh was light and airy and sent shivers down his spine. "No, of course not. Go on, Miss Page. I doubt our discussion will be of any great amusement to you, anyway."

"So," Gideon said once the chaperone was situated in a chair beside the window, "how did you find Lord Callingswell's party? Did you remain much longer after giving me the painting?"

It was none of his concern how Miss Sagewick spent the evening. Yet, the thought of her in the company of Lord Callingswell—or that of any other gentleman—longer than necessary bothered him, although he could not explain why.

She frowned in thought before responding, "Let me see if I can come up with the right words to describe my experience. Fascinating? No, that is not the right word. I found the viscount kind and intelligent. And his company was captivating. Yes, that is the best word I can use. Captivating."

She said the last with a sly smile, and Gideon had to wonder if she was teasing him. Could she be telling the truth? Had she found Lord Callingswell's company enjoyable? No, she had to be teasing him! Either way, this woman was more intriguing every time he saw her!

"If you did spend more time with this... captivating man as you put it, what time did you eventually leave the party?" He tried to make his tone uninterested, but it came nowhere close.

Her playful smile caused him to grin. "Hmm, let me think. Midnight? No, it must have been one." She tapped her lips. "No that cannot be right, for I returned just as the sun rose. That is how late I stayed."

Gideon glanced at the chaperone to make sure she was still occupied before whispering, "Why so late?"

"It's difficult to explain, my lord," she replied, her eyes twinkling like beautiful diamonds beneath a bright light. "But to find a true gentleman these days with so many rogues about is not an easy quest."

Gideon grinned. Oh, but she was a wild one. And he found that trait surprisingly attractive. "Rumor has it that some ladies prefer rogues."

Miss Sagewick glanced in the direction of her chaperone, leaned forward, and dared to touch his arm. "Trust me, my lord. That is no rumor."

His body felt awash in fire. Her words ignited a passion deep inside him. Or perhaps it was the smile that played upon her lips. Regardless, their banter was enjoyable, and he wished to continue, but Collins entered with the tea tray.

Once the butler poured and left the room, Miss Sagewick said, "Now, I know you did not invite me here to discuss Lord Callingswell. Or any other rogue with whom I've become acquainted. And since you did not answer my earlier question, I must conclude that you have not yet solved your riddle."

Her boldness should have had him scorning her, but he secretly enjoyed it. "That is untrue," he said, placing a fist on his thigh. "I solved it the very same night..." His words trailed off, and he glanced at the chaperone. He had no idea how much the woman knew about what had occurred at the party on Friday. "The same night you attended Lord Callingswell's party."

"Then you must tell me," Miss Sagewick said. She turned to Miss Page and added, "Lord Hainsley is a brilliant man. You really should listen to him." She settled back into her seat. "Go on, my lord. When you are ready."

She was a tormentor! And by the sparkle in her eyes, she relished in that torment. Again, he should have been offended, but he was not. He could spend the rest of his days enjoying her repartee.

"I would not wish to offend you with my vast knowledge, Miss Sagewick," he said, crossing his arms over his chest. "After all, women do tend to be less informed than their male counterparts."

To his delight, she let out an angelic laugh. "Less informed? I suspect you have many guesses but have come to no viable conclusions. You know, my lord, admitting your shortcomings is not so terrible. After all, every man must admit to failure at one time or another."

How could one woman possess both wit and beauty? Most conversations he had ever had with ladies of the aristocracy would have put him to sleep if he had not made a point of forcing his attention to remain on them. But not his Miss Sagewick. She was different...

He paused. *His* Miss Sagewick? They had only been acquainted recently. What made him come to the odd conclusion that she now belonged to him? Perhaps all this treasure hunting was making him go mad. Or was it the kiss they had shared that had him creating scenarios that were not yet true?

"Very well," he said, deciding to bring the banter to an end. "I have a few theories, though I would welcome any you might have."

He stood and offered his hand, which she took without hesitation. He loved the way it disappeared in his as he helped her stand and walked her to the painting.

She studied it for several minutes, tapping her chin and pursing her lips in a very lovely manner. "Could you repeat the clue?"

"'Two by two, whether sitting room or parlor, both remain together.'"

Miss Sagewick frowned in thought, but she continued to study the painting. "And where did you find this clue?" she asked.

"In a family journal," he replied. "Why?"

"May I read it?"

"I don't see how that can help. I've dictated it exactly as it was written."

She lifted her head. "Shall we argue, or will you set aside your pride and allow me to aid you?"

Gideon chuckled and opened the book to the correct page. "Here," he said, handing the book to her and pointing to a particular part. "It begins with this line."

Miss Sagewick read it over, looked at the parting, and then reread the line again. "'Two by two, whether sitting room or parlor, both remain together.'"

"You see? Exactly as I dictated it to you. It's clear that it speaks of the bond between men—in this case between the knights. But where should I begin? Which two knights in the painting does it refer to? There have been far too many knights throughout history to focus on one particular pair."

She set the journal on the table and returned her attention to the painting.

After a full minute and no comment from her, Gideon chuckled. "See? There is no answer. Perhaps my father had this all wrong. What if this was meant as a practical joke and not a clue?" Even he thought that idea far-fetched.

"I have solved it," she said.

Gideon let out a sigh of relief. "What does it say?"

That mischievous smile crossed her face again. "Before I answer, tell me what treasure this clue leads to. And the symbols for these knights, as I know little about them."

Rather than responding immediately, he paused. By her own admission, Miss Sagewick had been an experienced thief for many years, having taken anything of value from horses, coins, jewelry, and even fabled paintings. If he told her the truth, would she consider helping him steal the treasure once they found it?

She pursed her lips. "Very well. Tell me nothing. What does it matter anyway? I suppose I should just leave now."

"No, wait," he said. He had no choice but to trust her. At least a little. "For hundreds of years, stories about the Knights Templar have been passed down through every generation of my family. You see, the Knights helped to protect those who were on pilgrimages to the Holy Land. But they were not simply knights. They were well-versed men, men who were bankers, important military figures, and men of renown."

"They sound very brave, my lord. But what does that have to do with the treasure?"

"According to legend, a distant relative of mine was the protector of a vast fortune—jewels, silver, and enough gold to fill every room of this house."

Her eyes widened at the mention of each item. "Riches beyond belief!" she breathed.

Gideon nodded. "There is one more thing. My grandfather told me a story told to him by his grandfather. Apparently, one of the items is the very cup of Christ."

"The Holy Grail?" Miss Sagewick asked.

"Yes. My grandfather claimed that he who wields the Holy Grail will receive everything his heart desires—fortune, fame, power to rival any king. I want it all, yes, but I want to honor my father's wishes more by finding it."

The room fell quiet as Miss Sagewick shook her head in wonderment, the excitement he felt glowing in her eyes. "Thank you for sharing, my lord. I shall keep my end of the bargain." She took the painting off the easel and set it face down on a nearby table. "The clue is in the painting."

"But I've spent hours searching every inch of it and found nothing."

She smiled. "No, not in that sense. I mean 'inside' the painting. If we remove the backing, I believe you will find whatever it is we need."

"Do you think I've not taken the painting from its frame?" he asked, irritated that she would think him so simple.

With a swift step, she came to stand in front of him. Having her so near made him realize just how small and precious she truly was.

But her eyes were ablaze, even as she batted her eyelashes at him. "Lord Hainsley," she said in a soft voice, "there are times in a man's life when he must listen to what a woman has to say." She placed a hand on his chest, and his heart skipped a beat. "And this is one of those times."

How bold she was to be so forward while in the company of her chaperone! Granted, his larger frame blocked the other woman's view, but still, he appreciated her boldness. She was clearly afraid of nothing.

He placed a finger beneath her chin. "Such determination may get you another kiss, Miss Sagewick. If that is what you desire, then please, continue."

Her smile lit up her face. He wanted to kiss her right there and then, but lucky for them both, she returned her attention to the painting.

When she removed the backing, he stood in triumph. "You see? Nothing."

"My lord, knights engage in warfare. They do not take tea in a sitting room, or drinks in a parlor. At least, they would not be depicted doing so in a work of art. Which means there is more to this painting than meets the eye." She slid a fingernail along the edge of the canvas and nodded as it separated into two. "There we are. 'Two' does not mean two people but rather two paintings. They are joined together within the same frame, which hangs in whatever room, sitting or parlor, its owner chooses."

Chapter Twelve

Gideon was dumbfounded as Miss Sagewick peeled back the layer of canvas to reveal another hidden behind it. The second painting depicted a priest holding a scroll in his right hand, on which were words written in Latin. He never expected his university lessons in the language would be of any use. Until now.

He translated it silently:

Every winter day at noon,
At St. Paul's dome,
Eight archers gather,
At the place they call home.
The sun shows the doubter,
The light of the one most loved.
And in return he shall show you
The path which is true.

Excitement filled Gideon. He did not entirely understand this new clue, but at least he was one step closer to his prize. And closer to wiping away the shame of being caught stealing. Whatever the treasure was, he would restore his family's name as well as the wealth. And all to honor his father.

"Is that Latin, my lord?" Miss Sagewick asked.

He nodded. "It is, indeed."

She gasped. "What does it say?"

A twinge of sadness came over Gideon as he turned to Miss Sagewick. Although she had been a great help to him, it was time for them to part ways. This lovely woman was a master thief. If she learned the meaning of this next clue before he was able to puzzle it out, what would keep her from stealing it from right under his nose?

He would have preferred her to remain at his side, but he had no reason to trust her. Therefore, he had a tough decision to make.

"It's a complicated passage, I'm afraid," he replied. "Unfortunately, it does not translate well. I must study it later when I have the time. For now, I believe luncheon is waiting for us."

They went to the gardens, where their food and drink sat at the same tables as before. Today, they dined on cold ham, cubed cheese, and a variety of fruits. Sitting across from Miss Sagewick, Gideon struggled to look her in the eye. He was not obliged to tell her the truth, but he felt guilty that he had not.

Gideon believed everyone deserved a chance to walk a straight path. After all, did he not want the same for himself? But every time he thought of including Miss Sagewick in that group, he feared she would be unwilling to give up her long history of thievery. As much as he wanted to be the one to give her the second chance she needed, he could not. For he could not risk dishonoring his father's wishes, even for someone as beautiful as Miss Sagewick.

What a hypocritical man you are, Gideon, he thought to himself.

The conversation began with the usual small talk and soon worked its way around again to the Callingswell's party.

"The nerve of Callingswell to talk to you as he did," Gideon said. "How disappointed will he be when you refuse his offer of accompanying him on an outing?"

Miss Sagewick selected several cubes of cheese and set them on her plate. "I'm not sure I should refuse. Would you prefer I did?"

Gideon found her response odd. Was she baiting him again, or was her tone truly as serious as it seemed? It was becoming difficult to tell. Still, he could not confess his growing attraction to her. Not if he wished to keep away from her.

"I don't care what you do, Miss Sagewick," he replied offhandedly. "We are merely friends, are we not?"

"Are you saying that you would not mind if I accepted an invitation from him?"

Gideon sat his glass of wine on the table. "I care enough to say that some men are great collectors of things they enjoy. Some collect books, some great art, and others collect horses. Callingswell collects lovers. Therefore, do what you must." He could not tell her how he felt, but at least he could give her warning. "Such company would be dangerous to a lady like yourself. Choose as you will, but don't say I did not warn you."

Rather than be shocked by what he said, Miss Sagewick simply shrugged. "Then, I'll take what you say under advisement."

Under advisement? Gideon thought with a silent groan of frustration. If she were to see him on the street, she should consider running as far away from the viscount as she could!

"He seems decent enough," she continued, breaking off a morsel of cheese and popping it into her mouth. "I might even go so far as to say he's gallant."

She brought the rim of her wineglass to her lips. Images of kissing her appeared in his mind, and he had to grip the table to steady himself. Then he thought of Lord Callingswell partaking of her, and he stopped himself just short of turning over the table in a rage. He had to protect her!

"My lord?"

He shook his head to clear it. "I know we are just friends, Miss Sagewick, but please tell me you are teasing me. You cannot truly be considering allowing Callingswell to call on you, can you?"

Her eyes went wide. "Teasing you? Of course, I'm not teasing you. I simply don't know what I will do."

Gideon pushed away his unfinished food. "Do as you will. I, however, must make a copy of the clue. I would like to return the painting as soon as possible. Before the sun goes down if I can. But I'm afraid I have a business meeting I must attend. I'll see you out." Her surprised expression was rather satisfying.

Walking her to the carriage, he felt a twinge of regret. How could she do this to him? Did she not understand that her choosing Lord Callingswell over him made him angry? That if word reached him that the pompous viscount had upset her in any way, Gideon would hurt him?

"When shall I see you again?" she asked as Miss Page stepped into the carriage. "Or shall I ever?"

Her question was unexpected. Was it possible she knew his thoughts? No, how could she? No one could hear the thoughts of others. Still, her blue eyes called to him, and he wanted nothing more than to pull her into his arms.

But as tempting as it was to see her again, he knew he could not. He was already far too intrigued by her. Her beauty coupled by her sharp mind made him easy prey for her. Master thieves did not use their skills to create romance. Not unless they could use it to get what they wanted. He could not stand it if he turned around to find his treasure missing and the woman whose company he so enjoyed gone, too.

"I'll be busy for the foreseeable future, I'm afraid," he said, despite knowing he was sending her into the arms of the viscount. "I cannot make any promises as to when I'll have the time."

"And what of the treasure? Will you need any further help in finding it?"

There it was. Miss Sagewick was already plotting how to steal what was rightfully his. Perhaps that was the true reason she smiled at him as she did at this moment, a smile that made his heart race. Then again, the pout she wore begged him to kiss her. Could it be that she was as enamored with him as he was with her?

You are a fool, Hainsley! he thought. She probably had more wealth earned from her thievery than both Gideon and the viscount combined!

"I'm sure I will find it one day," he said with a nervous chuckle. "Unfortunately, hunting for treasures is more a pastime than honest work, but you'll be the first to know when I've found it. You have been of great help, and for that, I'm eternally grateful. But for now, I must focus my time on more important matters."

"Yes, of course." Was her tone dark? "Then I'll await a card from you."

Once the carriage was out of sight, Gideon hurried back to the drawing room. Honoring his father's wishes was in his grasp. Would there be great wealth as was told by the Hainsleys before him?

Yet there was no joy in those thoughts as before. His mind went to Miss Sagewick. Was he treating her too harshly? Was he being too careful? Why was admitting what he felt for her so difficult?

With a sigh, he sat down on one of the leather chairs, doubting his decision to never see her again.

Chapter Thirteen

Catharina had spent hours pacing her bedroom upon her return to Ivywood Manor, rage boiling inside her. And she was no less angry the following morning. She was no naive girl. Lord Hainsley had acted like a spoiled child with his outright lies to her!

Like most ladies of proper upbringing, she had been schooled in both French and Latin, which made reading the words in the painting easy. The only reason she had asked him to translate the text was to keep from embarrassing him, in case he had not learned the language. Men's pride could be as fragile as rice paper, after all.

But he had thrown her act of kindness back in her face!

To make matters worse, he had said the riddle was too complicated to explain. Too complicated for whom? Him or her? Did he believe that she was too feebleminded to understand? Not after she had worked out the first riddle.

Then he had lied to her again by saying he had a business meeting. Why invite her to luncheon only to throw her out of the house before they had finished their meal?

What Catharina needed was someone in whom she could confide. And who better than Lena? After swearing her companion to secrecy, she revealed everything that had happened. Including the part she played in stealing the painting.

"You must understand," Catharina insisted, "I know stealing is wrong, but I believed it was for a good cause. Please, don't think poorly of me."

Lena stood with her hands clasped in front of her. "I could never think poorly of you, miss."

Catharina gave a relieved sigh. "Thank you. And please, do not tell Lady Whitmore." She chuckled. "No, of course you would not, for then it would not be a secret."

Lena's face took on a solemn look as she sat on the bed, and she patted the space beside her.

"Lena?" Catharina asked, sitting. "Have I upset you in some way?"

"It's not that, miss," Lena said. "But I need you to understand something. What you say is true. Theft is wrong. But given the circumstances, I understand why you helped steal the painting. That is the only reason I'll not inform her ladyship about what you've done." Then her chaperone smiled. "Plus, how fun would it be to be a part of finding a great treasure? If I tell Lady Whitmore, she may forbid us from hunting. And that would be no fun at all."

Catharina sighed in relief. "I'm so pleased."

"But there is one more thing," Lena said. "Though I agree to look the other way when needed, there are certain instances when I cannot. You are a lady and are to remain one at all times. I don't think I need to elaborate on what I mean. Remain virtuous, and I shall help you in this endeavor. But betray that trust, and I will be forced to tell her ladyship immediately."

Oh, yes, Catharina understood exactly what Lena meant. Lord Hainsley would have to control his masculine urges, and Catharina would have to resist them. "I agree."

She stood and began to pace again. "What I cannot understand is why Lord Hainsley would lie to me. And why won't he allow me to continue helping him? It makes no sense."

She stopped her pacing and blew out a heavy breath. The earl was proving to be more complicated than any riddle. Did he not see how attracted to him she was? She had batted her eyelashes like the heroines in the best romantic novels. Her smiles had been flirtatious. She had even allowed the rogue to kiss her!

And his reaction to having Lord Callingswell call on her had been unexpected. Rather than make him jealous, he had been unconcerned. And that had hurt worse, for now she understood that he had used her. How can he believe that she would allow him to kiss her only to fling her aside afterward? She had been so certain that he shared her admiration, which only made her current problem all the more frustrating.

"It's my opinion, miss," Lena said, "that most men are stubborn. Perhaps they all are. I have no idea why, but men have far too much pride. They will never admit when they need a woman's help. That could be why he seemed so dismissive of you."

Catharina considered Lena's words. How many polite conversations had she shared with gentlemen who scoffed at her thoughts on one subject or another, especially when she believed their points to be wrong? Most laughed or said outright that she was mistaken.

"Yes, that makes sense. I would even wager that he cannot solve the next riddle without me. I should return to his house right now and inform him that he needs my help. Berate the pride right out of him. What do you think?"

Lena chuckled politely. "From what you've told me, miss, and judging by what I've seen, perhaps it would be best not to. If he's unable to solve the problem, he'll come and ask for your help again. Would you not prefer that instead?"

Catharina grinned. She was right. Let Lord Hainsley come and beg for her aid. "Thank you for your sage advice. And more so for your confidentiality."

Lena smiled. "You're most welcome. Though I must ask. Are you sure you wish to pursue a romantic entanglement with him?"

Lord Hainsley might be stubborn, but Catharina found his company delightful. Plus, the current adventure made turning away difficult. She had not had this much fun for as long as she could remember!

"I could use some fresh air," Catharina said. "Let's take a stroll through the gardens."

As they reached the bottom of the stairs, Lady Whitmore greeted them in the foyer. And she was not alone.

"Miss Sagewick," Lord Callingswell said with a deep bow. "We were just speaking about you."

Her heart leapt to her throat. Did he suspect her of stealing the painting? Had Lord Hainsley not returned the artwork as he promised he would?

No, of course he did not, she thought. He was likely off in search of the next clue and had either forgotten or did not care.

"About me?" she asked, offering him a smile in hopes of currying his favor. "I trust it was good." She could not have him accusing her of thievery, not after she had worked so hard to clear her name. Even if she was guilty of such a crime.

Oh, why had she allowed Lord Hainsley to talk her into this asinine venture?

The countess gave her a sad shake of her head. "Let's go to the parlor. Lena, please ask Hornsby to have a tea tray brought up and then leave us. I'm sure you have something to keep you occupied until we're done."

So, the viscount had pieced together what had happened after all. How could he not? After all, he had caught her in the library alone with the painting. And with the window open. Did he also suspect she had an accomplice outside? Most likely.

She sighed. Now she would be exiled from Lady Whitmore's home and her name would be further ruined. Not only would her father be irate, but he would likely sell her off to the highest bidder!

Catharina sat on the couch beside the countess, as Lord Callingswell sat across from them in one of the leather armchairs.

"Well," Lady Whitmore said with an air of reluctance, "perhaps you should be the one to tell her, Lord Callingswell."

The viscount nodded. "Yes, that would be best." He sat forward in his seat. "Miss Sagewick, last week at my party, a painting was taken from the library of my home."

"How terrible!" Catharina gasped, covering her mouth in hopes of showing convincing surprise.

"Yes, well, be that as it may..." He cleared his throat. "I do not like accusing someone without absolute proof."

All the air seemed to leave the room. At least he had the decency to accuse her to her face. And he had not yet called the magistrates. But he would eventually. She would hang for sure!

"I believe the thief was Lord Hainsley."

"L-Lord Hainsley?" she asked, feeling a mixture of relief and discomfort. "But he seemed like such a nice man."

Lord Callingswell shook his head. "He attempted to steal it in the past, but I managed to catch him before he could get away. I knew I should have done something about it then, but I made the mistake of showing him mercy. Sadly, he's desperate for attention. Or perhaps stealing is a favorite pastime of his. Either way, I'm certain he's the culprit."

"And what has this to do with me, my lord?" Catharina asked, finding it difficult to swallow.

"Did you happen to see Hainsley at the party?"

Catharina opened her eyes wide. "At the party, my lord? Why... why I don't know how I could have."

"Hmm. It's just that I cannot seem to fathom how he gained entrance into my home."

"I see." Catharina wanted nothing more than to leap from her seat and run as far away as possible. Yet that not being an option, she forced her muddled brain to come up with a plan to get her out of this situation. She had to give him some sort of answer, but she would not lie. Not outright. "I was with Lady Whitmore most of the evening, my lord, and not once did I see him in the ballroom." There, that was the truth. "If you would like, I can ask him if he did it."

The viscount smiled. "There is no need. I confronted him yesterday, and although he denied it, the painting miraculously appeared on my doorstep this morning."

"That is good news," Catharina said. "Perhaps he wasn't the culprit after all."

Lord Callingswell sighed. "Unfortunately for him, one of my servants witnessed him returning it." Lady Whitmore murmured her disapproval, but the viscount did not seem to notice. "I cannot understand why that painting is so important to him. It's been in my family since I was a boy. Still, I should be grateful that it was returned."

As frustrated as Catharina was with Lord Hainsley, she also did not want him to get into any trouble. Drawing in a deep breath, she let it out slowly and said, "I'm pleased you have your painting back, my lord. You were a gracious host. Perhaps that was why it was returned. The person who took it must have regretted doing so, or he would have kept it."

"You are a kind lady, Miss Sagewick," the viscount said. "And your ability to see the good in such a terrible situation is commendable." He crossed an ankle over the opposite knee. "Now that we have that sordid business out of the way, I must admit that I have another motive for calling on you today. We spoke previously of an outing together. Does that still interest you? But be forewarned, I shan't take no for an answer. Not after all I've endured with my painting."

Although she suspected that accepting the invitation for this outing would be a betrayal to Lord Hainsley, she also wished to ease the guilt that filled her. A sense of melancholy surrounded the viscount, and she was partly responsible for it. He might have been stubborn by refusing to adhere to his father's promise to return the painting, but that was not a good reason to hurt him.

Yet even though her reasoning was valid, was it not still betrayal?

Betrayal? she thought wryly. Lord Hainsley had made it clear it mattered not one whit if the viscount called on her. Then an idea occurred to her, one that would have been seen as underhanded but well worth the risk. Perhaps if he learned of their outing, Lord Hainsley would make his intentions with her clearer.

"Yes, I would like that very much," she replied.

Lord Callingswell stood. "Excellent. I'll come by to collect you at ten on Monday. There is a lovely brook on my estate that I believe you will appreciate."

Once the viscount was gone, Catharina let out a sigh of relief.

"So," Lady Whitmore said with an arched eyebrow, "do you think Lord Hainsley took the painting? Given that he was the one who returned it."

"At least it was returned to its rightful owner," Catharina replied, skirting the question. "That is the best thing to come out of the situation."

The countess smiled. "The Hainsleys and the Callingswells have been rivals for a long time now. Their fathers were very close at one point. I do hope they find a way to bridge the gap between them."

Lady Whitmore was right. This dispute between them had to come to an end. Perhaps during her outing with Lord Callingswell on Monday, she could begin construction on that much-needed bridge.

Chapter Fourteen

For nearly a week, Gideon struggled to work out the clue from the second painting to no avail. St. Paul's Cathedral was an architectural marvel. It had burned down twice, but the English were never ones to give up hope. In 1668, the great architect, Sir Christopher Wren, was commissioned to rebuild the cathedral—one among 50 great churches that had been destroyed in the Great Fire of 1666. Now, St. Paul's touted twin towers and a domed roof, making it far grander than its predecessors.

From his understanding, The Right Reverend Henry Compton, Bishop of London at the time, had preached the first sermon when the building reopened, based on the text of Psalm 122: "I was glad when they said unto me: Let us go into the house of the Lord."

Although Gideon had never experienced it, it was said that a man could stand inside the dome, whisper on one side, and his voice would carry around to a listener on the other side as if the pair were standing next to one another. He would one day see if that was true. But now was not the time.

He had visited the cathedral several times, but the place was so large that he had no idea where to begin. He had deciphered one part of the clue, which spoke of the winter sun. It was clear that the light from it would shine upon either the location of the next clue or another step. He even went so far as to take a small hand mirror with him, hoping to catch the rays of the sun so they could point in the right direction. He had tried moving around the dome, reflecting the light in attempts to see if it shone on anything worth inspecting. Yet, all he accomplished was making a man in the nave below shield his eyes from the reflective light.

Frustrated, Gideon reread the clue.

Every winter day at noon,
At St. Paul's dome,
Eight archers gather,
At the place they call home.
The sun shows the doubter,
The light of the one most loved
And in return he shall show you
The path which is true

Gideon crumpled the piece of parchment where he had translated the clue and shoved it into his pocket. "This is madness!" he growled. He should have been able to work this out by now. The treasure was so close that he could almost touch it.

Gideon paused. The clue spoke of "the doubter." He had no doubts that the treasure was real. Was belief in its existence not enough?

And what about "the one most loved?" Then he paused as a thought came to him. Taking out the paper once more, he smoothed it out and reread the inscription.

Every winter day at noon,
At St. Paul's dome,
Eight archers gather,
At the place they call home.
The sun shows the doubter,

The light of the one most loved
And in return he shall show you
The path which is true

Then it occurred to him. It was only the start of summer, but the clue indicated he needed the winter sun. But where did it arrive at noon? He knew a retired professor who spent his nights observing stars and such, and Gideon would call on him.

The fact remained that "the doubter" and "the one most loved" meant two people. Did that mean he would also need two people to figure out the clue? One each with his or her own mirror? But one could not ask a passing stranger to help. And the idea of bringing his butler, Collins, was ludicrous at best.

This left Gideon with only one option. He had to ask Miss Sagewick to aid him once again. After all, she had been more than willing to help him before. Furthermore, she was already aware of his quest, so he would not need to waste time explaining.

He sighed. As much as he hated to admit it, he had missed her company. No, he longed for it. Pushing the lovely woman from his thoughts had been an impossibility, no matter how he tried. From the way her blue eyes sparkled to their shared banter, he found her enthralling. Yet could she be trusted?

His father had once caught a servant stealing a silver spoon. They had later learned that the man had stolen from his previous employers as well. How they had never learned of Charles's previous pilfering, Gideon never knew, but he was dismissed the very day he was caught. And he was fortunate. The idea of seeing a man hanged for a petty crime did not sit well with his father, so he had not called the magistrates. But neither did he write Charles a letter of reference. Instead, Gideon's father had threatened to give testimony if the footman was caught again. Charles had promised to go on the straight and narrow, and they never heard from him again.

"Once a thief, always a thief," his father had said.

But could he apply that same logic to Miss Sagewick as well?

Closing his eyes, he considered the choices he'd made as of late.

Had Lady Whitmore not said that Miss Sagewick had put her ways behind her? And was it not Gideon who asked her to steal for him?

He opened his eyes again. There was one thing he understood. Not only had he judged her for her past, but he had refused to extend the very mercy he coveted for himself. He had used her for her skills as a master thief and then silently judged her for it.

Although Gideon would never admit it to a passing stranger—or to a friend, for that matter—Miss Sagewick was right. His own pride had blinded him. But no more. He would extend her his trust, and somehow, he knew, she would not betray it. That is, if she accepted his invitation.

Yet she would not approach him first, which meant it was up to him to apologize to her first and pray she would accept it.

Nearly three hundred steps led from the dome to the ground level. Once there, Gideon moved through the nave and out the front door. Taking a moment to reflect, he considered Lord Callingswell's call two days earlier. The viscount had leveled accusations at Gideon, and he was not wrong. Gideon *had* taken the painting. But he had also sneaked it back into Lord Callingswell's home, praying that it would be enough to keep the viscount from sending the magistrates after him. Granted, Gideon could claim Privilege of Peerage, but that did not mean he did not feel guilty for his crime.

"Lord Hainsley?"

Gideon turned and was surprised to find Lady Madeline approaching.

"Why, it is you," she said, smiling brightly. The hem of a pale-yellow dress peeked out from beneath her green pelisse, and strands of dark hair flitted across her face just under the brim of her green and yellow hat. In her arms was a Bible, which she pressed against her generous bosom. "What a wonderful surprise running into you here."

Gideon bowed. "Lady Madeline, what are you doing here?"

She let out a melancholy sigh. "I've realized as of late that I should spend some time in careful contemplation. I'm sure you've heard the unsavory rumors that are being spread about me."

"Oh?" A twinge of guilt tugged at Gideon. He had assumed those rumors to be true, but apparently, he was wrong.

"Indeed. Mother says I should ignore them, but Father is quite upset, and rightfully so. I've spent every night this past week weeping in my bed. But here, I find peace. And you? What brings you to this place of sanctuary?"

The guilt turned to shame. He was no better than his peers, misjudging this fine lady as he did. Even going so far as to avoid calling on her because of the rumors he had heard about her.

"Like you, I'm searching for answers. I believe I'm very close."

Was her smile a tad too wide? No, of course not. He was still allowing the rumors of her to cloud his judgment, and that was unfair of him. Had he not already promised to stop judging her? Perhaps he was the one who could not keep his promises.

"Tell me, are the pews set out today?" she asked.

Gideon thought back to the nave and nodded. "They are."

She gave a relieved sigh. "Good. I would like to pray before I study, and sitting is preferable to standing. The best of luck on your endeavors, my lord." She turned to the mousy maid who stood behind her. "Come along, Emma. Father insists that I return home within the hour."

With words of farewell, Gideon returned to the carriage, which was parked just down the street. Lobbs opened the door, and Gideon gave him instructions to take him to Lady Whitmore's house.

The traffic was light, and he arrived at Ivywood Manor in no time. He rang the bell and was surprised when Lady Whitmore herself answered the door. Then again, she could be unconventional at times.

"Why, Lord Hainsley," she exclaimed. "What a wonderful surprise. Do come in."

"Forgive me for coming unannounced, but I would like to see Miss Sagewick. It's a rather urgent matter."

Lady Whitmore closed the door. "You should know by now that you're always welcome to drop by whenever you would like. As for Miss Sagewick, she's out for the day. Lord Callingswell invited her on an outing of some sort."

A twinge of jealousy tickled the back of his mind. No, not a tickle, an entire wave. And with it came frustration. Not because of the outing but rather for his stubbornness pushing her into Lord Callingswell's company. It was a mistake he would never repeat.

"You seem distressed," Lady Whitmore said. "Come, let us have some tea. Hornsby, have a tray sent to the drawing room."

Gideon had not noticed the arrival of the butler, and he allowed the man to take his coat and hat.

"Please, sit," the countess said. Once they were seated, she continued, "We've been friends for a very long time, you and me. Now, tell me what is troubling you. Is it Miss Sagewick and her outing with Lord Callingswell? Would you prefer it if she were in your company rather than his?"

His mind screamed, "Yes!" but he could not admit this truth to Lady Whitmore. Yet, nor could he lie to a friend. Especially when she was a countess.

"I enjoy Miss Sagewick's company, yes. But what concerns me is any time she spends with that man. After all, his reputation is less than stellar. Especially when it comes to women."

The butler returned, poured the tea, and left the room before Lady Whitmore responded. "Miss Sagewick is much stronger and more intelligent than you give her credit for." Gideon went to argue that he had not meant to imply such a thing, but the countess raised a hand to forestall him. "I know you don't think of her as feeble, either in body or mind, but I am certain she will not succumb to any of his charms."

"How can you be so sure?" Gideon asked.

"Because she has her sights set on another gentleman." She raised her teacup, pausing before taking a sip to add, "One who mysteriously disappeared for nearly a week."

Gideon let out a frustrated sigh. Once again, he could not argue. He had not considered that pushing away Miss Sagewick would send her into the arms of another man. But he was a fool. What had he expected to happen?

"I have never been able to keep anything from you," he said. "I do have an interest in her." That was true. He needed her help with the clue at St. Paul's Cathedral. It had nothing to do with any romantic entanglement the countess implied. "But with her past, I have found it difficult to trust her. Now, however, I see what a mistake that was. Do we not all deserve a second chance?" He sighed. "Forgive me. I don't mean to speak ill of your friend. Nor burden you with my troubles."

Lady Whitmore smiled. "I cannot tell you who you can or cannot trust. What I can tell you is that you are right. Everyone deserves a second chance. Even a professed thief."

Gideon nodded. "Miss Sagewick has told me more than once that I'm stubborn. At first, I thought she was wrong, but now I see how right she was. I've developed a great interest in her, but my recent behavior has me worrying that she will refuse to ever speak to me again."

As always, Lady Whitmore's smile made him feel at ease. "I cannot promise anything save this. Speak from your heart. By doing so, I believe the listener can look past any loutish behavior you may have displayed."

As their conversation turned to other matters, Gideon considered the countess's words. He would admit his faults and hope that Miss Sagewick would forgive him. It really was all he could do.

But as the minutes ticked by, a sense of discomfort filled him. What if she refused to listen? Or simply told him to leave and never return? The idea of not being with her bothered him greatly. He had suffered a week without her company, and the idea of experiencing that for a lifetime brought about a loneliness like none he had ever known.

Chapter Fifteen

Lord Callingswell had no doubt that Lord Hainsley had stolen the painting. He also was certain that Miss Sagewick had abetted him. Clearly, she had slipped the artwork, frame and all, out the library window the night of the party. And although the thievery irritated him, he was much more angered that he had not been able to uncover the clue before that saddle-goose did.

He had sent a servant to follow Lord Hainsley. The servant had returned to say that the earl had visited St. Paul's Cathedral every day over the past week. Now, that was an interesting turn of events. What had Lord Hainsley learned in that painting that Alister had not?

Alister had spent a small fortune hiring educated men to study the painting and research the various knights it depicted, but none of what they learned pointed to St. Paul's Cathedral. He had even gone so far as to hire a witch to perform a spell over the painting, but it elicited nothing. Not that he had expected it to, but the waiting was becoming taxing.

And now, having Lord Hainsley do all the work was working for Alister far better than he could have imagined. Let the fool use his resources to decipher the clues. He, Alister, would reap the benefits. And if no treasure came from it, he would not have lost anything.

What troubled him was how Lord Hainsley had arrived at his conclusion. He had spent countless hours staring at the blasted painting, had even removed it from its frame to see if anything was hidden behind the backing, but he had come up empty-handed.

Well, how the earl came to his conclusions did not matter at the moment. For now, Alister's attention was focused on the ravishing beauty beside him.

Miss Sagewick had arrived an hour earlier, her companion with her to act as her chaperone. And what a bothersome woman this Miss Page was! She kept so close to him and Miss Sagewick that they could not whisper without her overhearing.

"The brook is lovely, my lord," Miss Sagewick said in that silky voice he had come to appreciate. "The sound of the water flowing over the rocks is calming."

Alister smiled. The brook was more an annoyance to him than something enjoyable. As vital as the water was to the tenant farms that surrounded this illustrious patch of land, Alister preferred uniformity and order. Yet the brook cut through an otherwise unmarred field in the middle of his estate, which invited the growth of unwanted trees and bushes.

However, he had learned long ago that others found the brook enchanting, especially the young ladies he pursued, thus he had not had it rerouted. Instead, he used it to his advantage. Just as he did everything else he encountered in his life. He had always been very good at taking the unpleasant and using it to his advantage. Or in Miss Sagewick's case, the pleasant.

Today she was as stunning as ever. She wore a pale-green walking dress and dark-green pelisse jacket. Despite her large hat with its multitude of green feathers and yellow daisies, he wondered what it would be like to run his hand through her dark hair. Of course, he would do far more given the chance. Which, if he earned her trust, he just might be able to do.

He leaned over and picked a blue violet. "It matches your eyes," he said, offering her the flower.

Miss Sagewick put the flower to her nose and inhaled deeply. "Thank you, my lord. It's lovely."

"Not as lovely as you," he said, reveling in her blush. "I do hope I've been able to charm you more than Lord Hainsley. Did you not say he's boring?"

Frustration made his temples throb. He had hoped the comment would encourage her to speak more. Thus far, she had said little. What he wanted was to catch a glimpse of that spark he had seen from her at the party last week. But she might have been made of wet wood. Lovely wet wood, certainly, but wet wood, nonetheless.

Did she have feelings for Lord Hainsley? If so, he had to guard his words. Any disapproving remarks might have her become as silent as a monk.

Then an idea came to mind. Alister, like any other member of the aristocracy, was privy to gossip. Had he not heard that Miss Sagewick had been caught stealing from a house party several months ago? Perhaps he could use that information to his advantage.

He offered her his arm, and they continued their stroll. "You know, having my painting stolen reminds me of a time when one of our servants, a stable hand if I recall correctly, was caught stealing a swatch of leather left out by the stable manager. How my father handled that situation changed my way of thinking about thieves."

Miss Sagewick's grip tightened slightly on his arm. "What did your father do? Did he terminate the man's employment? Or did he call the magistrates and have him hanged?"

Her shiver made Alister smile. His father would have personally beheaded any man who dared to steal from him. But he could not say that to Miss Sagewick, so, instead, he lied.

"Father told the man that if he confessed, he would be lenient with him. So, he did. Father gave him a warning to never steal from him—or anyone—again. You see, people make mistakes, Miss Sagewick, and deserve a second chance."

"And the stable hand? Did he steal again?"

Alister shook his head. "No, he went on to become a model citizen. He now has a position in the King's personal stables. So, you see, sometimes showing mercy allows others to reach their full potential."

Miss Sagewick dropped her gaze. "I would like to show Lord

Hainsley mercy. But first, he must confide in me. I'm not sure he is willing to do that. But if he did, we could become friends again."

"Do you believe he would confess?" Alister asked, bracing himself for her confession of stealing not only Lady Langley's pearls, but of his painting as well. But to his chagrin, she simply drew in a deep breath and smiled.

"I cannot say, my lord. The truth is, just because he returned the painting does not mean he stole it. Until he confesses, all I can do is be happy that your property has been returned to you."

Any doubts that Miss Sagewick had any romantic notions in Alister dissipated. Her parted lips and glowing cheeks gave away what she felt for Lord Hainsley.

So, her flirting with him the night of the party had been nothing but a ruse. The fact that he had fallen for it only made her deception worse. He would not be surprised if the two had not been working together. Now he had two people who he would see pay for humiliating him. Lord Hainsley would lose everything, and Miss Sagewick would become his to use as he saw fit. Not as a wife, of course. He would never marry a woman who was willing to steal. But he did not have to marry her to take her to his bed.

But to have that happen, he had to keep her close.

"I fear the hour is growing late, my lord," Miss Sagewick said, interrupting his thoughts. "I really should be going."

"Yes, of course," Alister replied with a smile.

They said little on their return walk to the house, and it was not long before he was helping Miss Sagewick into her carriage.

"Perhaps we can see each other again," he said.

"Of course. Please send a card." Her curtsy was polite enough, but there was also a curtness to it Alister did not like.

Once inside the house, Alister slammed a fist against the wall, ignoring the pain that radiated up his arm. Retreating to the parlor, he poured himself a hefty measure of brandy. That treasure belonged to the Callingswell family, not the pathetic Hainsleys. A family who, by all accounts, had been teetering on the edge of bankruptcy for years. And now the earl was one step closer to what belonged to Alister!

Something more raised Alister's ire. Miss Sagewick. He had yet to meet a woman he could not seduce, yet she seemed immune to his charms. Which confused him no end. Any sensible woman would find him attractive. Not only had many ladies declared him the most eligible—and the handsomest—bachelor in all of England, but he was also wealthy. Wealthy enough to buy anything a lady could want. Was that not what they all hoped for in life?

He poured himself another glass of brandy and nearly jumped when he heard a soft voice behind him.

"Good afternoon, my lord," Lady Madeline said from the doorway.

Where was that blasted oaf of a butler? But he pushed down the anger and forced a smile to his lips.

"How lovely to see you again," he said, kissing her hand. She was a handsome lady with deep-brown hair and eyes. The previous week, he had been given the privilege of being her first lover. And twice since then. He would likely have her again within the hour.

"I have news for you," she said in silky tones.

Alister poured her a glass of red wine. "Tell me everything. Leave out nothing."

She took a sip of the wine and went to the gold and blue velour couch to sit. He had not invited her to do so, but he made no mention of her impropriety. She was not there for propriety's sake. "I ran into Lord Hainsley. He was at St. Paul's Cathedral, just as you indicated. He was up in the dome, carrying a hand mirror that he used to deflect the sun's rays coming in from one of the upper windows. When he descended the stairs, I hurried outside, so he would not see that I was watching him. He was discontented, I'm sure of it. And after careful questioning, I learned that he still had yet to find whatever it was he was searching for."

Impressed, Alister could not help but smile. Lady Madeline was proving herself as competent at spying as she was in his bed. Perhaps he would keep her around. At least for the time being.

"You've done well, my dear," he said, refilling her glass. "Soon, I'll have my family's treasure returned to me."

"And then we shall marry?" Her look of innocence stirred him.

He touched her cheek with the back of his hand. "We shall have a wedding that will rival only that of the King himself. Think of all the rings that will grace your fingers. The many estates to visit. You can shop to your heart's content. You will have the life you deserve."

Of course, Alister had no intention of marrying her. What gentleman in his right mind would have as his wife a woman so easily coaxed into a man's bed?

"I will need your help in the coming days," he continued. "Are you willing to do as I request?"

Her nod was immediate. "Mother is away, and Father is so occupied with business that he'll not notice my daily activities."

The door opened, and his butler entered. "My lord, the maid you summoned."

"Send her in."

A young girl of eighteen came into the room, her uniform and mob cap impeccable. He recalled her name only because he had invited her into his bedchamber a fortnight ago. Bits of her blonde hair peeked from the cap, but he recalled all too well how silky it felt as he ran his fingers through it.

"Ah, Carrie," he said, smiling broadly as she bobbed a curtsy, "thank you for coming. I need your help."

"Yes, milord," she said, her eyes bright. She was smitten with him and thus would do anything he requested of her. Of that, he was certain.

"There is a man who has risen against me. I would like you to go to him and give him a tale of woe…" For several minutes, Alister explained his well-thought-out plan to the maid.

When he was finished, she readily agreed. Just as he had expected.

"You are to report everything you see or hear to either me or Lady Madeline. No matter how insignificant you believe it is. Can you do that?"

Her nod was eager. "Yes, of course, milord."

He positioned himself closer and lowered his voice. "Good. And I'll see you rewarded well for your troubles. Now, go."

Of course, her reward would be another night in his bed. If what she told him warranted it, he might even give her a glass of the wine he reserved for his parties. Not his best, of course, but better than the cheap swill to which the servants were accustomed.

"Why not simply steal the clue from Lord Hainsley yourself, my lord?" Lady Madeline asked. "You're far cleverer than he is and would be able to puzzle it out far quicker."

Alister smiled and offered a hand to help Lady Madeline stand. She, like all women, was a simple creature who did not understand the art of warfare. For this was a war. And the treasure was the spoils.

He drew her close and wrapped an arm around her waist. "My dear Madeline, would my time not be better spent with other more... important pastimes? We'll let Hainsley do all the work, and once he's led me to the treasure, I will steal it from him. Just like he did to me."

Chapter Sixteen

Not for the first time, Catharina swore she would have nothing more to do with Lord Callingswell. He had been nothing but an insufferable flirt both times she was with him. At first, she suspected he was simply a rogue any lady in her right mind would see coming from a mile away. And perhaps their encounter at his party had been just that.

Now, however, she was certain his attentiveness came from the fact that he believed she had something to do with his painting being stolen. Granted, his suspicions were correct, but did he truly believe her so dim-witted as to admit the part she played in that crime? She liked her neck as it was now. Unbroken. She had no reason to believe he would not see her hanged the moment she admitted guilt. Nor would she implicate Lord Hainsley.

"That story Lord Callingswell told was nothing but rubbish," she told Lena, who sat across from her in the carriage. "It was nothing more than a manipulative tool to get me to confess to stealing that painting, but I saw through his trickery as easily as the lace on my pelisse. My friend, Lady Olivia, would have been appalled by such terrible storytelling."

Her chaperone nodded. "I couldn't agree more. It appears he's full of rubbish himself." This made them both laugh.

The carriage slowed for a turn before picking up speed again. Catharina was determined to never see the viscount again, which made her think of Lord Hainsley. Should she write to him? Or would it be best to take Lena's advice and wait for him to call?

When they arrived at Ivywood Manor, Catharina was surprised to find Lord Hainsley in the drawing room with Lady Whitmore. What could he be doing there? Was Lena correct, that he would come asking for her help again? Although she wanted to give him a stern lecture about using her, deep down, she knew the truth.

Whatever request he made, she would oblige. But not before the oaf apologized.

Her heartbeat quickened as he stood. He was as handsome as ever, and she found herself imagining what it would be like to untie his white cravat and unbutton that dark coat...

Lady Whitmore also stood. "I'll see Hornsby brings a tea tray," she said with a small smile playing on her lips. "Lord Hainsley, it has been a pleasure talking with you again, as always. Until next time." Her skirts swished around her ankles as she left the room.

Always the discreet and accommodating chaperone, Lena took a seat on one of the benches in front of a window and opened a book on her lap.

"And what brings you here, my lord?" Catharina asked the earl as she sat in the place Lady Whitmore had just vacated.

He cleared his throat before replying, "I heard you were with Lord Callingswell. Judging by the clock, I take it that the excursion was... entertaining."

His voice dripped with jealousy. Although Catharina was sure he would deny it if she asked. But she would get him to admit that he wanted her for more than an accomplice.

"Oh, very entertaining, indeed," she said. "But I suspect you did not call to ask about my outing."

Lord Hainsley retook his seat and went to speak, but the butler entered with the expected silver tray and an assortment of tiny pastries. Once he poured, he bowed and exited the room.

Catharina gave the earl an expectant look. "So, your reason for coming to see me, my lord?"

"I came to say... That is, there are times when a man must admit..." He dropped his gaze and sighed heavily.

Catherina's heart went out to him. She put aside her teasing. For now, anyway. "My lord, there is no shame in what you wish to tell me."

"I judged you," he said, "for your past as a master thief. Which is quite incredible seeing as I have done the same."

Catharina nodded. Although she wished to confess that she was no such thing, she feared doing so would hurt their already strained relationship.

That thought caused a start. Relationship? They were friends at best. Yet even friends had to trust one another.

"Therefore," he continued, "I apologize for the way I treated you last week. Though it's hard to admit when I act foolish, in this circumstance, I do confess as much."

Catharina smiled, his words causing her heart to fill with happiness. "I would never steal from you, my lord. And in regard to your apology, I accept."

His smile erased the tension that filled the room. In fact, she found it handsome and could admire it all day.

The butler served the tea, and Catharina directed the conversation to the riddle. She was fascinated about what he had discovered thus far.

"I believe I've solved the St. Paul's Cathedral riddle," he said. "But it will take two people to find the next clue. Therefore, I shall need your help."

Catharina glanced at Lena, who appeared captivated by the novel in her lap. But she knew the chaperone was soaking up every word she and Lord Hainsley were saying. And what did it matter? Catharina had already explained everything she knew up to this point.

"I would be happy to help," Catharina replied before a new thought came to mind. Lord Hainsley had dismissed her as easily as a deer would a marigold plant in the middle of a lettuce patch. He may have apologized, and she did believe him, but there certainly was no issue in making sure it would not happen again. After all, she was not the type to throw herself at any man, no matter how handsome she thought he was. "But I have certain conditions if I'm to agree."

Lord Hainsley tilted his head and frowned. "Conditions? What sort of conditions? If you wish for a portion of the proceeds, I'll gladly share in the spoils."

Catharina smiled. "I have no interest in your treasure, my lord. But I am interested in the adventure that comes with finding it. If I agree to help you with this clue, you must promise to allow me to join you for the remainder of your hunt. Even if the next step only requires one person."

"I would like that," he replied.

"That is not good enough," Catharina said with a mischievous grin. She really could not help herself. "Swear on your good name. After all, I must learn to trust you again."

Lord Hainsley had just taken a sip of his tea and now was hacking into a handkerchief. Quite satisfying.

"You'll make me swear?" he asked once he had regained his breath. "I'm an earl! My word should be good enough."

Catharina pursed her lips. If men could be trusted on their word alone, then why was he here? But to point out such logic would only make him more stubborn than he already was.

"I don't mince my words, my lord. I must know that you'll not discard me as you did before."

Setting his teacup in its saucer, Lord Hainsley furrowed his brow in thought for several moments. Catharina wondered if his pride would get the best of him, and he would simply get up and walk out.

But to her surprise, and pleasure, he sighed. "I swear upon my family name that you may remain by my side for the duration of this hunt." He then smiled. "In fact, I would appreciate your company when it ends."

Catharina's mouth became as dry as a desert at the thought of them being together beyond this grand adventure. Images of him courting her came to mind. Then a wedding, a honeymoon, and enough adventures to fill a dozen books. She, too, would enjoy his company.

"I'll consider it," she said with a grin which he returned. "Now, for my second condition." His jaw dropped open. "There are three, so you may as well prepare yourself now. And stop looking as if you've been defeated at a game of whist."

The corner of his lips twitched, and a tingling ran down her spine. This was the banter she had come to enjoy with him. The kind that would continue for years to come. There was no more questioning it. After his apology today, Lord Hainsley was the perfect match for her. "I know very little about you. Nor do you know much about me. In exchange for my expertise, I expect outings, luncheons, and any other excursion where we are able to learn more about one another."

The earl did not hesitate. "Agreed. I have to admit that I'd like the same. And what will you do about Lord Callingswell?"

Catharina shrugged. "If I'm with you, I cannot be with him now, can I?"

To this, Lord Hainsley threw his head back and laughed. "No, I don't suppose you can. Miss Sagewick, I don't think I've ever encountered a woman with a mind as keen as yours. I look forward to the vast amount of time we will spend together."

The room began to spin, and Catharina thought her head would float into the air. She glanced at Lena, who flashed her a quick smile. So, she approved? That was fortunate, indeed.

She returned her attention to Lord Hainsley. "You've agreed to my first and second terms. Now for the third. And yes, they are my terms. Bruised ego or not, you must accept it."

"It appears I have no choice," he said, grinning from ear to ear. "And what is the third demand?"

A wave of mischievousness washed over Catharina. "You must wait to hear the conditions of third."

His eyebrows rose. "You want me to agree before knowing the condition?"

Rather than answering, she nibbled playfully at her lip.

"Agreed," he blurted out before clearing his throat and saying, "Very well, then. I agree."

Catharina lifted her teacup to her lips. "Now, why don't you tell me more of what you learned concerning the cathedral."

She listened closely as he detailed what he believed the clue meant and how he came to solve the riddle. Taking the parchment, she read over it.

"I do not understand who 'the doubter' is," Lord Hainsley said. "Does it speak of faith?"

Catharina nibbled her bottom lip. Something tugged at her mind. Then, with a smile she said, "It must refer to Thomas. There is a statue of him on the south end of the roof. He was the doubter."

Lord Hainsley clapped his hands together. "And the one most loved is John. That is how he is referred to in the Gospels. His statue is opposite to that of Thomas if I recall correctly."

"Yes!" Catharina gasped. "We are making progress. But what about the winter sun? We are in June. What shall we do about that?"

"I hope to speak to a friend who studies the stars and sun. He can explain to me about the position of the sun, how to account for the differences in where it is today, and where it would be in the winter."

Catharina had to force her heart to calmness. "And what if we still are unable to find the treasure? Or the next clue if that is the case?"

Lord Hainsley shook his head. "My father meant everything to me. I will do whatever it takes to honor his final request. I cannot fail him."

Catharina's heart clenched with sadness. Not for the first time, she could see the true importance of this quest. It was not just about the riches but also about honoring the wish of a dying man. Knowing this, coupled with his apology, made the respect she had for Lord Hainsley all the stronger.

"And I believe you will succeed," she said. "Your father would not have given you this task if he thought you would fail." She set down her teacup. "Was he aware of your adventurous life? Is that why he entrusted such an important task to you rather than leaving it to a hired man?"

The earl gave her a blank stare. "Adventurous life? Oh, yes, my adventurous life. Of course, he knew."

What an odd response. Had he lied to her about his secret life? Then the truth dawned on her. Surprise was a natural reaction to inquiries about a life one wished to keep hidden from others. As Lord Hainsley continued to speak of his father, Catharina began to see a clearer picture of what the previous earl had been like. Stern, yet kind; demanding, yet patient. She suspected they would have gotten along swimmingly.

"My father is very much like yours," she said when he was done. "My mother, however, was the opposite. I never understood what she saw in my father."

"Tell me about her."

Catharina smiled. "She was very clever and was never afraid to speak her mind." A sense of melancholy washed over her. Four years was a long time to miss someone. "After I took Lady Langley's pearls, I knew immediately Mother would be disappointed in me. That bothers me the most about what I did."

Unbidden, a single tear rolled down her cheek. Lord Hainsley was quick to brush it away.

"Though I've never met her," he said, "I suspect she would be proud of who you are regardless of what you've done. All I've seen thus far is a woman determined to do good. Granted, your means may be a bit... unconventional, but you're willing to help someone like me."

Catharina let out a small laugh. All she ever wanted in life was to find a man of adventure. Now she had found him, and he was handsome, to boot. With a smile, she wondered what the next step in their adventure would be.

Chapter Seventeen

Gideon sat at his desk, lounging back in his chair, and staring at nothing in particular. After visiting with his former professor, he had tried to work on his accounts, but his mind refused to remain focused on the entries. Instead, they wandered to the lovely woman who had consumed his thoughts since their first meeting.

For all the choices he had made in life, and the many paths he had taken, asking Miss Sagewick to join him on this quest was among the greatest. Today, he would collect her at Ivywood Manor, and they would go straight to St. Paul's Cathedral to begin the arduous—and, he had to admit, adventurous—search for the next clue.

The sound of a woman sobbing made Gideon hurry from his study to the foyer, where he found Collins berating a young flaxen-haired woman of perhaps eighteen. She had a heart-shaped face and hazel eyes that were now rimmed with red.

"I won't tell you again," Collins was saying to the woman, "Move along!"

"What is this?" Gideon demanded of his butler.

"My apologies, my lord," Collins said, embarrassment etched on his features. "This girl is seeking employment. I was just informing her that we currently have no positions available. I'll see she's gone from your doorstep immediately." He turned a glare on the girl. "And if she does not leave, I'll send for a constable to see that she does."

The girl's eyes went wide, and she dropped into a deep curtsy. "My lord, I can't tell you what an honor it is to meet the son of the gentleman who showed my mother such kindness."

"Your mother?" Gideon asked, frowning. "What do you mean? How did he show her kindness?"

"Many years ago, Mama was..." her cheeks reddened, "Well, she was in the family way, you see. With me. One day, as she was on her way to do the shopping, she collapsed on the side of the road, and your father, the great Earl of Hainsley, stopped to help her. Not only did he help her up, but he also made sure she got home safely by taking her in his carriage. Gentlemen don't do things like that often, my lord. Especially for those of us from the working class. No offense."

Gideon smiled. His father had been a great man with a wonderful heart. He would help anyone he encountered who was in need. Although Gideon had never heard this particular story, he did not doubt it happened. It was too much like many of the other stories he had heard.

"That's why, when his lordship, Lord Callingswell, spoke badly about Lord Hainsley—or rather the former Lord Hainsley—I just had to speak up." She dropped her gaze. "But when I did, he threw me out and told me to never come back. Now... now I'm without a position or a home."

"Lord Callingswell?" Gideon said, his fist clenching of its own accord. "What did he say?" The girl gave him a frightened look, and he lightened his tone. "You've nothing to fear from me."

She shifted on her feet. "Well, you see, he said your father was... was a drunkard. And a womanizer. But above all, he was a coward. I don't believe any of those things myself, my lord. Those kinds of men don't care about women like me or my mother."

Images of wrapping his hands around Lord Callingswell's neck until he no longer breathed came to mind. Perhaps it was for the best that he, Gideon, had been banned from returning to the viscount's house, or he would likely do something he would regret later.

"Mama always said that if you find yourself in dire straits, you can always go to a Hainsley. And that's why I'm here, my lord. I need help."

Gideon had informed Collins and Mrs. Plotts just last week that it would be some time before they could hire any new staff. But what was he to do? Throw this girl, who had defended his father's name, out into the streets? Lord Callingswell would not have given her a letter of reference, not with the circumstances of her dismissal.

"How long were you employed by Lord Callingswell?" Gideon asked.

"Four years, my lord."

Gideon sighed. At least she had experience. "What is your name?"

"Carrie, my lord."

"I'm sure there is something we can find for you to do," Gideon said. "The servants' entrance is down the stairs to the right. Collins, there must be plenty of work to justify taking on a new maid. Introduce her to Mrs. Potts and see that she's situated." He turned back to Carrie. "You have today to get settled, and tomorrow, you'll start work."

The girl's face shone. "Oh, thank you, my lord! Thank you so very much. Mama was right! The Hainsleys are angels on earth!"

The carriage Gideon had requested pulled up in front of the house as soon as the new maid was gone. He pushed aside his rage at Lord Callingswell's harsh words. It would do him no good to be snappish when he met with Miss Sagewick.

He donned a coat belonging to one of the footmen. It should be simple enough to keep anyone from recognizing him once they entered the cathedral. Luckily, he spent little time there, but the disguise would keep anyone from paying him much attention. Then, he collected his purse with the coins he would give to the priest and a satchel that contained two hand mirrors—one he had borrowed from Mrs. Potts—and returned to the waiting carriage.

Soon, he arrived at Ivywood Manor to collect Miss Sagewick. As she sat across from him, her chaperone at her side, Gideon soaked in her beauty. Today, she wore a brown pelisse over a peach-colored dress. Brown and peach trimmed her deep-brimmed bonnet.

Beautiful she might be, yet it was their conversations and playful banter that he enjoyed the most. It could not be denied Miss Sagewick was a unique woman. Although he trusted her more now than before, he continued to keep alert. Just in case the temptation of her old ways overcame her. He could not have her using her charm and wit to steal the treasure from right under his nose. If she managed to refrain from that temptation, he knew their relationship would continue to grow.

Which begged the question, where did they stand now? They would be spending a great deal of time together, but they were not courting. They had kissed, yet they were not lovers. He would have readily agreed to become a suitor, but... Was she willing to set aside her old ways and settle down if they were to marry? And what of this adventurous life she believed he lived? If she learned the truth, would she run away? Surely, she would not want to marry him.

Then a peculiar thought came to him. "Marriage? What am I thinking? It's far too soon to even consider such a commitment."

Immediately, he clamped his mouth shut. Had he actually said those words aloud? And had Miss Sagewick heard them?

Judging by her grin, she had. "Excuse me, my lord, but would you repeat that? I thought you said something about marriage."

Oh, but she was a wicked, wicked lady. And he enjoyed her wit so very much! "Oh, it's nothing. I was just reciting a riddle from my childhood." He waved a dismissive hand. "It's quite silly, really."

Miss Sagewick clasped her hands in her lap and smiled. "Silly? I doubt that. You are an earl and a man. Surely, there is nothing you can do that would be considered ridiculous. Or am I mistaken?"

Oh, yes, she was wicked indeed.

"I cannot argue with you there," he replied, his nose tipped upward. "Men are not silly. Women, however, are another matter altogether. In fact... No, we shan't speak of it."

Gasping in mock demureness, Miss Sagewick covered her mouth with a gloved hand. "Well, I've never been so offended in all my life, my lord! Perhaps Miss Page and I should walk the rest of the way to the cathedral!"

Gideon raised an eyebrow. "Perhaps you should. The exercise will do you good. It can be quite refreshing, really." He added a wink for good measure, which had them both laughing.

They arrived at St. Paul's Cathedral a little after eleven, giving them time to situate themselves. Once the clock struck noon, it would be the perfect time to manipulate the sun's rays from inside the dome. With luck, there would be few people visiting at noon, allowing them the opportunity to move freely through the building.

No sooner had they emerged from the carriage when a familiar voice said his name.

"Why, Lord Hainsley," Lady Madeline said, "how wonderful to see you here again." She wore a yellow wrap over a deep-green walking dress banded with yellow ribbon along the bottom hem that matched the ribbon on her hat.

"Good morning, Lady Madeline," Gideon said, hoping his disappointment did not sound in his voice. "May I introduce you to..." His words trailed off. How should he introduce Miss Sagewick? A friend? A woman he was courting, yet not officially? "My dear friend, Miss Catharina Sagewick. Miss Sagewick, Lady Madeline Johanson." There, that would do. It would honor whatever their relationship was without offering too much information.

Miss Sagewick gave Lady Madeline a polite nod. "It's a pleasure to meet you."

"Likewise." Lady Madeline's nod was also polite, but it seemed more formal. And much less friendly. "Forgive me for being rude, but may I speak with you alone for a moment, my lord? It's rather important."

It was rude. Yet Gideon remembered how he had unfairly judged the lady in the past. He. at least, owed her a few minutes of his time. "I'll only be a moment," he said before following Lady Madeline to a statue of Charles Marquis Cornwallis a few paces away. "What is it?"

Lady Madeline drew in a deep breath. "You must forgive me for being so forthright, my lord. But I have an appointment I must keep, so I'll simply say what I need to say." She glanced past him before continuing. "You see, Lord Callingswell informed me that the rumors that have been circulating about me originated from you. I'm not sure what I could have done, but if I've angered you in some way, please accept my deepest apologies. And I would like to appeal to your good graces—if you possess any—and ask you to please stop."

Gideon stared at her, dumbfounded. He was not the type of man to gossip! Blast that man! He and his family were nothing but trouble.

"I assure you that you've done nothing to anger me. Nor have I said anything unfavorable about you. In fact, I find you an enchanting and admirable lady." Perhaps that was stretching the truth a bit, but he had no reason to speak poorly of her to others.

She dropped her gaze. "Yet, every time I request that you call on me, you do not. Why is that?"

Gideon stopped himself from pinching the bridge of his nose in irritation. It served him right for listening to rumors in the first place. "I have my reasons, but you must understand—"

"My carriage is here, so I must go," she interrupted. "But perhaps you can join me for dinner tomorrow evening. Say seven? That way I will know for sure that we are friends."

How did he get himself into these situations? The last thing he wanted to do was to dine with this lady alone, but if he hoped to clear his name—and his conscience—what harm could one little dinner do?

"I'm unsure if I'm available tomorrow, but I will send a card."

Lady Madeline's smile was one of triumph, and it unsettled Gideon. "Then I shall wait with bated breath, my lord." With a quick curtsy, she turned and hurried away.

Gideon sighed and turned to join Miss Sagewick.

But she was gone.

Frantically, he looked around him, but she was not there. Where had she gone? He hurried into the cathedral and found her sitting in the back row of pews, her chaperone behind her.

"My sincerest apologies," Gideon whispered breathlessly as he hurried toward her. "I did not mean to be so long."

Miss Sagewick sat with a stiff back and a jutted chin, looking straight ahead. Had she heard him?

Gideon raised his voice slightly. "I'm truly sorry, Miss—"

"I heard you," she snapped. "And there is no need to apologize. I understand your kind far better than you give me credit for."

"My kind?" Gideon asked. "And what kind is that?"

"Men who cavort with any willing hussy who comes their way. I suppose I should thank you for having the decency to not speak of your intentions in my presence."

Gideon shook his head. How could such a perfectly good day have gone so awry? Well, there was only one solution. He had to tell her the truth.

Therefore, he took her hand in his, but she tried to pull it away.

"Please, let go," she said in a harsh whisper as she turned toward him.

"No. I must explain what happened."

She narrowed those lovely blue eyes at him. "If you do not release me this instant, I may have no other recourse than to slap you. And what would happen to your precious treasure if you were banned from ever returning here?"

He refused to be bested. "Hear me out, please. I promise what I have to say will make you change your mind about me."

She nodded, albeit reluctantly, and he explained the conversation he and Lady Madeline had shared. "And although she has been pursuing me like a cat after a mouse, I'm not attracted to her in the least."

Miss Sagewick chuckled. "I highly doubt that. Few men would find her unattractive."

Gideon sighed. "I did not say she was homely, but I have no interest in her—romantically or otherwise. I only wish to be honest with you, which is why I agreed to only share one dinner with her." The moment the words left his lips, he knew he had said too much. Even one evening with Lady Madeline could be more than Miss Sagewick liked.

Rather than rant and rave like some women might, a small smile played on her lips. "I don't know who the bigger fool is. You for telling me of your plans to dine with another woman, or me for trusting you enough to allow it to happen."

Gideon could not help but laugh. "Allow?"

She clicked her tongue. "Oh, you know very well what I mean. But I understand why you agreed."

With a relieved sigh, he gave her hand a gentle squeeze. "Thank you. And once again, there is no need to worry. I assure you that my intentions with her are pure."

A small laugh escaped her lips as she rose from the pew. Then she leaned over him. Surely, she was not considering kissing him right there in the middle of a church!

"And one more thing, my lord," she whispered so quietly that he had to strain to hear her. "I'm not the one who should be worried. For if you do anything untoward with that woman, anything at all, I will find a way to poison you." She stood, giving him a wide grin, and said in a more appropriate level, "Now, let's find that next clue."

Chapter Eighteen

Catharina was never one to gauge a woman's ability or judge her character on her appearance alone. Pretty women were capable of making mistakes and did as many good deeds as their homely counterparts. Unattractive women could be just as devious and spiteful, or as kind and compassionate, as those who possessed great beauty. Any woman, lady or maid alike, had to be judged by her own merits.

But none of those women were Lady Madeline.

Lady Madeline was an extremely handsome woman. Catharina suspected she turned many heads by simply walking into a room. But being handsome gave her no right to flirt so openly with Lord Hainsley. No right, whatsoever. Although Catharina was curious about what the pair had discussed during their private rendezvous, she did not care.

What she wanted to know was what Lady Madeline intended with Lord Hainsley. Granted, the earl had not yet asked Catharina to court, but he would soon enough. Two people could not spend the amount of time together as they did without developing certain feelings for one another. Unfortunately, Lord Hainsley's pride—and his extremely inflated sense of self-importance—got in the way of him recognizing that fact. Once he came to his senses, he would see they were meant to be together.

Regardless of their current standing, however, Catharina did not appreciate Lady Madeline's blatant disregard of her. The woman had treated her like a servant, pushing her aside like a tree branch on a woodland footpath. Which was why Catharina had gone inside the cathedral. She would not stay where they had left her like some trained puppy.

Plus, catching partial conversations could create more questions to which she was uncertain she wanted the answers.

When Lord Hainsley had joined her, she once again decided to trust him. Why? It is hard to say. She had heard enough stories of women losing their senses because of some man to whom they were attracted. Catharina just never thought she would be one of them. Still, doubt tickled the back of her mind. Or perhaps that was her senses.

The truth was, Lord Hainsley was adventurous, and few women could resist such a man. But if his tongue was loosed by only a glass or two of wine with Catharina, what would happen if he consumed more with Lady Madeline? Stories of exploring caves and searching for lost treasure would sweep her away, just as Catharina had been upon hearing the stories.

She could not deny the growing affection she had for him. Not love, certainly. It was far too soon for such a strong emotion. But she did have an undeniable admiration for him. And how could she not? He made her laugh. Her breath caught whenever he ran his hand through his hair. And his scent made her feel heady...

Shaking the cascade of thoughts from her mind, Catharina turned her attention to the earl beside her. He could say that he was disinterested in Lady Madeline, but Catharina knew full well what a beautiful woman could do to a man's mind.

From her seat in the pew, Catharina leaned in close to the earl and whispered a warning. "I'm not the one who should be worried. If you do anything untoward with that woman, anything at all, I will find a way to poison you." Standing, she grinned and added, "Now, let's find that next clue."

Catharina and Lena had agreed that being in a church gave her a little more freedom than most places would. As long as Catharina did not try to leave the building, and if Lena knew exactly where Catharina was, she would remain in the pews while Catharina and Lord Hainsley went on their hunt for the latest clue. Given the size of the cathedral, and with few clergymen about, Catharina was not worried about arousing suspicion. People came from every corner of the country to gape at the wondrous architecture. What difference would two more visitors make?

"I've given this a great deal of thought and made several calculations as to the position of the sun," Lord Hainsley said.

Catharina raised her hand, and he fell silent. "My lord, did you forget that you confided in me about speaking to your friend?" She adored the way his jaw fell open. His pride had taken a hit, but it was welldeserved. "There is no need to try to impress me."

A wry grin crossed his face. "Are you saying there is no need because you are already impressed?"

Oh. But he was a smug one! But it thrilled her, all the same. She clicked her tongue in mock vexation and pointed an accusatory finger at him. "That is enough boasting from you, my lord."

He smirked. "And your tormenting of me? Will it ever stop?"

Catharina sighed. "I cannot lie. Tormenting you brings me a great deal of pleasure. For when I do, you become more handsome."

Lord Hainsley looked like he wanted to scold her. But instead, he said, "As hard as it is for me to admit it, I enjoy our banter. But when you are angry, I find you even more beautiful."

Catharina felt as if her feet had left the ground. His words rang through her mind, and she felt as if they were the only ones in the cathedral.

But they were not.

"Enough of your flirting," she said, although she could not stop herself from smiling. "This is a place of worship. Now, what is our next step?"

He nodded. "Here is what I suggest we do." Lord Hainsley walked up to the front of the nave. "You will stand here, facing north. The statue of John is on the roof above you. I'll go upstairs to the south beneath where the statue of Thomas stands and reflect the light down to you." He pulled out a hand mirror from the leather satchel he carried. "Hold this against you at about this height." He demonstrated by placing the mirror against his chest with the glass facing outward.

She took the mirror from him and did as he instructed. "Like this?"

He glanced above them and shook his head. "A little higher, I think. And point it down just a mite. Yes, there. Now, don't move. When I send the beam down to you, it should reflect off your mirror and go directly to where we will find the next clue. So, pay very close attention to where it points. Do you have any questions before I go?"

"No," she said in a low growl. "But hurry before someone asks me what I'm doing. I cannot imagine that standing here with a mirror in my hands is commonplace."

Lord Hainsley frowned, although the corner of his lips twitched. "You've become quite demanding in your tone, Miss Sagewick. Don't forget, I'm an earl—a lord of the land!—not some country bumpkin you can order about."

Catharina pursed her lips. "And perhaps you should remember that I'm a woman and thus easily annoyed." When he smiled, her heart skipped a beat. Oh, but he was handsome! "Now, hurry along, *my lord.* Save your complaining for later."

He shook his head and chuckled before walking to the staircase that led to the dome.

As Catharina waited, an elderly woman walked past, frowned, and, to Catharina's relief, continued on her way without comment or inquiry.

Catharina caught sight of the earl as he moved along the landing that ran along the edge of the dome, and she silently urged him to hurry. A moment later, she cried out and shielded her eyes from the beam of light he sent down to her. She shot the earl a glare, and he shrugged.

Great oaf!

She returned the mirror to her breast but closed her eyes to slits, just in case he tried to blind her again. This time, he managed to hit the mirror directly. With a sense of anticipation, Catharina searched for the end of the light beam. It pointed directly at the organ that sat just ahead and to the left.

The light disappeared, and Catharina hurried to meet Lord Hainsley at the bottom of the staircase.

"So? Did you see where it went?" he whispered, gasping from his haste in coming down the stairs.

Catharina nodded. "I did. But first, catch your breath."

She handed him the mirror, which he returned to the satchel.

"I can catch my breath when we've completed our task," he said, although his tone held no sharpness to it. "Now, tell me."

And he accused her of being demanding! "It pointed to the organ."

With a quick nod, the earl placed a hand on the small of her back to guide her forward. Catharina found the touch intimate, and she enjoyed it immensely.

"It's beautiful," Catharina said as they approached the instrument. "A fitting piece for such a grand building."

Lord Hainsley nodded. "The man who built it was indeed a master craftsman."

"That he was," came a voice from behind them.

Catharina turned to find a balding robed man approaching, his smile welcoming. "Quite," she replied.

"I'm Reverend Elbert, one of the priests here." He ran a loving hand along the wood of the organ. "Bernard Smith was the master craftsman you mentioned. We were fortunate to have had him build this for us. The Knights Templar," he said the name with an air of disapproval, "had tried to avail of his service, but in the end, he chose us."

In her history lessons, Catharina had learned about the history of the Templar Church, located between the Thames and Regent Street. Although, the true Templar Knights had been killed off centuries ago.

"Are there any interesting engravings on the organ?" Lord Hainsley asked. "Inscriptions, artwork, anything of any significance?"

The old priest smiled. "I'm afraid not."

"Excuse me, sir," a boy in a white tunic said, hurrying up to them. "I've been sent to give you an urgent message."

The priest smiled. "Alas, the Lord's work is never done." He bowed. "If you'll excuse me."

As soon as Reverend Elbert was gone, Lord Hainsley began looking over the instrument, running his hand along any place he could reach. Given the height and size of the organ, there was much that was out of his reach.

"Nothing," he growled. "Not a single etching or marking. Not even a scratch. I just pray the clue wasn't buffed away from years of polishing!"

Lord Hainsley was correct. Although she did not voice it aloud, she was afraid their wonderful and exciting adventure was drawing to a worthless end. Yet upon seeing his dejected look, she was reminded of the man he was.

Therefore, she said, "I'm sure you have been baffled more than once during your past adventures. You cannot give up now. Give the matter some more thought."

Sorrow flashed in his eyes, but it was gone as quickly as it came. And of course, he would be sad. He had hoped to impress her with his skill and intelligence. Well, she would not allow him to fail!

Taking a step closer, she lowered her voice and said, "You can solve this puzzle, my lord. I know you can. You may just need to rethink the riddle."

A smile spread across his face. "Yes, you're right. I can." He turned to face the organ. "Where could the clue be? If I were a master organ builder, I would wish to make certain the instrument worked well. And to do that, I must sit."

Several older women whispered disapprovingly behind them as the earl sat upon the wooden bench.

"He would not have tea here," Lord Hainsley mused. "He may play, but only long enough to make sure the keys are working correctly. Once I've rested, what would I do next?"

Lord Hainsley's method for solving riddles was odd, but who was Catharina to argue? He was a seasoned adventurer who had solved plenty of puzzles, including those that had sent him to the ancient caves in Scotland.

"'Eight archers gather'," he murmured to himself. "Archers. Arch...

ers." He stood there for a full two minutes before his eyes lit up. "Archers? What if they meant arches?"

"My lord?" Catharina asked, knitting her brows.

"Look at the bench?" he asked. "What do you see?"

She studied the seat for a moment. "I only see a bench, my lord."

He grinned. "But look at the legs of that bench. Each leg is connected by a set of arches. Four legs, two arches each..."

"'Eight archers gather'!" Catharina said, excitedly. "Well, aren't you clever!"

"I've been told as much," he replied, flashing her a smile. "I'm just glad you recognize it."

Catharina pursed her lips. "Your arrogance knows no bounds, my lord. Now, why don't you put aside your pride and see if you are as clever as you believe yourself to be?"

Lord Hainsley hurried over to the bench, dropped to his knees, and ran a hand along its underside. "Yes," he grunted. "There is a hidden compartment... just here."

Catharina thought her heart would leap from her chest, for it was pounding so hard. When Lord Hainsley stood again, he held a folded piece of parchment in his hand.

"This is old," he said. "I'd guess at least a hundred years old. The parchment is brittle. I'm afraid to open it."

"You there," Reverend Elbert shouted as he hurried toward them, "what have you there? Anything you find belongs to the church."

Lord Hainsley put an arm around Catharina's waist, and several of the women made the sign of the cross. "Forgive me for being so bold, Miss Sagewick, but we really should leave. And quickly."

Shame filled Catharina. Stealing pearls, paintings, and now a message from a church... What was she thinking?

His strong arm around her waist, although far too intimate for any setting, but even more so in a church, was the most wonderful feeling in the world.

"Stop, thieves!" the clergyman cried after them.

"Sorry, sir," Lord Hainsley called over his shoulder. "It belongs to my family."

To Catharina's relief, Lena was waiting at the front doors when they arrived, and all three hurried from the church into the now busy street.

"We must hurry," Catharina told the chaperone. "I'm afraid we've made someone very unhappy."

"Stop them!" came the clergyman's voice. "Thieves have stolen from the cathedral!"

"Lower your head, Miss Sagewick," the earl said, pulling her in closer. "Bury your face against me so no one will be able to recognize you."

Without hesitation, and without concern for Lena's disapproval, Catharina did just that. His chest was as firm as she imagined it to be. That realization made the blood thump in her ears, drowning out the voice of the priest calling after them.

Chapter Nineteen

Five days had passed since Gideon had fled St. Paul's Cathedral. And in that time, he had kept away from Miss Sagewick. They had agreed to keep out of sight to allow time for the incident to pass from people's memories. They had been fortunate. He had not seen a familiar face that day, except for that of Lady Madeline. But she had no reason to connect him to the thief Reverend Elbert would be searching for. The last thing he needed was to further tarnish his already damaged reputation.

Although his current financial situation was hastening that process on its own.

Gideon sat in his study with Mr. Richard Burton, a member of the gentry who had a sharp mind for numbers. He was well respected by everyone, aristocratic as well as the less noble, for his ability to forecast the wealth of any given person. Or their fall into financial ruin if that were the case.

"With the collapsing wool trade," he was explaining as he ran a hand through the gray wisps of hair on his head, "coupled with the falling rents in Dorchester... and let's not forget that your mines have dried up. I fear the only recourse you have at the moment is to sell your Cornwall estate. Doing so would give you enough funds to last you perhaps a year. If it sells for the right price, that is."

Gideon dropped his head in shame. He had already sold one property three months after his father's death to make good on one debt. Besides Coventry House, a few tenant farms, and collecting rent from two inns, the estate in Cornwall was the last of the properties he owned. And it was also where his mother now lived.

"I cannot take away the one thing that brings my mother happiness, Mr. Burton. And even if I did, what then? Should I have her live on the streets?"

The older man sighed and leaned back in his chair. "You would be able to make repairs on your inn in Kent, my lord. At least that gives you some income. Far better accommodation is popping up all over the country. You can no longer compete unless you make extensive renovations on the place."

The man was right. Families with new money had invested in a string of hotels and inns, all with buildings so fine, they made his inn look like a stable. He had considered selling the inn, but it would be like tossing a thimbleful of water on a raging fire. If it could just get through until he and Miss Sagewick found the treasure, it could be worth the trouble.

"How long do I have to make a decision before my hand is forced?" he asked. "At least six months, I'm sure."

Mr. Burton shook his head. "I'm afraid not, my lord. I'd say you have four months at the most. But it may be nothing more than a bandage on a gaping wound. You're heading toward bankruptcy as sure as the sky is blue."

Four months? That was all the time he had left? He was tempted to take the clue he had found and run out the door. Yet he could not do so for two reasons. The first was that he had promised Miss Sagewick that he would not continue without her. The second was that, although they had studied the clue, neither of them had been able to decipher it. He had spent the last five days reading and rereading what had been written on that fragile piece of parchment, but to no avail.

"My lord," Mr. Burton said, standing, "if you sell the estate now, as well as the inn, perhaps the price of wool will have risen again before you lose everything."

"Thank you, I have much to consider."

Gideon walked the man to the front door and bid him a farewell. He then retreated to the parlor, where he would drown his sorrows in brandy. The idea of writing to his mother and explaining the situation made his head ache. But he could no longer avoid it. She had to know what the future might hold.

He paused, thinking of Miss Sagewick. She had believed in him. Granted, it was all based on a lie, but she had encouraged him at the cathedral. It was because of that encouragement he had solved the second clue. If he were to invite her over again, would his luck change once again?

Yes, he would delay informing his mother for the time being. He would instead call on Miss Sagewick in two days, so they could confer on the next step. He had hoped to call on her sooner but was informed she would be spending time with Lady Whitmore. Once she was available, they would solve the riddle together.

Yes, that would work out perfectly.

Pouring himself another brandy, Gideon reminisced about the time he had spent with Miss Sagewick thus far. Stealing a kiss had been his favorite moment, even above finding the first clue to the treasure. Surprisingly, that did not even come in second. That place was reserved for the unexpected thrill of running away from the priest, of all people.

Gideon's life had become an adventure. And he was relishing every minute of it.

"Lady Madeline Johanson, my lord," Collins said, jarring Gideon from his thoughts.

Standing, Gideon cursed himself inwardly. He had completely lost track of time. Dining with Lady Madeline had been the furthest thing from his mind. And the last thing he wanted to do this evening. But he had committed to it, and he was never one to break a commitment.

"Good evening, Lady Madeline," he said, giving her a bow and kissing her hand. "I trust your journey here was without incident?"

"The streets were relatively clear," she said, the skirts of her bronze gown rustling as she gave him a small curtsy. "I must thank you again for inviting me to dinner."

As if he had any choice in the matter.

"It was my pleasure," he said, smiling. "Please, have a seat."

He indicated a place on the couch, but as he went to sit in the leather armchair across from her, she pushed out her bottom lip and said, "Why don't you sit beside me, my lord, where we can hear one another far better."

Swallowing hard, it suddenly occurred to Gideon that she had no chaperone. Typically, her companion accompanied her everywhere.

"Have you no chaperone this evening?" he asked.

Lady Madeline gave him a sad shake of her head. "Emma is in the carriage, grieving. She received word just as we were leaving that her brother was killed in a farming accident of some sort. I told her she could leave for home immediately, but she refused. At least I was able to convince her to remain in the carriage. There, she can be alone to deal with this terrible tragedy."

"How horrible for her," Gideon said. Although her reason for the chaperone not being present made sense, it also meant that they would be alone for the evening. And that did not sit well with him.

Lady Madeline must have sensed his uncertainty. "Do you wish me to leave, my lord? I trust that you're always a perfect gentleman. but if you hesitate to be alone with me because of the rumors... If you believe I will act inappropriately with you... If a man of your character feels this way, then my name is truly ruined."

Tears glinted in her eyes as she clearly struggled to speak her thoughts. He had not meant to offend her.

Gideon smiled and patted her hand. "Don't fret. You are my only guest this evening. And because your chaperone is grieving, I'll have my housekeeper help serve, thus eradicating any suspicion that you were in my company unchaperoned. Now, let's discuss Callingswell and how he is lying to you."

For some time, he went on to explain that he was not the inventor of the rumors and how Lord Callingswell despised him. By the time he was done, he let out a relieved laugh. "So, you can see that our problems stem from years of disagreement. For more years than I've been alive, certainly."

Lady Madeline laughed. "I cannot explain why, but I suspected that Lord Callingswell was not being completely honest with me. Now I know the truth. Thank you, for now I can see that you are a friend and not the enemy I was led to believe you to be."

Now that the crux of their problems was settled, their conversation turned to more mundane topics. By the time Collins announced dinner, they had covered important articles in the Morning Tribune, the Queen's latest portrait, and Sarah Green's novel, *The Fugitive*, which both had enjoyed.

As the first course was being served, it occurred to Gideon that although he and Miss Sagewick had spent a great deal of time poring over clues and enjoying luncheons, they had yet to share a proper dinner together. And the guilt of that realization tugged at him. Well, he would soon rectify that error by providing her with the best meal she had ever experienced.

A footman refilled their glasses when the second course was served. Despite what had brought them together this evening, Gideon found conversation with Lady Madeline pleasant enough. How could anyone, himself included, believe she was a woman of loose morals? The idea was absurd. The gossip mill was truly out for blood with that rumor.

Once the meal ended, they returned to the drawing room, where they partook in a glass of sherry. Gideon was already lightheaded after consuming too much wine, but he was enjoying himself enough to not be concerned.

"Well," Lady Madeline said after they had finished their second glass of sherry, "I really must be going. I've thoroughly enjoyed myself this evening, my lord. I truly have. And as for Lord Callingswell, I realize he is an arrogant man, but I believe he has a good heart. I'll continue speaking to him in the hopes that, one day, he might change his ways. I've witnessed it often enough to have faith it can happen. Even for a scoundrel such as he."

Gideon admired her confidence. "Perhaps you're right. But please, do be careful. He may make unwanted advances. He has done so with a host of other women."

She smiled warmly. "Thank you for your sage advice, my lord. And I'll be vigilant." She let out a heavy sigh. "These last few months have been a dark time in my life. But it's comforting to know that I now have a friend to whom I may go when trouble arises. Your wisdom has helped me immensely, my lord."

Gideon could not help but grin. Although he did not throw himself at women, he was aware of his handsomeness. And now two lovely ladies, Miss Sagewick and Lady Madeline, had commented on his intelligence. To be considered wise before reaching his thirtieth birthday was a great compliment indeed!

"You may rest assured that if any trouble of any kind arises again, I'm here to advise you in any way I can."

Her sigh had a tinge of awe to it. "Thank you, my lord."

He escorted her to the waiting carriage, and once she was secured inside, he returned to the parlor. With that out of the way, he could now focus on Miss Sagewick and finding the treasure. And it occurred to him that both were proving to be equal in value.

Chapter Twenty

Catharina reread the missive she had received this morning from Lord Hainsley. Initially, they had agreed that he would call on her at noon, but his letter instead invited her to dine with him this evening.

He will finally ask to court me properly! she thought, her heart filled with anticipation.

Thus far, their relationship had been filled with adventure and excitement. If they were to add romance into that mix, what they already shared would be all the more exhilarating.

As she sat at the vanity table, Lena brushing her hair, Catharina wondered whether his dinner with Lady Madeline had gone well. Although Catharina trusted Lord Hainsley completely, she was not well enough acquainted with Lady Madeline to say for certain that she could trust her. Yet she felt in her soul that there was no need to worry. After all, the two had dined together and still, Lord Hainsley wished to see Catharina. No, not only see her, but dine with her.

And now that he had fulfilled his obligation to Lady Madeline, he had no reason to see her again. Especially if Catharina had anything to do with it...

Catharina had never been the type to be jealous of a man, but neither had she considered any she wished to claim for herself. Now she understood why so many women dreamed of pulling out the hair of a woman she saw as competition. Well, if Lady Madeline did not stay away from Lord Hainsley, Catharina would teach her a lesson!

She recalled a friend, one Miss Cora Hamilton, who was taken with Mr. Luther Glassgrow. When Miss Cora learned that Miss Darina Wirrington had attempted to spirit him away, Miss Cora had come weeping to Catharina.

Catharina knew exactly what to do.

One evening, Mr. Glassgrow hosted a gathering, to which all the parties in question were invited. Catharina had confronted Miss Darina directly, issuing her a warning. If she did not keep away from Mr. Glassgrow, Catharina would ensure her reputation suffered.

Whether Catharina would follow through on that threat was beside the point. Miss Darina turned her attention elsewhere, leaving Miss Cora and Mr. Glassgrow to marry six months later.

"Ah, there you are, Catharina," Lady Whitmore said as she entered the room. "May I have a quick word with you before you go?"

"Yes, of course," Catharina said, noting with trepidation the newspaper the countess carried. "Is there a problem?"

"Did you and Lord Hainsley not visit St. Paul's Cathedral last week?"

Catharina nodded. So, it was as she feared. Lady Whitmore suspected that she and the earl were involved in the story in the paper. "It was lovely. Did you know—"

"I would keep away from there for the foreseeable future," Lady Whitmore interrupted. "It may not be safe."

"What do you mean?" Catharina asked, praying the countess could not hear her pounding heart.

The countess held up the newspaper. "Let's begin here. Although the document that was stolen is not stated in the article, it was taken, all the same." She opened to a particular page and began to read aloud. "'One Lady Goodlock, who has attended services at the church for seventy years, said that the thief grabbed a young woman in a most unsavory manner in front of an entire group of ladies before spiriting her from the building.'"

Catharina's cheeks burned as she was reminded of how that was not the first time that Lord Hainsley had grabbed her "in a most unsavory manner." His hold had been firm, and she desperately hoped he would do it again.

Then her breath caught in her throat when the countess read the description of the young woman. "That sounds a great deal like you, Catharina."

Fear overtook Catharina as her mind scrambled to find a way out of this predicament. However, there was no excuse or lie she could tell that would do her any good. Perhaps she should simply tell the truth. But what if the countess sent Catharina right back to her father? Not only did that mean being away from Lord Hainsley, but it also likely meant marrying any gentleman willing to take her.

Lady Whitmore shook her head. "Of course, many young ladies have dark hair and blue eyes. And we both know you would never do something so foolish, don't we? To even consider that Lord Hainsley would be capable of such tomfoolery is outright ridiculous. But that does not mean people who have read this article will ignore the fact the two of you were there that day and resemble the description of the culprits. Which is why I insist you keep your distance from that place for the time being. You don't want anyone believing you were a part of that incident now, do we?" The last she said with a wink.

"No, we would not," Catharina said in a small voice to hide her relief.

"Good," Lady Whitmore said with a sense of finality. "Now, I do hope you enjoy your evening."

Once the countess was gone, Catharina stood and began pacing. "Oh, Lena, I thought for sure she knew it was me!" She paused and worried her bottom lip. "Unless she knows and chooses not to say so. But that makes no sense. If she believes I'm guilty, why not accuse me outright?"

Lena chuckled. "You should be relieved that you're not in trouble. Don't you think?"

She was right. Catharina was safe from the countess's scrutiny. For the time being, anyway. Still, the encounter brought another question to mind.

"Lena, may I ask you something."

"Of course, miss," Lena said, pinning a rose-shaped brooch to the bodice of Catharina's dress.

"The countess trusts you completely, correct?"

"She does."

Catharina knitted her brows. "Then why did you not tell her the truth about what happened last week?"

Lena sighed. "It's because she trusts me that she doesn't make demands on what I tell her. What happened at the cathedral was not ladylike, but it was necessary. It isn't as if whatever he found has any value to the church. Yes, some lines should not be crossed, but my duty to you remains the same—to make sure you find love. If that means helping a man take what rightfully belongs to him, then so be it."

"So, you believe I may love him?" Catharina asked. Her cheeks had to be the color of ripe apples.

Lena smiled. "Do you doubt you do?"

Catharina shook her head. "No, but I have wondered if I was being too hasty in my admiration for him." She embraced her companion. "Thank you. Perhaps when my love is secured, I can help you find yours."

Lena shook her head. "That is a kind offer, miss, but my work is here with Lady Whitmore. And although the man I love is gone from this world, he remains in my heart. There is no room for another."

Those words had to be the most heartwarming Catharina had ever heard. Did she care for Lord Hainsley to such a degree? Perhaps. But if not yet, she would soon enough.

The sky was a dark gray, and thunder rumbled in the distance, promising rain. Catharina wished now that she had worn her pelisse rather than a lace wrap. But she had been more concerned about her appearance than utility. By the time she and Lena arrived at Coventry House, the first spats of rain ticked on the roof of the carriage. At least she did not have far to walk to reach the front door.

To her delight, the earl was waiting for her in the foyer. His dark hair had been neatly combed forward in the latest fashion, and his suit had been carefully pressed. Oh, but he was delightfully handsome!

"I feel as if it's been an eternity since I last saw you," he said as

Collins took her wrap and hat. "We really should not remain apart for so long again."

With a flutter in her stomach, Catharina said, "I agree. I suppose we've added another term to our agreement."

With a chuckle, he led them to the dining room. A silver candelabra lighted one end of the long table, which could easily accommodate a dozen people. Once they were seated, Lord Hainsley at the head and Catharina and Lena to his right, the soup course was served.

A peal of thunder made Catharina start, and Lord Hainsley glanced at one of the tall windows, frowning. "I hope this storm does not cause too much damage. The last thing I need is to delay making more repairs."

Catharina frowned. She knew he needed the treasure, but was he so desperate that he would put off important house repairs?

Before she could give it much thought, however, the earl laughed. "What I mean to say is that I tend to be stubborn and try to make the repairs myself. My father gave me more than one stern lecture about taking away opportunities from skilled tradesmen. Now, Miss Sagewick, tell me. Is there any exciting news this week?"

Catharina could not help but laugh as a footman removed her soup bowl. "All has been quiet. Well, except for an article Lady Whitmore pointed out to me this evening. It had to do with our little adventure at St. Paul's last week." When Lord Hainsley groaned, Catharina gently placed her hand on his. "Don't worry, my lord. We're safe. Lena has been sworn to secrecy, and Lady Whitmore is convinced that we were not involved."

The earl pursed his lips and glanced at Lena. "Are you sure?"

Was he deaf? "Completely." She grinned. "Lena swore a blood oath, did you not, Lena? Now, let's talk about other matters."

The conversation moved to more pleasant topics. Once dinner was finished, they retreated to the drawing room, where they sipped coffee and looked over the parchment taken from the cathedral.

Catharina reread the riddle for the fifth time:

The first duke built it twice,

then his heir turned away.
Taken from the fireplace
in a tested hand it stayed.
Then the Pharaoh's cat arrived
in checkered wrap doth pray.
What you seek is inside
if it were able to rise from the grave.

She sighed. "This makes less sense than the previous clue," she said. "'Taken from the fireplace?' Does it mean a fire poker or a similar tool?"

Lord Hainsley shook his head. "I'm still baffled by that first line. The first duke? Does that refer to an actual dukedom or does it perhaps have to do with one's father? And what did he build twice?"

"His lineage?" Catharina offered. "Perhaps he lost his first wife in a tragic accident and was compelled to remarry." She laughed and carefully set down the paper. "Or another son after the first died? I have no idea. Perhaps he built a house."

The earl stood. "That's it! Why had I not considered it before?"

Catharina frowned. "Considered what? I cannot hear your thoughts."

"Montagu House. The Duke of Montagu had it built twice. Then his son sold it. It's now a museum."

Catharina clasped her hands in delight. "The clue was in one of its fireplaces but was removed when the building was sold. But where was it hidden after that?"

"That is a good question." Lord Hainsley poured himself another brandy. When he offered Catharina more sherry, she nodded.

"The Pharaoh's cat?" Catharina said thoughtfully. "Pharaohs are from Egypt. Do you think it means we must go there?"

Lord Hainsley shook his head. "That would be too far away." Then his eyes went wide. "But there is a collection of Egyptian artifacts in the museum. Perhaps we will find a statue or a painting of the cat there."

Catharina's heart quickened. Truly, she had never met a man so intriguing. And not for the first time, she imagined a life at his side. One filled with more adventures like the one they were on now. "Have I mentioned how clever you are?" she asked, rising from her seat to join him beside the sideboard that held his liquor decanters. She glanced at Lena, who had taken out an embroidery hoop, and lowered her voice. "I must say, my lord, you are unlike any man I've ever known. The life you lead stirs something inside me. I may find myself unable to control it if I'm not careful."

The sherry swayed in the glass he offered her. "There is nothing more thrilling than knowing how equally skilled you are in the art of thievery, Miss Sagewick. I, too, must restrain myself, for what is inside me is more potent than the storm raging outside. How much longer I'm able to keep it from erupting remains to be seen."

Men had propositioned Catharina before, but none left her feeling breathless as she did now. She wanted so very much to kiss him, but Lena would only allow so much. Kissing was most definitely nowhere on that list.

Plus, if she did do something so forward, a man as pompous as Lord Hainsley would likely pick her up and take her straight to his bed.

Well, perhaps he was not *that* bold, but he was an exhilarating gentleman. Tonight proved to be one of the most exciting she had ever had. To make matters even more wonderful, they were now one step closer to finding the treasure. And one step closer to courtship. Both of which were of equal value as far as Catharina was concerned.

Chapter Twenty-One

Not for the first time, Gideon was grateful for the day he and Miss Sagewick had met. And all because of his dear friend Lady Whitmore and her insistence on introducing them. The thrill of solving the next clue, dining together, and sharing in drinks all added up to a very pleasing experience indeed.

And the conversation they had shared only moments ago, meant for lovers, replayed in his mind. He had wanted to take her in his arms at that very moment and kiss her thoroughly. But even if he were certain she would not protest, he could not have gone through with it. He was a gentleman, not a rake who took advantage of any willing young lady. Therefore, he chose not to succumb to such acts of debauchery.

Plus, Miss Sagewick had to understand that just because she was full of wit and was as beautiful as a field of flowers, it did not mean he would simply kiss her whenever the mood struck. Unlike other men, he could show restraint. At least, he prayed he would.

Thunder rumbled outside, but Gideon ignored it. Returning to the sideboard, he poured himself another measure of brandy. He should restrain himself there as well, but he needed it to calm the rising desire.

"I know the hour is late," he called over his shoulder, "but we shall have one last drink in celebration before you go."

He nearly jumped out of his boots when Miss Sagewick seemed to appear out of thin air next to him. "You are not plying me with wine like some rogue in hopes of lowering my guard, are you, my lord?" Her playful smile told him that this was not coquetry but rather the playful banter they had come to share. That he had come to adore.

"I imagine there is no need, Miss Sagewick," he said in retort, grinning, though his voice was just above a whisper. It would do neither of them any good for Lena to hear them and mistake their wit for something more sentimental. "We both know you would not resist if I tried to kiss you again." His body heated. Then again, anyone in their right mind would make that mistake.

Her jaw fell open, and her eyes widened. "Such beastly talk, my lord," she whispered. "I should leave right now, but then I would miss out on this splendid sherry."

"So, you are using me for my sherry?" he asked with a laugh.

She jutted out her jaw. "Of course, I am. Do you think I enjoy spending my time listening to your dull conversation? Now, we have something important to discuss."

"Do we?" he asked, surprised at this sudden change in conversation. "And what would that be?"

"This relationship between us, will you be asking to court me or simply string me along like some puppy?"

He nearly spit out his brandy. Courting? He had considered that situation and, in fact, wanted it. Yet what sort of man was he if the woman he had come to care about had to be the one to broach the subject? It was his responsibility and therefore would not deter from it.

"I would never compare you to a puppy, Miss Sagewick, but I see your point. I..." He glanced at the chaperone, praying she could not hear what he was saying. "I have come to enjoy your company, Miss Sagewick." He swallowed, trying to work moisture back into his dry mouth. Why was this so difficult?

From her beauty to her sharp mind, she overflowed with perfection. Her past no longer mattered. She was a changed woman; he was sure of it. And, he thought with a great deal of pride, it all boiled down to his shining example.

"I must admit," she said. Oh, how he loved it when she blushed! "I have new feelings I've never experienced before. It would be an honor to have you court me, my lord."

There were a thousand things he wished to say to her at that moment. How she fascinated him at every turn. Her laughter, her beauty, and the way she spoke her mind, everything about her added to her allure.

Yet she believed him to be someone he was not. What she had pointed out before was closer to the truth than he cared to admit—he led an extremely dull existence. If the treasure had no value, he would be forced to sell much of what he owned to pay off his debts. There was a chance that his mother would be forced from her home, and he might even lose Coventry House. But now was not the time to address these issues with her, for the treasure just made those points moot.

"I'm pleased you feel that way," he said instead. But then he frowned. Why was she not smiling?

"You are a stubborn man, Lord Hainsley," she said, her nose crinkled as if she had smelled a foul odor. "Your pride is such that it keeps you from being honest with your feelings for me." Placing her hands on her hips, she mimicked him. "'I enjoy your company.'" She sighed. "Still, it's clear you do have feelings for me, so I shall be content with your request for courtship for now."

For a moment, he was taken aback. Men did not go about spouting words of love and admiration. Only poets spoke such drivel, and he certainly was no poet. But once again, she wore that playful smile. Oh, but he enjoyed their repartee!

"Assuming you are correct," he said, laughing.

"I am."

"And how can you be so sure?"

Miss Sagewick's lips curved upward. "Contrary to what most men believe, women are the superior of the two sexes. We are wiser and more mentally pliant, but your kind refuses to acknowledge that fact."

Gideon waved his hand. "My kind, is it? Well, perhaps I'll allow you to believe that is true. Still, you assume I agreed to the courtship. What if I refused?"

She folded her hands together. "That would mean you have a choice. And we both know you do not." Her grin was mischievous.

"It is customary—and proper—for the man to ask," he said. "Though I suppose I can make an exception."

Catharina quirked a small smile. "Please, do hurry, my lord. I promised Lady Whitmore that I would join her for the Christmas Eve service."

Gideon roared with laughter. "Very well, I accept."

"That was not so difficult now, was it?" she asked smugly. "And now that our courtship is settled, our time would be better spent making plans for the museum."

After much discussion, they decided the best time to visit Montagu House was two days later. Gideon could not help but wonder if this would be the final clue or if another would be waiting for them. Then again, if the treasure was something at the museum, would they be able to confiscate it? Not likely.

Despite the uncertainty of the hunt, Gideon was pleased that he and Miss Sagewick had taken the proper step toward becoming something more than treasure seekers. The fact they were moving rather quickly mattered little to him. As unconventional as their relationship had become, he enjoyed it immensely.

Besides, it appeared Miss Sagewick would not have it any other way.

Other than the dinner with Lady Madeline, Gideon had not had much more than a passing conversation with a woman in years, and usually that was simply out of politeness. Few women had enough wits about them to hold a proper conversation, and those who did were overly opinionated to the point of offense. No matter how much they would argue the point.

Thinking of Lady Madeline reminded Gideon that he should assure Miss Sagewick that she had no reason for concern. She had denied any feelings of jealousy, but her ability to hide it had been as weak as a winter sun. He was not an arrogant man, but he knew women found him dashing. He received many appreciative glances and flirtatious smiles, but they no longer mattered. Only Miss Sagewick did.

He set his now empty glass on the sideboard and smiled. "Miss *Sagewick...*" He paused. Why had he said her name like that? "*Mish Sagewick...*"

Dash it all, I'm drunk! He thought with horror. *Get your thoughts in order, man! You don't want to make a fool of yourself.* He frowned slightly. *What was I going to tell her? Oh, yes, that's right.*

"You see," he would not attempt to say her name again, "I'm a handsome and desirable gentleman. And though my dinner with Lady Madeline was pleasant enough, as was the conversation, I'm glad it happened because it reminded me of you." When she did not give him the look of elation he had expected, he pinched the bridge of his nose. This was not going to plan. "What I mean is, there I was, an extremely agreeable-looking man, having dinner with a handsome woman, and I invited you to nothing more than a simple luncheon. It was unfair, really. You deserve at least a dinner."

Miss Sagewick took a polite sip of her sherry before setting down her glass beside his. "Twice, you've boasted about your handsomeness. I suppose men tend to think much of themselves. But learning that Lady Madeline reminds you of me is... interesting. I suppose I should be pleased by such praise."

Gideon frowned. Was she angry? She certainly sounded as if she were. But why would she be? He had given her a great compliment.

Her following statement solidified his suspicions. "Tell me, my lord, what else has Lady Madeline done first with you? But be warned. If it includes a kiss, you shall never see me again."

"Kiss Lady Madeline?" Gideon asked dumbly. How could she have misunderstood him so dreadfully? If only his brain did not feel as if someone had replaced it with thick, wet cotton stockings. He had no desire to kiss Lady Madeline. But how could he word his intentions better?

Then the words came to mind. He would explain that there was no other woman on earth he wished to kiss, only her, Miss Sagewick. And he was grateful that he had been honored to do so already.

To his horror, however, rather than that sentiment, this is what he said: "There are plenty of women in this world I could kiss. But know that when I do, I'll honor you by thinking of you and no one else."

Miss Sagewick pressed her lips into a thin line before saying, "Lena, we're leaving. Please have our carriage brought around, my lord. Immediately." And with that, she spun on her heel and left the room.

"But wait!" Gideon called after her. "Please, listen!"

"I believe I've heard enough, my lord," she said as Collins helped her with her wrap. "Thank you, Collins. Will you see that my driver is ready with the carriage? It appears Lord Hainsley lacks the ability to follow simple instructions."

When the butler was gone, an awkward silence fell over the foyer, and Gideon knew he would have to apologize again tomorrow.

Collins returned, but he wore a distressed expression. "I'm sorry, miss, but your driver is struggling to keep the horses under control. He says they are unnerved by the storm." To punctuate his point, a loud clap of thunder made the windows shake in their frames. "He also says that he is concerned about your safety if he must drive in such conditions."

Gideon pinched the bridge of his nose again. Either they had to wait out the storm or have Miss Sagewick and her chaperone remain here for the night. The trouble was, neither was favorable. They had no idea how long the storm would remain, and having her stay for the night was improper. If word got out by way of a servant's loose tongue, her reputation would be ruined. Yet he refused to send her out in such terrible conditions. The driver was right. It was too dangerous.

"You will remain here for the night," Gideon said finally. He turned to Collins. "Please see that Mrs. Plotts has a room readied for her."

Miss Sagewick was not at all pleased. "This is ridiculous," she said, her hands firmly on her hips. "What kind of storm prevents horses from pulling a carriage?"

Before Gideon could reply, she grabbed the handle and yanked open the front door. The moment she stepped beneath the portico, sideways-falling rain pelted her, followed by a gust of wind that caught hold of her wrap and sent it flying out into the night. Not only that, but it was pulling at her dress and hat—and at her. If he did not do something soon, she would be joining her wrap.

With quick steps, he rushed to her side, grabbed her ceremonially by the waist, and pulled her inside. He and Collins both had to push their weight against the door to close it.

"You were saying, Miss Sagewick?" he asked, perhaps with a bit more smugness than he had intended.

She narrowed her eyes at him. The anger only made her eyes sparkle even more. "I'm no fool, my lord. Any attempts to use the storm as an opportunity to woo me will fail. I've instructed Lena to defend me and my property with whatever force she deems necessary." Her smile was sly. "She carries a rather sharp knife on her person and is not afraid to use it." That last she said with a firm nod.

Gideon went to laugh, but Miss Sagewick's stern glare gave him pause. She was not teasing. In fact, he doubted he had ever seen her more serious.

"You have nothing to worry about." He raised a hand. "I swear to remain in my rooms until the morning."

"My lord, Miss Sagewick's room is ready," said a distinctive Irish brogue. Mrs. Potts was a short woman in her middle years who had been employed at Coventry House for more than ten years. Her gray-streaked dark hair was pulled into a severe bun at the back of her head. "I've set you up in the Green Room. It has a small room attached to it for your chaperone."

"Thank you," Miss Sagewick said, yet she did not move. Instead, she turned her scowl back on Gideon. "And what will Lady Whitmore say once she learns I'm staying here?"

"I'll speak with her tomorrow and explain," Gideon replied. At least he was no longer slurring. That was progress. "I'm sure she will understand."

"I'd rather have her hear it from the cobbler," Miss Sagewick said with a derisive sniff. "If the telling is left to you, you'll likely spend the entire time speaking of yourself!"

Gideon had no words of rebuttal. His tongue might have untied, but his mind was still jellied. "I'll walk you to your rooms," he said. "Miss Potts, lead the way."

Once they reached the door to the Green Room, Gideon said, "If you need anything, please let me know. My room is beside yours." He pointed to the double doors that led to his bedroom.

"You will be in the room next to me?" Miss Sagewick asked, her face turning pale. "Is there not a room in another wing available?"

"This is the only wing that is in use at the moment, miss," Mrs. Potts replied. "But if you would like me to open one of the rooms on the next floor—"

Miss Sagewick sighed. "No, there is no need to trouble yourself. This will be adequate, thank you."

Gideon caught her by the arm before she entered the room. "Wait, please. I cannot apologize enough for misspeaking earlier. I'm not quite sure how my words got so muddled."

To his relief, she let out a small sigh. "Well, you are a man and thus prone to silly mistakes. But we can discuss it further in the morning." And with that, she entered her room, Lena following on her heel and closing the door behind them.

As Gideon sat in a chair beside his bed, Halliway pulled off his boots. No matter what happened tomorrow, Gideon decided that watching how much he drank was something he needed to watch closely. Drunkenness served no one well, rather it caused problems when there need not be any.

Once Halliway had hung his coat in the wardrobe, Gideon dismissed him. He would finish undressing on his own to allow time to consider the evening. Replaying the conversation from earlier, or rather his absurd rantings, he prayed that tomorrow he could convince Miss Sagewick of his true intentions.

Throwing his shirt over the back of the chair, he went to unbutton his breeches when there was a gentle rap on the door. Bereft of his shirt, he rolled his eyes and said, "For goodness' sake, Halliway! Have I not told you time and again that you may enter my rooms without knocking?"

Flinging open the door, Gideon took a step back in shock. For the second time that night, his words had gotten the best of him.

Chapter Twenty-Two

The Green Room was aptly named. The bed covers and curtains, drapes, and round rug on the floor were made of one shade of green or another. Even the doilies on the top of the dresser drawers were the color of new spring grass.

But Catharina paid little attention to the room. Instead, she paced back and forth, ignoring Lena, who sat on the edge of the bed. "Why can we not just leave?" she demanded.

The rain pelted on the window, the wind howled, and a flash of lightning lit up the room as if it were daytime, mocking her for asking such a silly question. Despite her harsh tone, however, she felt more regret than anger. She had never been one quick to anger, but Lord Hainsley's words had sparked such ire that she was unable to contain it.

Now, however, with her temper cooled, reason had returned. "I had every right to be upset," she said. "Do you not agree?"

"Indeed, miss."

"Regardless of a man's inebriation, no woman should allow him to compare her to another. Especially since I gave him permission to dine with her." She came to a sudden stop upon hearing what she had said, and guilt filled her. "Oh, Lena, what have I done? He confessed to caring about me as much as I do him. Well, in his own stubborn way he did. Then he agreed to courtship. And only minutes later, we're arguing over another woman. Have I doomed our relationship even before it has begun?"

Lena rose to take Catharina's hands in hers. "Do you remember when I told you that the man I loved died?"

Catharina nodded. "I do."

"Well, early on, we had an argument of sorts about his mother. Apparently, they had a disagreement over me. She felt I was not good enough for her son. And no matter how much he argued, she refused to see reason. And I said some disparaging things about her to him."

"I don't blame you," Catharina said. "She sounds like a difficult woman."

Lena smiled. "Oh, she was much more than that, I assure you. But it doesn't matter now, does it? The point is all couples disagree from time to time. Their tempers flare and they say things they don't mean. As long as they can reconcile, all will be well."

"Yes, you're right. First thing tomorrow morning, I'll apologize for my hasty reaction. But what about the countess? She may be displeased that I'm staying in the home of a gentleman in whom I have a romantic interest. And I would not blame her in the least if she sent me back to my father."

"I'll take care of her ladyship," Lena said, patting Catharina's hand. "Her worries will ease, but we must leave as early as possible, so as not to arouse anyone's suspicion. It's one thing to be seen leaving before midnight and quite another to be caught in the morning. And the fact you did nothing improper won't make a bit of difference."

Lena was right. It was one thing to be caught stealing a painting or a piece of jewelry and quite another to stay at the home of a gentleman without benefit of a party. A full house meant she was not singled out as the only guest. But the only person's opinion that mattered was that of Lady Whitmore. Likely, she was beside herself with worry, but sending a messenger at such a late hour and in a terrible storm to boot was unfair to the messenger.

"Then we shall leave just before the sun rises." When Lena yawned, Catharina added, "You're tired. Maybe you should go to bed."

"But I should at least ring for Stella to help you to undress."

Catharina laughed and waved her off. "If you unbutton me, I'll undress myself and sleep in my shift. Then in the morning, you can call for Stella."

Once Lena was gone, Catharina sat on the bench at the foot of the large bed, the back of her dress open. She had to apologize to Lord Hainsley for being so sharp earlier. If she left before sunrise, would he be awake at such an early hour?

No, she had to make her apology at this very moment or be plagued with nightmares all night. If she went to bed with a clear conscience, she would have a much more restful sleep.

After managing to button at least the top button of her dress, she took the single candle in its holder. Slipping from the room, she made her way to Lord Hainsley's bedroom door, she gently rapped twice and took a step back. What she had expected was for him to greet her with a warm smile, not the words he shouted—nor his state of undress.

"Have I not told you time and again that you may enter my rooms without knocking?" The door opened and Lord Hainsley filled the empty space. Catharina's breath caught in her throat at the sight of him. With his hands on the door jamb and his arms raised, his near nakedness was far more pleasant than her imagination had conjured. Muscles rippled across his stomach, chest, and down his arms. He was perfect in every way possible.

Her mind begged her to turn away, told her that it was improper to so openly take in his manly form. After all, she was a lady, decent and pure.

Yet another, more sinister part of her fixated on every line, every angle, every bit of skin that she could see. Unfortunately for her—or perhaps fortunately—she preferred the latter opinion far more than the former.

"What are you doing here?" he asked, his eyes wide.

"I, my lord?" She swallowed hard. The words were sticking in her throat like a lump of soft cheese. "It's just that—" Then she caught sight of his insolent grin and her senses returned to her. "I'm certainly not gallivanting around half naked and yelling that I should enter your rooms whenever I please!"

Please don't let him notice my unbuttoned dress! What had she been thinking?

His laugh filled the air. "I thought you were my valet, Miss Sagewick. But I'm pleased you came. Regarding my strange attempt to explain myself earlier, I'm afraid my words came out in a jumble. What I wanted to say was quite different from what I actually said. Unfortunately, drinking in excess can have that effect on me."

Relief rushed through her. He had misspoken and nothing more. Just as she was ready to forgive him, however, the cocky oaf grinned and added, "Though, I must admit, it pleases me that my state of undress seems to delight you."

Catharina took a half step backward, glaring indignantly. "Why, I never!"

"You really should not tell lies, Miss Sagewick," he said, taking a step toward her. "You are wearing the most delectable blush I have ever seen on any lady, and your eyes are awash with wonder. Or perhaps it is something more?"

Only a moment ago, she was ready to give him a stern talking to. That had become a need to apologize. Now, however, she was ready to give him a right slap! "Well, I see the rogue in you has awakened for the night. Good night to you."

She went to turn to leave, but he put his arm around her waist and pulled her against him. "I accept your apology, Miss Sagewick. Do you accept mine?"

This was the most improper position in which Catharina had ever found herself. What was wrong with her? She had once been a young lady of good moral standing who would never even consider flirting with a man. Yet Lord Hainsley had awakened something in her she had no idea she possessed. She had enjoyed flirting and teasing the earl, and now she would pay the price.

And although every scrap of decency within her screamed that she should demand he release her, the mischievous side of her spoke on her behalf.

"I accept your apology, my lord." Did that breathy voice belong to her? And did he have to hold her so close? "And since it appears I have no choice in the matter, you may kiss me."

Before she had the chance to consider what she had said, he did kiss her—passionately and deeply. It was searching, persistent, and powerful.

When he withdrew, she put a hand on the wall to keep herself from toppling to the floor.

"We should retire to bed," Lord Hainsley said, backing away. "I would feel terrible if we were caught alone, and the truth came out."

"Truth?" Catharina asked, her thoughts a jumble. "What truth?"

"That you have once again thrown yourself at me and demanded I kiss you."

Catharina gasped as he closed his door. "You'll pay for that," she whispered. "Do not doubt me!"

The laugh from the other side of the door made her balk. "I would never doubt you with anything."

With a sigh, Catharina returned to her bedroom and lay on the bed, fully clothed. Tonight had been one of emotional turmoil. But at least they had apologized to one another for the part they played in their argument.

And as her eyes grew heavy, Catharina thought of the painting, stolen items, and the storm raging outside. But most of all, she thought of Lord Hainsley and the heated kiss they had shared. Perhaps, one day, they would be able to enjoy such a display of affection without keeping it a secret.

Chapter Twenty-Three

Gideon awoke just before sunrise the following morning, his mind fixated on Miss Sagewick. Their passionate kiss from the previous night had ignited a longing for more. Before he could entertain those desires, however, he had to uncover the mystery surrounding her. What circumstances had led her to a life of crime?

Pulling the cord to summon his valet, Gideon prepared for the day ahead. It had been ages since he had grappled with the decision of which coat and cravat to wear. Such decisions usually came easily to him. Yet on those occasions, Miss Sagewick would not have met him downstairs. After several futile attempts at tying his neckcloth himself, he gave up and allowed Halliway to step in and assist him. The valet handled it all with a composed demeanor. Just as he always did.

Gideon's unease stemmed not only from the anticipation of reuniting with Miss Sagewick before her departure but also from the looming task of accompanying her back to Ivywood Manor. He needed to provide Lady Whitmore with a credible explanation for her ward's unanticipated absence the previous night.

"You should have dispatched a messenger, you oaf!" he muttered under his breath.

"What was that, my lord?" Halliway asked from the chest of drawers.

Gideon sighed. "Nothing. No, not the brown breeches. I'll wear the white ones with the brown buttons. They should pair nicely with my coat."

Not that anyone will see them, he thought with a small chuckle. Why concern oneself with such trivialities when there were more pressing matters to attend to?

Once he was dressed, he made his way to the dining room. Several moments later, Miss Sagewick entered. Her dress was wrinkled, which meant she had chosen to sleep in it rather than taking it off and sleeping in her...

He swallowed hard, imagining her in her shift, and shook his head. He had no business thinking of her in such a state of undress.

He could see that Lena had attended to her hair. Women seldom ventured outside without at least a well-kept hairstyle, or so their maids ensured. Regardless of her fatigue and the disheveled state of her gown, she remained as beautiful as ever.

"Good morning, Miss Sagewick," he said, rising and pulling out a chair for her at the table. "Did you sleep well?"

She looked down at her dress and laughed. "I did, but my dress did not fare well, as you can see."

Gideon chuckled. "Are you hungry? Would you like something to eat? Mrs. Laughlin can prepare anything you would like." He was prolonging their departure, he knew, but it did not matter. The truth was, he wanted her to remain here forever.

He paused. What had brought about that thought? Of course. They had discussed courtship. Marriage was a typical event to follow such an association. And marriage was forever.

"No, thank you," she replied. "But a cup of tea would be lovely." After a footman poured for her, she sweetened it with a spoonful of sugar before taking a sip. "Lena and I discussed the impending conversation with Lady Whitmore. She's assured me that all will be well."

Gideon leaned back in his chair and sighed. "I truly hope she's correct. Our families have enjoyed a longstanding friendship. The thought of disappointing her troubles me. Still, she has always been one to listen to reason. If anyone were to understand our situation, it would be her."

Despite his bravado, the idea of Miss Sagewick facing any difficulties bothered him. No reasonable unmarried woman would spend the night as the sole guest of a man to whom she wasn't engaged, not unless she did not mind the prattlers singing by the end of the day.

He took her hand in his. "Should any issues arise as a result of your stay here, I shall act with honor."

A faint smile played on her lips. "And what, pray tell, is that?"

Gideon's heart pounded in his chest. Suddenly, the words caught in his throat. His tongue felt swollen. But he managed to say, "You understand precisely what I mean."

Her eyes lit up in that mischievous way he had come to relish. "I must confess, my lord, that I'm quite in the dark. Please, illuminate me."

They remained locked in each other's gaze for a few heartbeats before he mustered the courage to speak. "I would marry you. There, I've said it."

He had expected her to appreciate his candidness. Or at the very least offer a hint of a smile. But she did neither. Instead, she took a sip of her tea and said, "This is quite good, my lord. Did you have any part in its choosing?"

Gideon gaped at her. "I explicitly mentioned that I would uphold my honor and marry you if gossip jeopardized your reputation. Do you have no opinion on this matter?"

She delicately placed the cup back onto its saucer. "I suppose there are worse things in life."

He was taken aback. Had their encounter the previous night not been as he had thought? Had he misconstrued her response?

You're a fool to assume that this woman would be willing to forsake her dreams of adventure to be with someone like you!

Then, to his utter amazement, she winked at him. "Oh, very well. If the situation calls for it, I shall accept. With a few additional conditions, naturally."

Gideon nearly choked on his tea. "More demands? Have you not made enough already?"

She narrowed her eyes at him. "Are you saying that the terms upon which we already agreed have been demanding?"

He raised his hands as if to defend himself. "No, not at all. Please, continue."

"Good. I was beginning to worry that we might have to terminate this arrangement. Now, firstly, you must stop being so stubborn. I've yet to encounter a man as headstrong and opinionated as you. Occasionally adopting a more agreeable disposition would make things more palatable. Secondly, you are not only to continue with your secret life of adventuring, but you must also take me with you."

And there it was—the lie he had spun when they first met had returned to haunt him. He was no man of adventure, as she had rightly observed. And most people would have agreed. Gideon knew he certainly did.

"Forgive the interruption, miss," Lena said from the door, startling Gideon from his thoughts. "You asked me to inform you when the carriage was ready."

Gideon had never been particularly fond of the concept of chaperones. He grasped their necessity but did not relish the idea of another person constantly present, privy to his every conversation. Now, however, he thought Lena the finest chaperone on Earth. She had spared him the need for further deception in front of Miss Sagewick.

"Indeed," he said, standing. "The sooner we leave, the better. Lady Whitmore must be beside herself with worry."

Conversation was sparse during their journey to Ivywood Manor, much to Gideon's relief. The longer he delayed revealing the truth, the more time they could spend together. Once she discovered how mundane his life truly was, Miss Sagewick might end their odd courtship and search for a man more to her liking.

Wetness from last night's storm glistened on the walkway in the dawning sun as they made their way into the house. They were ushered inside and led to the drawing room. Lady Whitmore sat in a wingback chair, wearing a stoic expression that made Gideon feel like a boy called to his mother for a reprimand.

"Well, good morning," the countess said, her elbows resting on the arms of the chair and her fingertips touching. Not his mother. The Queen. "I hope that what I am about to hear will in no way strain our friendship. We've trusted one another for a very long time. I pray that trust does not waver today."

He cast a brief glance at Miss Sagewick, who looked every bit the remorseful child he felt. "Let me begin by saying that last night's storm was quite fierce, as I'm sure you know. I had dispatched my butler to fetch the carriage, but your driver expressed concerns about Miss Sagewick's safety, as the horses were unsettled by the thunder and lightning. Therefore, I suggested that Miss Sagewick and her chaperone remain at Coventry House for the night to ensure her well-being. I swear on my father's good name that there was no impropriety involved. Nevertheless, Miss Sagewick conducted herself as a lady at all times. If blame is to be assigned, it falls squarely on me."

He looked at Miss Sagewick again, who gave a small shrug. So, she recognized how precarious this situation was as much as he did. He had crossed a line and had earned Lady Whitmore's distrust of him. And who could blame her? After all, what sensible lady would accept such an explanation, even if it was the truth? This was not the countryside where storms could wreak havoc on travel. This was London.

You should have sent a messenger!

Lady Whitmore slowly rose from her chair. "Well," she said, her tone carrying the weight of finality, like the lid sealing a coffin. "Given the circumstances, I understand your decision to have her stay at Coventry House. After all, I, too, had concerns about anyone traveling in such a dreadful storm. But I suggest that we never speak of it again. We cannot afford for this indiscretion to become public knowledge, can we? Miss Sagewick's reputation already has enough... discoloration. We do not wish to add more. Are we all in agreement?"

Gideon gave a vigorous nod and was relieved when Miss Sagewick did the same.

"I believe it would be prudent for the two of you to spend some time apart," Lady Whitmore continued. "I assume Miss Sagewick could benefit from a period of rest after her recent experience.

Besides, she is my guest, and I would appreciate some time to spend with her."

Bowing deeply, Gideon agreed. Although he would miss Miss Sagewick's company terribly, perhaps some time spent apart was for the best.

"Would you care for some tea, Lord Hainsley?" Lady Whitmore asked, her stern demeanor dissipating, replaced by the amiable tone to which he was more accustomed.

"No, thank you," Gideon replied. "I have accounts and ledgers to attend to." He turned to Miss Sagewick and kissed her hand. "I shall send a card in a few days."

Once inside the carriage, he heaved a sigh of relief. Although no physical exertion had taken place, the past day had been exhausting. It appeared that he, too, could use time to rest.

Chapter Twenty-Four

Catharina couldn't help but find the countess's company utterly captivating. They had spent the past three days delving into conversations ranging from the countess's marriage to Lord Whitmore to her matchmaking endeavors. Despite the numerous hardships she had endured, Lady Whitmore had fashioned a meaningful and prosperous life.

Yesterday, Catharina had received a card from Lord Hainsley, indicating his intention to visit her at one o'clock tomorrow. The prospect of seeing him again filled her with anticipation. Today, however, she was exploring the vibrant streets of London in the company of the countess.

Following the recent tumultuous storm that had assailed London, the weather had taken a delightful turn. The sun graced the city with its warmth, occasionally tempered by a gentle breeze, preventing the temperature from becoming oppressive. The heat could be stifling in Town, which was why so many families spent the summer at their country estates. But Catharina did not mind. There was just so much to do here.

They spent a good part of the afternoon perusing various shops. They had ventured into a cobbler's, explored a millinery, browsed the haberdashery, lingered in a bookshop, and indulged in an assortment of confections from a sweetshop. Now, they meandered leisurely along one of the streets, with Lena, as usual, trailing not too far behind. Granted, Catharina had no need for a chaperone, given she was with Lady Whitmore, still she found solace in Lena's companionship.

"You mentioned that you trust Lena more than anyone," Catharina said. "May I ask why? I mean, I trust our servants, but only so much." When the countess frowned, she quickly added, "I don't mean to suggest that Lena is beneath us. She's a lovely companion. But I do find the depth of your regard for her rather unusual."

Lady Whitmore chuckled and stopped in front of a window displaying a selection of delicate music boxes.

"Catharina, you will discover that some of your dearest friendships can blossom in the most unexpected of circumstances. Lena and I, for instance, initially had a strained relationship at first, but we quickly bonded." A warm smile graced her features as she looked fondly at Lena. "Today, I could not ask for a better friend."

Although Catharina nodded, she still found the entire situation odd. Lady Whitmore was on friendly terms with every member of the aristocracy. In fact, Catharina struggled to recall a single noble who harbored ill will toward the countess. But to count a companion among her greatest friends was unconventional.

Well, it had nothing to do with Catharina, so she dropped the matter. If the countess kept Lena close, it was no business of hers.

"Well, it is you!" said an older lady with steel-gray hair and a fine cotton twill dress. Several rings decorated her gloved hands and gems sparkled from her ears and around her neck. The cost of the jewels could likely have funded a war.

Lady Whitmore smiled. "Why, Lady Wilberly, how wonderful to see you!" They kissed each other's cheeks. "Allow me to introduce you to a dear friend of mine. Miss Catharina Sagewick, this is Viscountess Wilberly."

As the two ladies exchanged pleasantries, Catharina studied the older woman. They had never met, Catharina was certain, but she also found the lady oddly familiar. Where had she seen her before?

"Did you hear about the incident at St. Paul's?" Lady Wilberly asked in a conspiratorial tone. "I was there, you know."

Catharina's breath caught. That was where she had seen the lady before. She was one of the women at the cathedral when Catharina and Lord Hainsley had searched the organ. Yet, Lady Wilberly showed no sign that she recognized Catharina.

"I read about it in the paper," the countess replied with an air of disapproval. "What a shame you were forced to witness such a travesty. And in such a place of sanctity. I do hope you are not scarred from it."

The older woman snorted. "It will take much more than that to scare me, as you should know. And the papers only told a portion of the story." She looked around them as if expecting someone to be listening in on their conversation. "The young man was with a dark-haired hussy. One moment he was crawling about the floor beside the organ like some drunkard and the next, he grabbed hold of her in a way no proper gentleman should handle a young lady. At least, not in public. Then again, if he was willing to act so indecently in a church, I fear what they do in private."

Catharina did her best to not bring attention upon herself. If Lady Wilberly studied her hard enough, she likely would recognize her as that "hussy." While certain aspects of the viscountess's story were correct, she was clearly embellishing other parts. And enjoying every minute of it.

"And she carried a mirror with her!" Lady Wilberly continued. "And not to look at herself. I believe there was a bit of sorcery at play there. She was likely casting some sort of spell!"

Catharina stifled a laugh. Sorcery? Spells? Clearly, the viscountess was as prone to storytelling as her best friend Lady Olivia was!

"A young lady with that type of behavior signals only one thing—she is in league with Lucifer!"

Catharina had never heard such absurdity! Thankfully, Lady Wilberly ran out of things to say and gave them a farewell before ambling up the street.

"Thieves and women making pacts with the devil," Lady Whitmore said, smiling. "Nonsense thrives in society, does it not?"

"I suppose it does at that," Catharina replied, surprised by the countess's quick dismissal of the things Lady Wilberly had said.

Their steps came to a halt in front of a dressmaker's shop. "I might be some time," Lady Whitmore said. "If you and Lena would like to take a stroll, you are welcome to do so. It has been awhile since my last visit, so I know Mrs. Fredek will insist on measuring me again." She glanced down at her dress. "I've managed to stay away from sweets, but cakes seem to call to me." She leaned in closer and added with a mischievous smile, "Perhaps Mrs. Null has cast a spell on them."

Catharina could not argue. The cook's cakes were rather tasty.

"There is a tea shop just up the street," Lena said as the door to the dressmaker's closed. "We can stop in there and have some tea if you'd like. But may I pop into the haberdashery first? I saw some ribbon in the window that will go well with my green dress."

"That does sound lovely," Catharina replied. "I'll wait for you there."

Just outside the door to the teashop, however, a voice made her stop.

"Miss Catharina?"

Catharina's jaw dropped upon seeing Lady Olivia fast approaching. "What are you doing in London?" she asked, giving her friend a hug.

"Father is here on business," Lady Olivia replied. "I insisted that he bring me. Oh, Catharina, I have so much to tell you!" She glanced at the shop they were about to enter. "Shall we have some tea?"

"Yes, of course," Catharina said. "I must run to the haberdashery to let my companion know first."

Olivia remained in front of the tea shop as Catharina hurried to the shop. Lena, who was still perusing the wares, said, "I hope you won't mind, but I'd like to remain here. I just caught sight of the loveliest buttons Lady Whitmore would like."

Catherina laughed. "No, of course not. But do join us when you are done."

When she returned to the tea shop, Catherina and Lady Olivia sat at a round table covered in a lace tablecloth. Not long after, they were sipping a wonderful blend of tea and snacking on tiny cakes. Lady Whitmore was going to be sad she missed out on them.

"You said you have much to tell me," Catharina said, smiling.

"I do! But before I share, I must know how everything is going with the matchmaker. How have the gentlemen she's chosen for you been? They haven't been horrible, have they? And the matchmaker. Is she as old and worrisome as we guessed her to be?"

Oh, if only Lady Olivia knew the truth about the countess! But Catharina would never divulge Lady Whitmore's identity. Nor would she reveal where she was staying. It was why her letter to her friend had divulged very little about her current circumstances. Instead, she told Lady Olivia about Lord Hainsley and their budding relationship. She also alluded to their adventures without giving too much detail. Lady Olivia was a friend, but who knew how she would react if she learned that Catharina was the famed "dark-haired hussy" who stole from St. Paul's Cathedral?

"I've enjoyed myself here thus far," she concluded with a sigh. "And now we are courting. I had given up hope that my dreams would come true."

Lady Olivia smiled. "Your story is wonderful, and it makes my heart happy. But you should prepare yourself for what I'm about to tell you. Do you remember Lord Twombly?"

Catharina nodded. Cecil Lord Twombly was a tall, nasally man who took orders from his mother like an obedient child.

"Father wishes for me to marry him."

Catharina nearly fell off her chair in shock. "No! Has he any idea the type of life he leads?"

"He doesn't care," Lady Olivia said, sighing heavily. "Lord Twombly's business ventures align with Father's. I'm not too worried, though. I'll simply have to run away. That should put a stop to the nonsense."

"Oh, Olivia, do be careful! You have no idea how much trouble that can cause you. And what would you do if you did succeed?"

Lady Olivia grinned. "I would return to London and seek out Mr. Paul Harrison. We'll perform on the stage together, and he will fall in love with me."

"And if he doesn't?" Catharina asked.

"He'll have no choice in the matter."

Catharina stifled a groan. Although Lady Olivia had no formal training, she was quite adept in theatrics and embellishing stories. Despite the fact that she had never met the stage actor, she was convinced that she was in love with him. All she knew about the man came from the newspapers.

Every story concerning Paul Harrison described him as a handsome and charming man with a multitude of women flocking to see him. Catharina had seen a sketch included in one of those articles and thought his looks highly overrated. But that did not mean he could not be considered dashing by other women.

It was unkind to say so aloud, but what if Lady Olivia found him plain-looking rather than dashing? After all, an artist can make a sketch look far better than the subject truly is. And face paints... well, they improved the looks of most women and, therefore, had to be equally useful for men who took to the stage. Lady Olivia went on to tell a few more stories from home, embellishing them all, Catharina was certain. Women who had fallen in love at first sight. Men jealous of the talents of their counterparts. One particular gentleman received two hundred letters, all from ladies wishing for him to call on them. But it was not long before she was gushing about Mr. Harrison once again.

In the past, Catharina would not have commented on Lady Olivia's stories. She did not want to hurt her friend's feelings. Now, however, she felt the need to at least offer her some sage advice.

"I can tell you from experience," Catharina said, placing her hand atop that of her friend, "that you cannot trust everything the papers say. Mr. Harrison may be a wonderful actor, but that does not mean he is a gentleman. I'm not saying you should ignore your dreams. But please, just proceed with caution."

"I appreciate your concern, my friend. Don't worry. I'm more than capable of using my wit to determine if a man is good or not."

Catharina frowned. Lady Olivia was in many ways a bright and intelligent woman. But she was even more headstrong than Catharina. Just last year, she had convinced a footman that he was the illegitimate son of a Spanish prince, and the poor man had gone about boasting his newfound link to royalty to anyone willing to listen.

Although Lady Olivia's heart was in the right place, for the man had been ashamed of not knowing his father's identity, it brought about a severe word from her father. Which, of course, begged the question. How would Lady Olivia know his plight to begin with?

Still, Catharina had to hope her friend would find a way out of her current predicament.

When they had finished their tea and cakes, Catharina insisted on paying, and they left the teahouse. "Just promise me you'll be careful," she said as she embraced her friend again. "And once I return home, I will be with my fiancé. I cannot wait for you to meet him."

"I look forward to that," Lady Olivia said. "And we shall all dine together as couples—you with your young gentleman and I with Mr. Harrison, for he will be my beau."

Upon returning to Ivywood Manor, Catharina wrote a letter to her father. It was time to inform him of the courtship between her and Lord Hainsley. At least he would be happy she had found someone she would eventually marry.

Lying in bed that night, Catharina's thoughts turned to her future with the earl and their wonderful life together. One filled with adventure. And truth. For she would soon have to tell him the truth—that she was not the thief he thought her to be.

Chapter Twenty-Five

Gideon silently prayed the search for the blasted treasure would not take much longer. How many times would he be required to steal? Or enlist the aid of Miss Sagewick?

As many as it takes, he supposed.

He paused. That thought did not sit well with him. Here she was, a lovely lady who endeavored to put her former life behind her. And how did Gideon react? By asking her to continue doing for him that which she wished to quit.

Perhaps I'm the rogue she has insisted I am.

The carriage stopped in front of the British Museum, formerly known as Montagu House. Located in Bloomsbury in the west end of London, it was a magnificent sight to behold.

As was the long line of people waiting to get in. Initially, entry for nobles was never declined. All one had to do was simply show up at any time and gain entrance. Yet that was no longer the case. Due to the overcrowding caused by its popularity, both lords and ladies were now required to have their names added to a list in advance to secure entry.

Gideon had forgotten this important piece of information until early this morning. And now, it was too late to have their names placed on the list. The chances of gaining entrance were thin, yet he had to try.

"I would have sent Hornsby had I known," Miss Sagewick said as she adjusted her hat, clearly annoyed. "Now, we'll have to beg to get inside." Gideon went to argue that he was not at fault but then caught sight of her sly smile. "Oh, don't worry so much, my lord. If the need arises, I'll use whatever means necessary to get us in. Lena, are you ready?"

The chaperone nodded, clutching the extra shawl to her chest. As the women walked toward the museum entrance, what Miss Sagewick had said finally sank into Gideon's mind.

He hurried to her side. "What do you mean, 'by any means necessary'?" he whispered. "What are you planning?"

Miss Sagewick pursed her lips as they joined the end of the long line. There had to be at least sixty people waiting to gain entrance. "Stop asking so many questions," she whispered back. "Just trust me."

Gideon pinched the bridge of his nose. Oh, he trusted her, all right. Trusted her to do something dotty!

"Once I tell them my name, how can they refuse?" he demanded.

Placing her hands on her hips, she turned a glare on him. "Did you not tell me that your name is currently in poor standing?"

"Well, yes, but—"

She leaned in closer. "If we plan to steal something today, do you believe it wise to announce that you were here today? Having your name missing from the list is a blessing, not a curse."

What choice did he have? He had used the last of his savings to begin repairs on the inn because of a fire. Then, just yesterday, he learned that several dozen cattle died from a disease on one of the farms he owned, thus furthering his losses. More than ever, he needed the next clue. Hopefully, it would lead them straight to the treasure.

Gideon drew in a deep breath and slowly released it. "You're right." It irked him no end to admit that. "I shall trust you."

"And trust is exactly what we need," Miss Sagewick said as the line moved forward. "After all, I'm risking my good name for you."

What they were doing today would indeed put her name at risk. Just as they had before. And not once did she complain.

"For all you've done for me, Miss Sagewick, thank you." And he truly meant it. He could not have gotten this far without her.

Although she said nothing in response, there was no need. Her smile said it all.

They remained quiet as the line inched forward. For every couple who exited, another entered. Soon, their turn came, and they approached a young man with a leather-bound book in his hands.

"Now, remember," Miss Sagewick whispered, "keep quiet. I'll handle this."

"My lord," the man said, his brown hair neatly combed forward. His suit was tailored, but it was not nearly as fine as Gideon's. "May I have your names please?"

"Lady Theresa Goodbank and my friend, Henry, Lord Montagu."

Gideon nearly swallowed his tongue. Of all the names she could have used, why would she give that of the former owner of the building they were about to enter?

"Montagu," the man murmured as he looked over his list. "Forgive me, but I don't see either of your names. And as you can see, we are quite busy today." He lowered the book. "Is his lordship related to the former owner?"

Gideon went to respond, but Miss Sagewick stepped on his foot. "Forgive my friend," she said. "He is feebleminded and cannot speak of his own accord."

Gideon clenched his fist. How dare she refer to him as feebleminded! And with a smug grin, to boot! He would make her pay. Oh, yes, she would pay dearly!

"His lordship is in fact third cousin to the duke," Miss Sagewick continued in a low voice. "And it would be a personal favor to me—and His Grace, I'm sure—if you let us into the home that had once belonged to his family. It would mean so much to him."

The young man gave her an awkward grin. "Forgive me, please, my lady, but I have specific orders to not admit anyone whose name is not on the list." He glanced around them. "I could lose my position here. And I rather enjoy it."

Well, there is nothing to do but admit defeat, Gideon thought dejectedly.

He would have to return later—after having his name on the blasted list. The treasure would have to wait another day.

"I understand your decision," Miss Sagewick said sadly. "I'll simply have to add today to my ever-growing list of bad luck. Why, just yesterday, a gentleman refused to call on me because he said I was too plain looking." She heaved a heavy sigh. "That is why you refuse me. I must make you feel ill by simply looking at me."

The young man's eyes went wide. "Not at all, my lady. You're far from plain. I'd say you're wonderful." His face went red to his ears.

Miss Sagewick pressed a hand to her breast. "Wonderful? You truly mean that?"

The man nodded.

"Sir, may I have the honor of knowing your name?"

"M-my name, my lady?"

"Yes, your name, if you please."

"Ben-Benjamin, my lady. Benjamin Drexel."

"Well, my dear Benjamin Drexel," she cooed, "know that on this day, you have given a lady hope. Perhaps one day we shall meet again. In fact, I hope that we do."

Gideon stared at her. Was she batting her eyelashes? She was! Well, this coquettish behavior was out of line and had to stop!

"I pray that day comes quickly," the young man said.

Gideon stifled a groan. Miss Sagewick was going to have every common man in London flirting with noble ladies at this rate!

"Until then, my lady," the clerk said, "please go inside. And I'll not even require payment for admittance."

"A gentleman among gentlemen," Miss Sagewick whispered. "Thank you." Then to Gideon's annoyance, she turned to him and added, "Come along." Like he was some sort of puppy! "That is it. Now remember, one step followed by another lest you fall again."

Once inside the museum, he grabbed Miss Sagewick by the arm and gently pulled her to the side.

But she spoke first. "Before you begin, know that I do care deeply for you. So much, in fact, that I would openly flirt with a man plainer than the buns your cook serves."

Gideon shook his head. "Mrs. Laughlin's buns are wonderful. It would break her heart if she heard you calling them plain."

Miss Sagewick smiled. "And it would crush mine if you scolded me for what I just did. Do you believe I'm proud of having to lie?"

His outrage cooled. "No, I suppose not. Just promise me that you won't do it again."

Her grin widened. "Oh, Lord Hainsley, have you not learned yet? I'm the one who decides the terms of this relationship. Now, set aside your jealousy, so we can go in search of the Egyptians."

It was so like her to answer as she did. And it was also one of the many reasons Gideon had come to adore her. As a matter of fact, he just might love her. That in itself was surprising, for he had not considered love before meeting her.

Of course, he was aware of love. Many women described it as a strong emotion, but he knew it was nonsense. Honor a woman, see that her needs were met, and give her children. That was love. Or at least that was how he saw it.

He nearly stopped in his tracks. He was not simply enthralled with Miss Sagewick. He needed her. Not to help him solve riddles or steal paintings. He needed her near him. She supported him in every way. Their talks on various subjects engaged him. And when she was not with him, he was left feeling something he had never truly felt before.

Lonely.

Although they were now courting, as much as they could be without her father's permission, he knew marriage would soon follow. The only thing that could stop that from happening was if he revealed the truth to her—he was no man of adventure.

What they did today bothered him greatly, for he was asking her to steal for him again. And by assisting her, he was just as guilty as she was.

Yet he had sworn to return the artifact once they got what they needed. Despite that promise, to say he was nervous would be a lie.

Making their way through the gallery, they came upon the area that housed the Egyptian artifacts. Vases dating back hundreds of years before Christ, scrolls filled with hieroglyphics, and other wondrous items sat on tables and pedestals. Then he caught sight of what had to be the location of the next clue sitting in the corner.

But there was a problem. A gentleman in a suit, no doubt employed by the museum, gave every person who approached the item a stern look. Which left only one question.

How would they escape with their prize without getting caught?

Chapter Twenty-Six

Catharina could not help but wonder if she had lost her mind. Her actions these past weeks had been quite exciting, yet it was not the act of thievery itself that made her heart thump like the beat of horses' hooves on a runaway carriage. It was the stealth, the gripping fear of being caught, the very risk of the act that excited her.

But this was not simple pilfering of a lady's necklace. This was stealing from the British Museum. Where her father had been able to call on the good graces of Lord and Lady Langley, that guard standing beside the display they meant to target likely meant criminal charges. Probably followed by a swift death by hanging.

In the corner behind a single rope dyed black stood four mummified cats. They were ghastly looking creatures that stood on their hind legs. Each was wrapped in what appeared to be some sort of fabric. How could anyone spend their days looking at them?

It was the checkered one that held the clue they needed. Or so they had figured. Yet the vigilant man watching everyone and everything would be difficult to get past.

Catharina glanced at Lord Hainsley and smiled. In all they had endured together, even if they were caught, it did not matter. He would marry her regardless, of that, she was sure. His tendency for jealousy was laughable, of course. Did he truly believe that she would be romantically involved with a boy as young as Benjamin? He had to be what? Eighteen at best? Far too young for a woman on the verge of spinsterhood. Only royalty entertained such notions. Not that she would mention that opinion aloud. Stealing was not the only offense that led to the gallows.

How strange it was to go from having a small admiration for a gentleman to caring deeply for him in the span of only a few weeks. She suspected that she might even love him.

No, it was far too early for love, but there was no doubt its seed was already planted in her heart. She adored the way Gideon's nostrils flared when he was angry. When he ran his hand through his hair or pinched the bridge of his nose when he was uncertain or flustered. Or the way he smiled at her when he thought she was not looking. But most of all, she was attracted to him most when he was simply being himself. A great man of adventure.

Each day they spent apart felt like a millennium, and she had counted down the minutes to when they would be reunited. Which was why she was here with him today. And why, yet again, she would use her skills as a thief to help him.

You're not truly a thief, Catharina Sagewick! She had to remember that fact. She was only playing a part. Lady Olivia would have been proud!

Although Gideon had promised to return the artifact, taking it did not sit well with Catharina. Oh, she may act like what they were doing was a daily activity to her, but she had convinced him of her prowess as a lady thief. There was no going back now.

Taking the shawl from Lena, Catharina loosely rolled up the shawl into a ball, leaving just enough of it to wrap around the outside. She would then hide the mummified cat inside the makeshift swaddling and cradle it in her arms. All that would be left was to pray that no one became suspicious of her "baby."

Then a realization hit her. How would she explain to Lena what they were doing? She had not questioned why Catharina had asked her to bring the shawl, but neither had Catharina given her any reason to do so. Now, however, the questions would abound.

"My lady," Lena said, "I'm feeling unwell and need fresh air. Do you mind if I wait for you by the door?"

Catharina studied Lena. She appeared well enough, but having her leave eliminated that particular problem. Now she could hide the hideous statue and wait until they returned to Coventry House to take it out. Yet Catharina suspected her motives. She was as observant as a mare with her fowl. She likely suspected what they were up to, no matter how quiet Catharina and Lord Hainsley were when they devised this plan. Still, Lena said she could be trusted, and Catharina would do just that.

Placing the bundle in her arms, she stood beside Lord Hainsley. "We are a loving couple with our baby. There is nothing abnormal about that, is there?"

The earl shook his head and snorted. "We're just stealing from the British Museum. Nothing abnormal about that in the least." He sighed. "Yet we have a bigger problem. Do you recall the clue? It seems to have disappeared from my brain."

Catharina had memorized it and thus whispered it aloud:

The first duke built it twice,
then his heir turned away.
Taken from the fireplace
in a tested hand it stayed.
Then the Pharaoh's cat arrived
in checkered wrap doth pray.
What you seek is inside
if it were able to rise from the grave.

A younger couple moved past them before Catharina went to take a step toward the display. But then Lord Hainsley whispered for her to wait. "There is another problem," he said. "Two of the cats are cloaked in checkered robes. How will we know which one it is?"

Catharina's eyes went wide. He was right. She had not noticed the second cat behind the first. Taking one was risky enough, but two was out of the question. Not without something large enough in which to carry them. Why had they not thought of that earlier?

They moved closer to the mummified cats. Although she could see how appreciated they likely were by their owners—after all, one did not mummify a pet they did not like—the sight of them made her stomach churn. Therefore, she closed her eyes to keep from sicking up. It would do them no good if her breakfast returned in full force. That was no way to remain inconspicuous.

"Are you well, Miss Sagewick?" Lord Hainsley asked, his tone drenched with worry. Then it changed to excitement. "There, that is the one! Its eyes are closed as if in prayer, just like yours are now."

Catharina forced open her eyes and looked to where the earl pointed. Indeed, the one in the far-right corner did appear to be praying. "You're as clever as always, my lord," she said in an excited whisper that matched his. "Now to get close enough to take it without the gorilla seeing us." She indicated the guard, and Lord Hainsley snickered.

"I doubt he would find your analogy complimentary," he said. "I imagine he believes himself to be a lion or a tiger."

She snorted. "More like a hyena, I would say." That was a perfect description of the guard. He had unruly black hair, a thick, black mustache, and a strong build. But he would likely leap as gracefully as any feline if the need arose.

Then we shan't give him the need to do so, she thought with a firm nod.

Behind them, a boy of perhaps five threw himself to the floor in a tantrum, which created the very distraction they needed. All heads turned in the direction of the crying child, and the guard left his station.

"Now is our chance!" Lord Hainsley said in a harsh whisper. "Wish me luck."

Catharina nudged him forward. "Do hurry, my lord. Or luck will not keep us from the gallows!"

As the child kicked and screamed, the earl ducked beneath the rope, grabbed the mummified cat, and returned within seconds. Catharina took a step back when he wrapped the cat in the shawl and tried to hand it back to her.

"What are you doing?" he hissed. "Take it. You must hold it, or this will all be for naught!"

She swallowed hard. "But he's horrid looking. You expect me to embrace what I cannot even look at?"

Then her heart leapt into her throat as the mustached hyena suddenly appeared to their left. His brow was scrunched, and it was clear he had become suspicious of them. Catharina rarely lost her ability to speak, yet now, her thoughts were a muddled mass, and her tongue had gone numb.

"Our son is quite plain looking," Lord Hainsley explained to the guard. "Which he has no doubt inherited from my wife's side. But I can assure you that she loves him, regardless. Do you not, my dear?"

Oh, the gall of him! Plain looking people on her side, indeed! Her family was made up of dashing men and beautiful women, all of them. But now she had a part to play. Summoning her courage, she tried not to flinch as she drew the bundle to her breast.

"My husband is right." She even managed to sound convincing. At least to her ear. "But the fact our son has a large head is not his fault, for he resembles his father in that way."

The guard's mustache twitched, and with a polite nod, he returned to his place against the wall. Not once did he glance at the display but instead began his survey of the crowd once more.

"Come along, dear," Lord Hainsley said, placing a much too familiar hand on the small of her back. "I would like to visit the books next."

Catharina was once again left breathless, but this time fear had nothing to do with it. "Now is not the time to woo me, my lord," she whispered. "And you *will* apologize for what you said about my family!"

"And what about my big head? You should take that back."

"Never," she said, although she could not stop the smile from forming on her lips.

They rejoined Lena, and the trio made their way outside and toward the waiting carriage.

"Well, that went much better than expected," Catharina said, praying the noise of the crowd around them would keep Lena from overhearing. She had not even glanced at the shawl Catharina carried. "You see? Luck is with us. We were able to get in and out without raising anyone's suspicions. I would say even the great thief Robin Hood would be impressed."

Her boastful declaration was short-lived, however, for a shout made her turn to find the bushy-mustached guard pointing at them.

"You there, stop!"

Lord Hainsley chuckled. "You were saying?"

Lena was already in the carriage when the earl helped Catharina inside. If Catharina had been annoyed by the number of people waiting to enter the museum, she was now grateful for the crowd. By the time the guard reached the edge of the street, Lord Hainsley's nondescript carriage was well on its way. And although the man gave chase, he gave up in no time.

"He's gone," Lord Hainsley said, settling onto the bench across from Catharina and Lena.

Catharina handed him the wrapped monstrosity. "Your son needs you, my lord."

Laughing, he took the bundle from her and rested it on his lap. "Now, what was that about a big head?"

"I was speaking of her stubbornness," Catharina replied with a grin. "And as I told you before, not one person in my family is plain looking. Well, there is my cousin Molly, but she is lovely in her plain way."

His grin nearly cut his face in two. "Miss Sagewick, I can assure you there is nothing plain about you."

Pushing out her chin, Catharina sat back on the bench. "Perhaps you should tell me something I do not know."

"And you call me arrogant?" he roared.

Catharina shook her head and smiled. "Thank you for the compliment, my lord. And you are a handsome man." She loved the way he smiled and how his eyes sparkled. "Even with your big head."

And most of all, she enjoyed it when he became frustrated.

Gideon waved her off. "Enough of that, you! Now, how about we find this next clue?"

Chapter Twenty-Seven

By the time they returned to Coventry House—Lobbs taking them down random streets and in various directions, just in case someone was following them—Gideon struggled to contain his excitement. They were able to remove the clue hidden within the cat without damaging it in any way.

Gideon read it aloud:

To find the reward, the pure swan will tell,
For its elixir is known all too well.
The descendants gather at half a man's height,
Their cups raised to the fallen knight.
In death he shows the prize they seek,
And the offering required sold on the street.

After discussing its meaning and being unable to come up with any interpretations that made sense, they decided to revisit it another day. Plus, it would give them another excuse to see one another again.

"I believe I should return to Ivywood Manor anyway," Miss

Sagewick said. "Word will travel soon enough about a lady and a gentleman stealing from the museum. Or at least a couple posing as such."

Gideon nodded. "Rightly so." He cocked his head. "I'm curious. How would you assess my thieving abilities?"

"Adequate," she said with a sly smile. "Though you would be better served leaving the thievery to me."

After dropping off Miss Sagewick and Miss Page at Ivywood Manor, Gideon instructed Lobbs to go straight to Coventry House. There was no need to hide the fact that they had spent time together. After all, he had accompanied Miss Sagewick back to Lady Whitmore's home on more than one occasion. Doing so again would not raise anyone's suspicion. There was no reason for others to connect their outing to the theft at the museum.

He wrapped the shawl tighter around the mummified cat. He would send it with a servant boy, who would say he found it in an alley. Any small reward they gave him he could keep.

Exiting the vehicle, he paused when he caught sight of a familiar carriage parked on the street. He had not expected his mother to visit. It was not that Gideon disliked her visits, for he enjoyed spending time with her. But she was not one to simply show up unannounced, which meant her coming here meant unfavorable news.

Collins greeted Gideon at the door. "Her ladyship arrived while you were away, my lord," the old butler said. "She awaits you in the drawing room."

"Did she say why she's here?"

"No, my lord."

Gideon sighed and handed the bundle to Collins. "Put this on my desk in the study. And do be careful. It is extremely fragile and highly valuable." He did not worry the butler would peek beneath the wrap. Just the mere suggestion of him doing such a thing would be seen as a betrayal to his honor.

Taking a deep breath, Gideon made his way to the drawing room, pausing at the doorway. His mother stood gazing out the window. Not a sliver of gray touched her dark hair, or at least not where it could be seen. She wore a red traveling dress with black boots, which said that she had not been there long enough to have gone upstairs to change. Either that or what she had to say was too important to waste the time.

"I understand you have a female friend, Gideon," she said, turning to face Gideon. She had always had a way of knowing he was there before he could make himself known. "Don't worry. Collins told me. But how the entire *ton* does not know already baffles me. Now, will you tell me her name, or must I correspond with the butler about every aspect of my son's life?"

Gideon chuckled and kissed her cheek. "Her name is Miss Catharina Sagewick. But what brings you here? Surely, my romantic entanglements have not reached you all the way in Cornwall. Not if the gossips here have not learned of it. And what else did Collins tell you?"

His mother went to the couch and sat, smoothing her skirts. "I'll tell you why in a moment. Tell me more about this young lady."

And so, Gideon did, leaving out any mention of stealing, of course. But it did not take long before his mother broached the subject herself.

"I heard that you stole a painting during a party hosted by Lord Callingswell," his mother said, frowning. "Is there any truth to that rumor?"

Gideon lowered himself into a wingback chair. "I cannot lie. I tried to steal the painting in question." When she clicked her tongue at him, he quickly added, "I had no choice, Mother! Lord Callingswell refused to honor a promise made by his father to sell the painting back to us if we asked."

She shook her head, disappointment filling her eyes. "There is always a choice, Gideon. Please tell me that was the only instance I should be concerned about." Rather than lying, he remained silent. "Whyever would you make such a choice? Your father and I raised you better than that!"

"But Father is the one who sent me on this quest," Gideon insisted. "He said he found a passage in an old family journal." He went on to explain about the lost treasure and the steps he had taken thus far to find it. When he was done, he offered her a smile. "The stories of the Knights Templar and the treasure, they are all true. That is why I tried to steal the painting. But it no longer matters because I've already found the first clue and more since then."

Gideon had seen his mother angry only twice in his life. Once, when one of the chambermaids was caught stealing a pair of earrings from her jewelry box. And again, when his father returned home, stumbling drunk, and began arguing with who he believed was a servant hiding in the shadows but was, in fact, the tall clock in the dining room.

And now her sharp tone said he was about to witness a third instance. "You know as well as I do that your father was in a great deal of pain during his last days. His great-grandfather, to whom that journal belonged, was well-known for his madness. He even claimed to be a direct descendant of one of the Knights Templar but never could provide proof of that fact."

"But I may have the proof he needed," Gideon said, excitement coursing through him. "The painting is a depiction of several members of the Knights Templar. Why would he have such artwork if it did not have specific meaning? My knowledge of the history of the Knights Templar might be limited, but I'm aware that they were men of great courage and honor."

His mother pursed her lips. "Your father also believed this, as did his father before him and so on. I hate to disappoint you, but I believe they are nothing more than tales told of men who wanted to be more important than they truly were. You would think that being an earl would be enough, but it never was." She sighed. "And while you were trying to decipher clues from the pages of a madman's journal, I come with distressing news. Last week, five of the servants walked out because they had not been paid."

Gideon stared at her. "That is impossible. I'll write to the steward this very moment and insist that he—"

"I've already spoken to him, Gideon. He has also not been paid for his services in several months, and he politely told me that he is withdrawing his services." His mother leaned forward, concern etched on her features. "Are you in some sort of financial trouble?"

Gideon heaved a heavy sigh. He could not lie to his mother. "I am. But please, don't worry. I'll redirect funds to the Cornwall estate, so you are able to replace the servants who have gone. Once I find this treasure, all will be set to rights. I promise."

"This is a great burden you are placing on yourself," she said. "I have no true need for the estate in Cornwall. I realize you purchased it for me, but you are welcome to sell it if you must, given it is the only property that is not entailed. I'm sure an apartment here in London will suit me just fine."

Gideon shook his head. "No, it is not fine. I know how much you love the house, Mother. You must trust me. I'll find a way to save it all."

"I have always trusted you, my son. But promise me that if you do not find what you seek, you will sell the house."

"I promise. But it will not come to that. I'm getting close, I just know it. Now, tell me what you've been up to since I last saw you." He chuckled. "Besides servants leaving, of course."

They spoke of more pleasant matters for some time. Gideon learned that his mother was staying with a friend who lived nearby and would be returning to Cornwall in four days.

"Will I get to meet this Miss Sagewick before I go?" she asked.

"Of course, you will," he replied. How that would come about within four days remained to be seen.

Once his mother was gone, Gideon went straight to the study, removed the shawl from the cat and set it beside the clue they had found. Then he sat in his chair to think.

What if his mother was right? Would he come to find out that the clues were nothing more than a game a distant grandfather created out of his madness? That thought worried him, but the shame of knowing the trouble his estate was in only added to that worry.

His thoughts turned to Miss Sagewick. There lay another problem. What if there was no treasure? What woman wanted to marry a man on the verge of financial ruin? Although he wished he could share his concerns with her, he could not do so. For it would give her another reason to leave him.

And the fear of losing her troubled him far more than the thought of losing his estate.

Chapter Twenty-Eight

Alister took a thoughtful sip of his brandy. When he had sent the young maid Carrie to spy on Lord Hainsley, he had been confident that she would return with good news. Unfortunately, what she had to say made little sense to him. Initially, he had considered having the girl lashed and sending her back to Coventry House with strict instructions not to return with anything less than the truth.

Listening to the maid's story, however, he realized that what she said was much more believable than he first realized.

"I didn't see myself, my lord," Carrie explained. "I caught young Saul running down the corridor, looking every bit like he'd seen the dead rise. When I stopped and asked him why he was so frightened, he told me that he was checking on the firewood in his lordship's study and found a dead cat wrapped in cloth on his lordship's desk. At first, I didn't believe him. Children tend to let their imaginations get the best of them. After sending him on his way, I went to investigate and found the boy was right. There was a strange cloth-wrapped cat on his lordship's desk. Beside it was a piece of paper."

Alister swirled the brandy in his glass. Dead cat? Had Lord Hainsley taken up witchcraft? And did this dead cat have anything to do with the British Museum, or was its presence in the earl's study merely a coincidence? "What was written on the paper?" he asked the maid.

Carrie dropped her gaze, her cheeks reddening. "I... I can't read, my lord."

Alister stood and placed a finger under the maid's chin. She was a striking young woman, and once this charade was over, he would welcome her back to his estate. And into his bedchamber.

"You've done well, Carrie," he said, smiling down at her. "I'm very pleased with you."

The girl's blush made her all the more alluring. Oh, yes, she would be a fine diversion once this was all done. And a means to celebrate his newfound wealth once the treasure was his.

"If there is nothing more, you may return to Coventry House."

"There is one more thing, my lord. Lady Hainsley arrived unexpectedly."

Although this was of little interest, he urged her to continue. Every seemingly unimportant piece of information might be what tied everything together. Or it was cast aside. A few more moments listening would make no difference.

"Go on."

As the maid continued, Alister could only smile. Lord Hainsley had informed his mother of his financial troubles? What gentleman would so willingly admit his shortcomings? He would rather die than to do such a thing, even to his mother! Then again, the fool was accustomed to disappointment. He, on the other hand, had experienced nothing but success his entire life. Anything else was unacceptable. Plus, clever men did not fail.

"She wishes to meet Miss Sagewick, you say?" he asked, returning to his seat.

Carrie nodded. "Yes, my lord. She was quite insistent about it."

So, this news had been worth the time. He could use the situation to his advantage. Perhaps an unexpected guest could arrive at just the right moment.

Alister placed a coin in the maid's hand, and she beamed. "Return there now," he said. "And remember, report back to me immediately if you learned anything new."

The girl agreed, bobbed a curtsy, and hurried from the room, but Alister barely noticed.

Lady Madeline rose from the couch where she had been listening to the entire encounter. "What will we do next, my lord?"

Alister pursed his lips to keep from chastising her. There was no "we" in this situation, only him. Still, Lady Madeline had proved useful to him in many ways. He was not ready to rid himself of her just yet.

"Four days from today, you will call unannounced to Coventry House," he replied with a sly smile. "You'll take with you tales about the museum theft, tales that you heard from me, a man you've come to realize is as villainous as *his lordship* said."

His lordship, indeed! If Alister had his way, the earl would be stripped of his title and cast out of England forever. He was an embarrassment to the *ton*. If only he had more influence over the King.

Lady Madeline frowned. "I don't understand, my lord. Why would I do that? I don't believe you're a villain."

Alister sighed. He glimpsed signs of an intelligent mind in this woman, but there were times when he questioned if she had any sense at all. Placing the back of his hand on her cheek, he smiled. "I realize that as a woman, a man's wisdom can seem complex. But if you remain quiet and pay very close attention, I shall explain my plan."

Her face darkened, but it only enhanced her beauty. "I'm not a child, my lord. Nor am I featherbrained."

He chuckled. "No, I suppose you are not." He sat beside her. "You will be an important player in this game, Lady Madeline. You are to continue earning Hainsley's trust. By doing so, he will take you into his confidence."

"I'm sorry, my lord, but I don't see how you can think he would confide his secrets to me. He barely sees me as a friend let alone a confidante."

"He may not tell you outright when he has found the treasure," Alister said, forcing back the annoyance that rose in him. "But I won't need you for that. Carrie will be listening for that particular news. No, if he truly trusts you, he will invite you to dine with him again. You will see that he does. Then, we will find a way to secure what is rightfully mine. Now do you understand?"

"Yes, my lord," Lady Madeline replied, her eyes wide with awe. "It's a clever plan, my lord!"

Alister smiled. "Of course, it is. I'm a clever man. Now, be silent while I think. I don't need a mindless woman prattling on and interrupting my thinking."

Now that he had formulated a plan for stealing what rightfully belonged to him, he allowed his thoughts to wander. He would become the wealthiest gentleman in all of England once he had procured the treasure! The things he could buy... the palms he could grease! Why, he could even sit at the right hand of the King himself!

Women would flock to him, gentlemen would bow down, his every whim would be pandered.

But above all, Alister could not wait to see the Hainsley name ruined once and for all.

Chapter Twenty-Nine

Catharina had spent hours wringing her hands and pacing the floor rather than doing anything meaningful. Whenever she took her embroidery hoop in hand or sat at the pianoforte—though she never had an aptitude for it, no matter how many hours she spent tapping at the keys—her thoughts returned to the letter she had received from Lord Hainsley a few days prior.

They had decided to maintain their distance from one another, agreeing to meet this evening. That would have been just fine to sit with him and discuss the clue—or to simply enjoy being in his company. But now he had included an introduction to his mother in that meeting. Now, all she could do was fret over whether she would make a good impression.

That was why she had spent the majority of the early afternoon preparing. After choosing—and discarding—a rainbow of dresses and gowns, Catharina finally settled on an amethyst-colored gown trimmed with intricate white lace.

She stifled a giggle, recalling a story that her mother had told her when she was younger. According to her great-grandmother, amethyst—the gem, not the color—could ward off drunkenness. If only it were true! Then she could indulge in as much wine as she pleased.

Unfortunately, she had learned on her own that the old wives' tale was untrue. The following day's aching head and churning stomach taught her that lesson.

From her ears hung amethyst earrings, which matched the teardrop-shaped pendant on her necklace. The jewelry had belonged to her mother and always brought her good luck. Perhaps they would keep her tongue from tying and her mind clear this evening.

She spent the short journey to Coventry House pulling at her white gloves and glancing out the window every few minutes. Terrible images of her misspeaking or offending the countess filled her mind. Perhaps she should feign illness and ask the driver to return to Ivywood Manor.

"It's unfortunate that Lady Whitmore was unable to attend," Lena said from the opposite bench. "But hopefully they will be able to make arrangements to see one another before Lady Hainsley returns to Cornwall."

"Indeed," Catharina replied absently. Lena had tried several times to initiate conversation but soon gave up when Catharina gave only short responses. Which only made Catharina worry more. If she could not hold a decent conversation with her companion, how could she do so with Lady Hainsley?

The moment she set eyes on Lord Hainsley, however, all her worries vanished. Catharina let out a soft sigh. Each time they met, he was more handsome than the time before if that were possible. His blond hair and blue eyes had always appealed to her, but tonight he was much more dashing. The way he wore his elegant dark-blue coat did little to hide the statuesque body beneath it. She could have stared at him for hours. He also stood taller this evening and seemed more self-assured, which eased her worries somewhat.

"Mother is waiting for us in the drawing room," Lord Hainsley said. "She is looking forward to meeting you."

Catharina nodded, but she struggled to swallow down the lump in her throat. "What if she does not approve of me? What will we do then?"

He chuckled. "That simply cannot happen, Miss Sagewick. Plus, she values my opinion, and my opinion is that you are too wonderful to find fault with."

A warmness coursed through her veins at his words. It was unfortunate that they were not alone, for she would have allowed him to kiss her. She glanced at Lena. Perhaps it was fortunate. They were not yet engaged, and here she was thinking of them kissing. Never would she have considered herself a harlot, but now she wondered if she did not have a bit of one inside her.

That thought only managed to make her cheeks burn. Proper ladies don't align themselves with women of that sort!

"Miss, may I make a suggestion?" Lena asked in her quiet voice.

"Yes, of course."

"Perhaps I should join the servants. Given that her ladyship will be in attendance, you'll have no need for a chaperone. A simple companion really has no place at the main table if there is no need of her. I think it would be for the best."

Catharina glanced at Lord Hainsley. "I doubt the countess will mind if—"

"I think that is a wonderful idea, Miss Page," the earl interrupted. He turned to Catharina. "And if Mother wishes to retire before you leave for Ivywood Manor, she may join us later."

"Well, if you both feel it would be best..."

"Oh, I do, miss," Lena said.

"Collins, take Lena to the kitchen and see she is served dinner."

The butler bowed deeply. "Yes, my lord."

Once the two servants were gone, the earl smiled at Catharina and said, "Well, let's meet my mother."

The countess was a striking woman, tall and imposing with dark hair free of any signs of silver, and smooth skin that belied her age. "My dear, it is wonderful to meet you," she gushed as she kissed Catharina's cheeks. "Gideon has told me so much about you that I feel as if I already know you."

Catharina felt the return of her blush. "It's a pleasure to make your acquaintance, my lady."

"Come, sit beside me," Lady Hainsley said, leading Catharina to the couch.

They engaged in small talk, which pleased Catharina. Thus far, the countess was an engaging lady. She did not make their first conversation into an interrogation, which was what Catharina had expected. Instead, they kept to pleasant topics.

Every so often, Catharina glanced at Lord Hainsley, who seemed as comfortable as Catharina felt.

"My son says you are staying with Lady Whitmore," Lady Hainsley said. "She and I have been well acquainted for many years."

Catharina smiled. "She and my father have been friends for some time now, so she invited me to stay. I've never experienced London in the summer."

Lady Hainsley chuckled. "You chose the best summer to be here. Usually it's stifling hot, which is why I spend the majority of my time in Cornwall. But this year has been much more pleasant than most."

Once they were called to dinner, the conversation continued, and Catharina felt her distress ease. Gideon had been correct. His mother did seem to approve of her. Her previous worries now seemed silly.

"You really must visit the Western Exchange," Lady Hainsley was saying. "I cannot imagine how you have not been there yet! One can find curiosities of all sorts and from every part of the world. I purchased a lovely Japanese folding screen several years ago that still adorns my boudoir. All my friends were so envious! And I was delighted." She paused and turned to Lord Hainsley. "That reminds me. Gideon, you were so occupied earlier, you missed this morning's news. Look at the paper there beside you."

Lord Hainsley picked up the newspaper, and Catharina caught sight of a headline that made her eyes bulge.

London Besieged by Thieving Couple

"I'm sure this is nothing but nonsense," Lord Hainsley said with a snort. "This rag tends to exaggerate even the least interesting story. They must sell their newspapers, after all."

"I'm afraid that is not the case in this instance," the countess insisted. "Apparently, the couple in question not only stole from the museum earlier this week, but they also took something from St. Paul's Cathedral." She clicked her tongue in vexation. "What has this world come to? And I'll not repeat what I heard they did while in the church! Decent people don't do such things in a house of God."

Catharina breathed a sigh of relief. So, no one had recognized them. Thank goodness! Giving a false name had helped immensely.

"Begging your pardon, my lord," Collins announced from the door, making Catharina start. "You have a guest who insists on speaking with you."

Lord Hainsley frowned. "Who would call during the dinner hour? Surely, they can wait to schedule an appointment."

The butler shook his head. "It is Lady Madeline, my lord."

Catharina gripped her fork so tightly, her fingers ached.

Lord Hainsley pushed back his chair. "My apologies, ladies. I shan't take long. Please, don't wait on my account. Continue enjoying your meal, and I'll return shortly."

Catharina watched him walk out of the room. What had brought that woman here unannounced? Although she claimed to be nothing more than the earl's friend, Catharina had her doubts. She had seen how some women looked at particular men, and that was how Lady Madeline looked at Lord Hainsley.

If she had her way, Catharina would lay the woman low with a single punch to her lovely nose!

"No one knows my son better than I," Lady Hainsley said with a knowing smile. "I can say with certainty that no other woman can draw his eye. Not even Lady Madeline."

Catharina sighed. "So, my jealousy is that evident, is it?"

The countess chuckled. "A lady has every right to be concerned when it comes to the men for whom she cares. What we mustn't do is allow our jealousy to misguide our perception."

"Misguide our perception?" Catharina asked.

Lady Hainsley set her utensils on her plate. "Indeed. Some women see deception at every turn. Any woman who even looks at the man for whom she cares becomes a target of her rage. But just because she's intrigued does not mean the man returns her interest. Ladies with any sense will give him the benefit of the doubt before allowing their jealousy to get the better of them."

Catharina considered Lady Hainsley's advice. The countess was right. Catharina could not make accusations without any proof of impropriety. The earl had been upfront with her about Lady Madeline and therefore deserved her trust.

That did not mean that Catharina trusted Lady Madeline. Which gave her cause to find out why the woman had called.

They finished their meal in silence. By the time the footmen had cleared the table, Lord Hainsley had not yet returned, and Catharina had to fight off the urge to go find him.

"I apologize for my rudeness," he said breathlessly, just as Catharina and Lady Hainsley were about to leave the dining room. His coat was wrinkled, and his hair tousled. "Our conversation went on longer than expected."

Conversation? Catharina could not help but wonder what sort of "conversation" could leave one looking as disheveled as he did right now.

"Mother, Miss Sagewick and I will meet you in the drawing room in a moment. Would you entertain Lady Madeline until we get there? We shan't be long, I promise."

Lady Hainsley glanced from her son to Catharina and back to her son again. "Just see that you're not."

Once the countess was gone, Lord Hainsley turned to Catharina. "I'm so very sorry."

"Your hair is mussed, my lord," she whispered. "Surely, you didn't allow Lady Madeline to run her hands through it. If so, I may have to shave it off your head."

Lord Hainsley laughed. "No, of course not." He peered into a nearby mirror and attempted to comb it with his fingers. "I tend to run my hand through it when I'm thinking."

Catharina sighed. He was not lying, for she had seen him do just that many times before. She clicked her tongue at him. "Would you stop that? You're making it worse." Standing on the tips of her toes, she did her best to put his hair back into place.

But when he caught her up by the waist, her breath caught. "What are you doing?" she asked, trying to sound demanding but doing a poor job of it. "Of all the times you should control yourself, now would be the most prudent. Your mother is just down the hall, and Lena is not here to chaperone. If either were to see you... manhandling me, my reputation would not survive."

His grin was mischievous. "I only wanted to help you retain your balance, Miss Sagewick. I'm well aware of how weak you are in my presence." He even had the gall to wink!

She slapped his arm. "Control yourself," she hissed. "And put me down at once!"

When he did as she bade, she settled back onto the soles of her feet, immediately missing his firm hold on her. To mask her volatile emotions, she smoothed out the skirts of her gown.

"Lady Madeline is here with news that affects both of us."

Catharina stopped midswipe and stared at him. "And what news is that?"

"It's about the museum," he said gravely. "Callingswell is spreading rumors that you and I are the culprits in the theft of the artifact."

"But how would he know it was us?" Catharina asked, mortified that anyone could place the blame on them. She was so sure no one had recognized them!

Lord Hainsley shrugged. "I don't know, but he has disparaged me for years. He wishes to ruin me and won't give up until he has done so. What troubles me is that he has dragged your name into it."

"How terrible!" Catharina gasped. "What are we to do?"

"We have an ally in Lady Madeline. She's agreed to continue to see him, so she can learn more about his plans. Then she will report what she learns back to me. This is a blessing, her coming to me, for Callingswell has the power and wealth to destroy me."

A maid entered the room and began wiping a rag across the table, yet Catharina paid her little attention. "But this makes no sense. Why is she so quick to go against Lord Callingswell in order to help you? Are you certain she's not using the situation to get closer to you?"

Lord Hainsley took an angry step backward. "What is this about?" he demanded. "The war raging between the Hainsleys and the Callingswells has gone on for decades. Are you saying that you don't trust me to be in the presence of another woman?"

How she wished to tell him that it was Lady Madeline she did not trust and not him! But doing so would only enrage him further. He simply would not understand a woman's intuition. Few men did.

She sighed. "I'm sorry. I do trust you."

"Thank you. Now, we should go before Mother thinks we've been doing something improper."

Catharina studied the maid, who had paused in her work. Had she been listening in on their conversation? When she noticed Catharina watching her, the younger blonde woman returned to her cleaning with vigor. Something about the maid did not sit well with Catharina, but she could not have explained what that something was if she were asked.

Just as she was about to tell Lord Hainsley about her suspicions, she stopped. He would just think she was acting like a jealous girl, and she did not wish to upset him again.

As they entered the drawing room, they found Lady Madeline speaking with Lady Hainsley. "And the woman had the nerve to say that I didn't know my gems!" she was saying. When she caught sight of Catharina and Lord Hainsley, she paused and smiled. "There you are. I was beginning to think you got lost in your own home."

Lord Hainsley laughed. "You remember Miss Sagewick?"

"Yes, of course," Lady Madeline said in a sweet tone that made the hair on Catharina's arms stand on end. "How wonderful to see again."

Catharina did not trust this woman in the least. No matter how much Lord Hainsley said otherwise, something was amiss. And it had nothing to do with jealousy.

Summoning a warm smile, Catharina replied, "Wonderful indeed. In fact, you've been on my mind often since we met last week. And now, here you are."

As they engaged in small talk, Catharina found Lady Madeline dull and her conversational abilities lacking. Who cared about the colors of the flowers in her father's garden or what she had for luncheon the previous week?

Then again, few women enjoyed adventure as much as Catharina did.

"It's as I told Christopher," Lady Madeline said before turning her attention to Catharina. "That is, Lord Sidley. He's a mutual friend of Lord Hainsley and myself."

"How nice for you," Catharina said, making a mental note to never attend one of his parties.

As Lady Madeline prattled on about nothing of consequence, Catharina prayed she would grow tired and leave.

When the woman finally announced her departure, Catharina had to force herself from leaping out of her chair and dancing a jig.

"I suppose you will be leaving soon as well," Lady Hainsley said to Catharina.

"Yes, I should return to Ivywood Manor before it grows too late."

"Then I'll say goodnight." She kissed Catharina's cheek. "My son adores you," she whispered. "No one can threaten that."

Relief washed over Catharina. "Thank you." She had developed a certain kinship with the countess, one she hoped would become true kinship.

After his mother left, Lord Hainsley returned from seeing Lady Madeline to the door. "Is all well?" he asked.

Although Catharina truly did trust him, the doubts that had consumed her about Lady Madeline returned. But his mother was right. No woman could ever steal him away from her. Not if he cared about her as much as she claimed.

"Yes, very well," she replied. There was one area in which Lady Madeline could not replace Catharina. "Now, are you ready to ask for my help in solving the latest riddle? Or do you plan to botch it up yourself again?"

Chapter Thirty

It was as if the weight of the world were upon Gideon's shoulders. How did Titan Atlas endure it? Fire had consumed one of his most productive tenant farms. An outbreak of a strange disease wiped out over a hundred sheep on another. And now, his mother knew about their financial troubles. Oh, yes, and Lord Callingswell was actively attempting to destroy him. Yes, things had become dire, indeed.

He had some sense of relief that Lady Madeline was willing to help.

"I shall remain close to his lordship and thus you will know his exact plans to destroy you. And trust me, my lord, that is precisely his plan."

That had been what she had said during their meeting. Her sudden appearance had ruined the wonderful dinner with Miss Sagewick, but the sacrifice had been well worth it. Miss Sagewick had understood; she had said as much. And why would she not? Lady Madeline's aid could benefit them both in the end.

Yet when he had rejoined the ladies in the drawing room, he was met with a frown from Miss Sagewick. She had made it clear that she did not approve of Lady Madeline, and he had no idea how to calm her worries. But he had to at least try to do so.

He led Miss Sagewick to the couch after his mother had gone to bed. "You do understand there is nothing to concern yourself with Lady Madeline, correct? Granted, I can see how you could worry. After all, I have dashingly good looks that turn every woman's head."

He grinned at her, but she did not laugh at his joke. She was far more jealous of Lady Madeline than he thought.

"Do you not trust me?" he asked.

She smoothed her skirts in that way women did when they were uncomfortable. Or annoyed. He suspected it was more the latter than the former.

"I do trust you, my lord," she said, sighing heavily. "But she is an entirely different thing altogether."

Gideon could only nod. Women were complicated creatures prone to jealousy. Therefore, he would have to approach the subject with care. "I can assure you that I have kept my wits about me. And I'll continue to do so." He chuckled. "It's not as if she were after my lack of wealth."

Miss Sagewick knitted her brows. "Is all well with your estate, my lord?"

Gideon cursed himself inwardly. He had not meant to reveal his money troubles to her. Now he had two women who were important to him who knew he was struggling financially. Which was unfair to them. The responsibility for keeping his estate in order was his, not the ladies in his family. Well, Miss Sagewick was not a member of his family, but she could be...

The question now was, did he tell her the truth? That his sleep was restless, his mind worried, and there were times he wanted to do nothing more than to give up and walk away from it all?

No, he could not do that. He could not allow any woman, especially Miss Sagewick, to turn and walk away in this situation. He was a man of adventure, or so she believed, which meant he needed to maintain the appearance of financial stability.

"Of course, all is well," he said.

Just then, Lena entered the room. "I hope you don't mind if I see to some of my work, miss," she said. In her hand, she held a sewing basket and what appeared to be a stocking.

"No, of course not," Miss Sagewick replied with a small smile.

Lena bobbed a curtsy and went to sit in a chair beside one of the lamps.

Her sudden appearance was a relief, for now Gideon would not need to expound on his reply about his finances.

After asking Collins to have more coffee brought up, Gideon sat beside Miss Sagewick on the couch. Reaching into his pocket, he removed a folded piece of paper. "I made a copy of the clue. I say we study it before you return to Ivywood Manor."

Miss Sagewick nodded, took the paper from him, and read the riddle aloud:

To find the reward, the pure swan will tell,
For its elixir is known all too well.
The descendants gather at half a man's height,
Their cups raised to the fallen knight.
In death he shows the prize they seek,
And the offering required sold on the street.

The sound of Miss Sagewick's voice mesmerized Gideon. It was soft and melodic; she might as well have been singing the clue rather than reading it.

She cleared her throat. "Perhaps you should focus on the clue rather than on me, my lord."

As if awakened from a trance, Gideon laughed. "Yes, I suppose I should. Well, what do you think? This bit about 'the pure swan' refers to eternal childhood, purity, in Templar lore."

"I am amazed at how much you know about their history," she said. "But what about the 'half a man's height'? Could that have anything to do with children?"

"Nothing in the lore pertains to children," he said. "At least what I know. No, it must be something else, but what?" For some time, they continued to study the words, each giving suggestions on what certain passages might mean, but none seemed very illuminating.

"I like your mother," Miss Sagewick said without warning. "I can imagine myself spending a great deal of time with her in the future. She's amusing and clever and has a kindness about her that appeals to me."

"I'm pleased to hear that," Gideon said, perplexed by her sudden change in subject. "And I can see that she likes you, too. She's returning to Cornwall at the end of the week, and I have no idea when she'll be back in London again. How long will you be staying with Lady Whitmore?"

Miss Sagewick sighed heavily. Lena coughed, but it sounded as if she were covering a giggle.

"What is it?" Gideon asked, perplexed. "Did I misspeak?"

Miss Sagewick pursed her lips and lifted her nose. Even her back straightened. "My lord, when the woman you are courting says she would like to spend time with your mother in the future, she typically indicates that she is thinking beyond their courtship." He must have appeared as blank-minded as he felt, for she sighed again. Why did women sigh so much? "You are a baffling gentleman, my lord. You can reason out clues about castles and caves with little trouble, but you don't understand what is right in front of your face."

Gideon closed his eyes. How could he have missed the obvious? She spoke of marriage. So, she hoped he would propose? He would have done so at that very moment, but without the treasure, he would have no means to properly provide for her. A cottage on a farm was no place for a countess. And such a home was especially not meant for the lovely Miss Sagewick.

Her look of disappointment tore at Gideon's heart. He had not meant to hurt her in any way. Reaching out, he placed a hand atop hers. "In due time, we *will* marry," he assured her. "I promise. But now is not the time."

His words seemed to placate her, for the rigidity in her shoulders seemed to soften and the worry on her features became a smile. "If that is true, I hope the time passes quickly, for you'll find that I'm impatient when it comes to engagements."

Gideon laughed. "Is that so? How many engagements have you experienced thus far?"

He had meant it as a joke, but she responded without hesitation. "Oh, yes. Twice, actually." Her face softened, and she smiled. "The first was a viscount. He was supposed to propose to me on a Saturday but canceled because a relative had died. He did return a week later, but I refused his offer. How selfish can a man be to put off proposing to the woman he says he loves?"

"Selfish?" Gideon asked, his jaw dropping. "I hardly think that the loss of a family member is cause to..." His words trailed off as Miss Sagewick began to laugh.

"You are far too easy to tease, my lord," she said, dabbing the corner of her eye with a handkerchief. "But truthfully, besides Lord Langley, whose engagement to me lasted a mere hour, I've received no other proposals. But I'm certain there were plenty of gentlemen who considered asking."

"And what about before your... incident with the Langleys?" Gideon asked. "Lady Whitmore mentioned you've spent little time in London. Did you not attend at least one Season? Surely you had every gentleman vying for your attention if you did."

"Oh, they were," she said, waving a dismissive hand. "But they were all insufferably tedious in every conceivable way. Every time I considered whether I could entertain affection for a particular gentleman, the answer was a resounding *no*." She arched an expectant eyebrow. "Now, out with it. Don't be selfish with your story. I imagine you've had all sorts of ladies hoping to catch your eye."

Enjoying her playfulness, Gideon slowly rose from his chair. Two could play at that game.

"Where are you going?" she asked, the mirth gone from her tone.

He sighed heavily. "You're right. I mustn't be selfish. In fact, it's about time I was honest with you." He turned to face the fireplace to keep her from seeing his lips twitch. "I've promised no fewer than five women that I would eventually propose marriage. Now, I must write and explain to them that I cannot marry them after all. I'll invite them to the wedding, of course. It's the least I can do for breaking their hearts. And I see no reason we cannot remain friends. With your permission, of course."

Her gasp was satisfying. "Well, if you invite any of your hussies to our wedding, I'll marry Collins instead."

The butler, who was gathering their empty coffee cups, turned a deep crimson.

Gideon, however, roared with laughter. "What do you think of that, Collins? Would you marry Miss Sagewick if the opportunity arose?"

"I... I'm a butler, my lord. If you required me to do so, I suppose I would."

To that, Gideon laughed so hard that his sides hurt. All his worries were gone, and that was due to only one thing. Or rather one person—Miss Sagewick. And suddenly, he knew for certain that he would one day marry this woman. No matter what it took, he would find a way.

"I don't think there will be any need," Gideon said, returning to his seat. "But perhaps you can help us in another way. Listen to this and see if any of it makes any sense to you. It's a riddle of sorts."

He read the clue aloud to the butler:

To find the reward, the pure swan will tell,
For its elixir is known all too well.
The descendants gather at half a man's height,
Their cups raised to the fallen knight.
In death he shows the prize they seek,
And the offering required sold on the street.

Collins stood straighter and wore a wide grin. "You are kind, my lord, to allow me to offer my opinion. One particular line, the reference to half a man's height, brings to mind a time when I was young. My father took me to a particular public house. I sat in a chair at one of the tables across from him. He was a very tall man, my father, but I shall always remember how much shorter he looked sitting in that chair."

Gideon frowned. What did that story have to do with the clue? "Thank you, Collins. You may go."

After the butler was gone, Miss Sagewick leapt from her chair. "That's it!"

"What is *it*?"

"The pure swan will tell, the raising of cups, chairs," she said excitedly.

Gideon also rose. "Yes! Pure. White. The White Swan! It's a public house that has been around for years. And the white swan is a symbol of the Knights Templar."

"'Their cups raised to the fallen knight,'" Miss Sagewick read from the paper. "What if the 'elixir' here means 'ale'?"

"It's also a gathering place, as the clue indicates," Gideon added, nodding vigorously. "And as Collins so aptly noted, if a man sits in a chair, he is then half his height. It makes perfect sense!"

Excitement filled the air. Tonight had proved to be a wonderful evening. Now they were a step closer to finding the treasure. And when they did find it, Gideon would ask Miss Sagewick to marry him.

Chapter Thirty-One

Three days after her dinner at Coventry House, Catharina wondered how far she was willing to go for Lord Hainsley. She had lied, stolen, and even flirted with other men, all to help the earl with his quest. And what had she received in return? A discussion about marriage without the benefit of a proposal!

Perhaps that was a bit harsh. She had not expected him to propose that night, but she had at least hoped that he would be the one to broach the subject. She had even given him a hint. But rather than noticing her subtle reference to the future, he instead left it to her to state the obvious. Were all men's skulls so thick when it came to matters of the heart?

Glassmore Street was by no means in the vilest part of London, but it wasn't a place a lady would frequent unless engaged in unsavory activities.

"And here I stand, in front of a public house that appears to be of ill repute," she said to Lena as they stood before a pub with dirty windows and a strange stench emanating from the door every time it opened. "Waiting for a man I've grown fond of to arrive. And yet again, he is late. I won't speak aloud the thoughts going through my mind at this very moment! Ladies refrain from using such language, even in a place like this."

They had arrived some twenty minutes ago—at the exact time indicated by Lord Hainsley. Only he was not there. And she would certainly not enter a public house without him. Not even with a chaperone! Proper ladies simply did not do such things.

"He'll be here soon, miss," Lena said. "Try to remain positive. I'm sure there is something nearby that we can appreciate."

The words had no sooner reached Catharina's ears than a man in tattered trousers stumbled out of the tavern, the stench of stale ale following behind him. As he walked toward them, Catharina stiffened.

"Beggin' yer pardon, milady," he said, removing his cap and pressing it against his threadbare coat. His breath reeked of whiskey, and Catharina had to stop herself from taking a step backward. Or from running away altogether. "This here's a bit o' a bad place ye be in, milady. 'Tis a shame ye ain't got no gentleman with ye. Now, if you'd be needin' one, Levi—that'd be me, milady—I'd be at yer service."

Relief washed over Catharina, and she smiled. "I appreciate the offer, Levi, but I do have a gentleman joining me momentarily. But if he fails to arrive, I'll gladly accept your kind offer of protection."

"Ye can find me at me house, milady," he said, pointing a grimy finger down the street to the left of the pub. "Five doors down." He frowned. "Or is it six? Well, it don't matter none. Just look for the red door. That'd be me place."

She gave a single nod. "I shall. Thank you."

The drunken man mumbled something about answered prayers, turned, and began singing a song that made Catharina's cheeks heat.

When he was gone, Catharina turned to Lena, who was worrying her bottom lip. "I know," Catharina said. "Decorum and all that. But he left singing. Is it a crime to bring joy to another?"

"Certainly not," Lena said. "You seem to have a gift for cheering people up. Look what you've done for his lordship."

Catharina looked down the street to where Lena indicated and laughed upon seeing Lord Hainsley taking long strides toward them. "My, yes, you're right. Now if I could only make him be on time."

Lord Hainsley approached with purpose. "No sauciness from you,

Miss Sagewick," he said, breathing heavily as if he had just run a race. "I realize I'm late. My meeting with the bank went longer than expected."

Catharina recalled how he had alluded to being in financial straits. And now he was meeting a banker? Although he had assured her all was well, she had her doubts.

"No need to worry, my lord," she said with a sniff. "I've grown accustomed to being at the bottom of your list of priorities." She grinned at his mock look of affront. "Are we ready?"

Lord Hainsley drew in a deep breath. "A public house is no place for a fine lady. And this one even less so. A woman of your innocence and beauty would only cause problems for the men inside. And although I'm certain I could defend your honor, I would prefer that you stayed clear of such terrible circumstances."

"My what?" she said, placing her hands on her hips and taking a menacing step forward, "My beauty will cause problems?"

"Don't be insulted, Miss Sagewick," he said, raising his hands as if to defend himself from her wrath. He was lucky she did not pummel him right there on the spot! Still, he continued with his nonsense. "If I need the men to be distracted, I'll return to get you."

Catharina managed a small smile, but her ire kept her from allowing it to form completely. "Allow me to explain a simple point to you. If you refuse to allow me to accompany you inside, other men will be the least of your worries. Now, shall we go together, or will you spend the entire evening wondering what I paid the cook to put in your dinner?"

Lord Hainsley threw his head back and laughed before taking her hand. "Miss Sagewick, you are a raging fire that cannot be quenched. Very well, because I value my life far too much, you may join me. But behave yourself. Keep your flirtation under control while we are there."

Insufferable man!

"Don't test me, my lord," she whispered. "Or I may just marry the first drunkard I see!"

That mischievous grin sent pleasant shivers down her spine. This banter they shared made all this worth whatever trouble they got themselves into. "We'll just see about that."

Lena was less pleased about entering the pub, but she followed dutifully behind them, nonetheless. The place was dark and dank with a long counter running down along the wall to the left with high stools, all empty except for one man, in front of it. The room was L-shaped, and tables and chairs filled the space, seven of the seats occupied by patrons.

Catharina followed Lord Hainsley to the bar where a bald man with a stern countenance greeted them. "What'll ye be havin', milord?"

The earl placed his hands on the counter. "Your finest brandy, good sir. And I would like to know a bit about your business. When did it come into ownership? If you are the proprietor, that is."

Catharina groaned inwardly. She might not have spent time in public houses or with the likes of the working men who frequented such places, but she knew that Lord Hainsley was so far removed from them that he would never get an answer. Not outright, anyway.

"Three ales will do us just fine, sir," she said to the barman. She looked around them and gave an appreciative smile. "You have a fine establishment here."

The stern look softened. "Why, thank ye, milady. It's been in me family fer more'n four hundred years. Or at least, that's how far back we can trace it with records bein' what they are 'n all. A few've been lost 'cause of fires, but me ancestors kept good records themselves."

She opened her eyes wide. "Is that right? Four hundred years? How fascinating! Why, I'm not sure I would get more than two hundred and fifty years of my family history. Quite remarkable."

The barman poured the ales as he spoke. "We're not sure 'xactly how old it is, but it be famous, ye know. Fancy lords, foreign kings, even descendants of the Knights Templar themselves tipped a mug or two at one time or 'nother."

"Tell me more about these knights," Lord Hainsley said. "What have you heard about them?"

With a deep frown, the barman placed the mugs on the top of the counter, collected the coins, and walked down to speak to the single patron at the other end of the bar.

"Perhaps you would like to flog him openly," Catharina said, shaking her head. At his blank expression, she added, "Why are you being so ill-tempered? You cannot feed him vinegar and expect to get wine in return!"

Lord Hainsley sighed. "He has information we need. And why are you ordering ale? I would prefer to drink something other than whatever swill they serve here."

Catharina pursed her lips. "Because we are in a public house, not a gentleman's club. Now, get off your high horse. If we are to build rapport with him, we cannot be putting on airs."

"I'm surprised you've not started flirting with him yet," he said with a snort. "You do realize that simple conversation can get us what we want."

Catharina laughed and laid a hand on his arm. "You know, you are so adorable when you're grumpy." Upon seeing the barman returning, she quickly added, "Now, let me talk to him. It would do you well to observe and learn." Before allowing the earl the chance to argue, she smiled at the barman. "What is your name, sir?"

"Donald, milady."

"Donald?" Catharina repeated. "That was my grandfather's name, and a handsome one at that." She took a sip of the ale. Not the finest drink but bearable. "I hope you don't think me nosy, but I'm sure you have some wonderful stories that have been handed down from your ancestors about the knights who drank in your fine establishment. I just find history so fascinating."

She batted her eyelashes for good measure. And, as expected, Lord Hainsley groaned, but the barman grinned. "'Tain't nosy, milady. A fine lady such as yerself only needs to ask, and I'll see it done."

Catharina smiled warmly. "A true gentleman." She glanced at Lord Hainsley. "A rare find these days." When his face darkened, her smile widened. Teasing him had proved to be a delightful addition to any outing.

The barman leaned an elbow on the counter and leaned across it. "Stories, they get handed down from father to son. There were always whispers of the Knights Templar 'round these parts long after they were disbanded or killed off. Haven't seen 'em meself, mind ye, but me papa, he told me a tale ye may find interestin'."

Catharina nodded. "Oh, yes, please! Go on."

"We've a tradition here that started years ago—centuries, really. The knights, they'd come in here to drink to one of their fallen comrades. They'd raise their glasses, and each of 'em would speak of the other's bravery 'n such."

Catharina glanced around the dark interior. Were they toasting to a particular part of the pub? Perhaps an engraving or a mark on one wall that has since been removed. Or a painting of some sort that had to be put away after the group was disbanded. Hopefully, he would include such information in his telling.

Unfortunately, he did not. He stood back up and began to rub the counter with a rag. "It's just a tale, milady. Papa said he saw it once when he was young. Five maybe? I'd like to believe him, but he was fond of the drink, so his tales could be a bit fanciful." He sighed heavily. "The Knights Templar's gone now, killed off so long ago, there ain't no one left to tell what the real truth is. All that's left are the stories."

Catharina glanced at Lord Hainsley, who looked ready to burst at the seams with excitement. They were drawing closer to what they needed to know, and it was clear he was doing his best to not interrupt.

She turned her attention back to the barman. "Your tale is so fascinating! I'm sure you have many more stories to tell, but do you mind if I ask you a question?"

"Of course, milady."

"You said they raised their glasses to a fallen knight. Was this done in any particular direction? Or was it done in general?"

The barman scratched his bald head. "Well, I don't know 'bout a direction exactly. There was a paintin' that hung here at one time, but Helga, she be me wife, she thought it was too ugly and had me get rid of it. I might be willin' to face off with a drunkard, but not her." He chuckled at this.

So, there it was. The next clue had been long since discarded. Their adventure had come to a sad end. "I see," she said. "You're a very good husband to discard a piece of history to appease your wife."

With a chuckle, the barman shook his head. "She only thinks I got rid of it, milady." His grin was reminiscent of a boy stealing a pie from the window of his mother's kitchen. "I stored it away. Beggin' yer pardon for saying so, but ye can't always give into a woman's every whim."

Catharina nearly leapt from the stool to throw her arms around this man. "I could not agree with you more, Donald. We often follow our hearts rather than our minds." She looked around them conspiratorially. "Would you be willing to show it to me?" Lord Hainsley cleared his throat, and she amended her request. "Us? If it's nearby, that is."

"Absolutely!" Donald chuckled and bent a finger to beckon them. "Come 'round here to this side, milady."

She and Lord Hainsley followed the barman to a door behind the counter, which led to a dimly lit hallway. They stopped at an old door.

"It's in here, milady. But if ye're wantin' me to sell it, I won't."

"We wouldn't think of making such an offer," Lord Hainsley said. "But I, too, am intrigued. Would you mind if we take a look at it?"

Donald paused and looked behind them. "Well, I s'pose it'll be all right, milord. Just put it back when yer done. I don't want Helga to find it and use it for firewood." He opened the door and lit a lantern that hung from a peg. "It's there in the corner, behind that pile of crates. Helga, she don't come in here much except to get somethin' for the pub, so I know it's still there."

Once they were alone, Catharina followed Lord Hainsley to the place the barman had indicated. Indeed, the painting was still there, covered with an old cloth. It depicted four knights carrying a casket toward a large church. On the lid of the casket was a long sword with a lamb lying at its hilt.

"That is the symbol of the Knights Templar!" Lord Hainsley said in an excited whisper. "This must be the final clue." He unfolded the paper with the clue. "That must be the fallen knight, and the others are carrying his casket to the Templar Church for the last rites."

Catharina brought the lantern closer and squinted at the shapes. "There," she said, pointing to the knights. "Look at their hands. They are each clutching the stem of a rose."

Lord Hainsley nodded. "Yes, that was a requirement. They were to bring four roses to this fallen man's grave." He turned toward her.

"There are tombs inside that temple, Miss Sagewick. We did it! We found where the treasure is located!"

Happiness bubbled inside Catharina, and she threw her arms around Lord Hainsley. Never had she experienced such excitement. She could not have smiled any wider than she did right now! "I'm at a loss for words, my lord," she said.

He gripped her waist, and her breath came in short gasps. Her eyes searched his, and she could see the desire that matched hers.

"You may kiss me," she whispered.

Lord Hainsley lowered his lips toward her but suddenly stepped away. "Let's return the painting so we can leave."

Catharina was stunned. Why had he denied her a kiss? But then she heard a familiar voice from behind her and understood.

"Is everything all right?" Lena asked. "When the barman returned without you, I thought it would be best if I at least stood in the hallway. But I could not do so forever. If Lady Whitmore found out—"

"Of course," Catharina said, smiling. And wanting to throttle her at the same time. Which was unfair. She was only doing what was required of her. "We found what we needed and were just about to join you."

The kiss would have to wait for another day.

On their journey back to Ivywood Manor, they agreed to meet again in two days' time, so they could go to the temple.

Once there, Gideon would complete the quest given to him by his father. And if all worked out as it should, he would finally tell her what she wanted to hear.

Chapter Thirty-Two

Gideon had purchased five roses from an old woman with a cart in Covent Garden. Four he would take to the Temple Church, and the fifth he would give to a lady so deserving. And as he stood outside the massive temple, he smiled upon seeing Lady Whitmore's private carriage approaching. Inside would be Miss Sagewick, whom he had looked forward to seeing these last two days.

How fortunate he had been that the countess had introduced them. Yet there was still the question of Miss Sagewick's past that continued to prick at the back of his mind. She was a master thief, proved true by her actions over the past few weeks.

She insisted that her old ways were behind her and that she had only taken them back up to assist him. Now he was in her debt, and the rose would be the first of many gifts to come. Once the treasure was secured, he would lavish her with whatever her heart desired.

The driver set out the step, and Gideon smiled as Miss Sagewick alighted. Her blue dress brought out the color in her eyes, which were set deep inside the brim of her bonnet. She was more beautiful than ever.

He stepped forward and offered her one of the roses. "For you,

Miss Sagewick," he said. "Yet it pales in comparison to your perfection."

Her cheeks turned the color of the petals as she brought it to her nose and inhaled deeply of its fragrance. "Thank you, my lord. Like you, it means a great deal." With a sigh, she handed the rose to Lena, who set it inside the carriage. "My father wrote and said he will be coming on Monday to collect me. And he wishes to meet the man who is courting me."

Gideon smiled. "I'll be sure to make the best impression on him. Now, let's go inside."

The afternoon sun shone brightly as they made their way to the entrance of the temple. It was quite distinctive with its rounded wing at one end, said to have been modeled after the Church of the Holy Sepulchre in Jerusalem.

The moment they stepped inside, the temperature cooled significantly. The floor was of white marble with large black squares at even intervals down the center. Stone columns became distinctive arches that filled the domed ceiling of the circular nave.

"How magnificent," Miss Sagewick breathed beside him. "The draperies, the artwork, I've never seen anything so wonderful."

Indeed, gold tasseled red tapestries the height of ten men hung from the walls. Most depicted simple crosses, but one showed a swan and another a single sword. Stained glass windows filled the wall behind the altar in the chancel, which was common in most churches. What differed was the placement of the pews. Rather than rows facing the altar at the front of the nave, these were set up like seating in the House of Lords—vertically along both walls, so they faced the center. Perhaps they had been used for the choir at one time, for that of what Gideon was reminded, but there was no other seating for the congregation.

"What are those?" Miss Sagewick asked with a gasp.

"Those are called 'grotesques'" he replied. And no wonder. The stone carvings of faces that dotted the walls of the nave were indeed grotesque to behold. With tongues sticking out and twisted expressions, all were bizarre.

In the middle of the circular room was a grave surrounded by an iron fence. Gideon's heartbeat quickened.

"Look at the inscription!" he said in an excited whisper.

She joined him at one corner of the fence and gasped. "'Hainsley'," she read aloud. "'He who honors the Oath and protects the Grail, his name shall be forever remembered.'"

A thousand thoughts flashed through Gideon's mind. "My grandfather was not as mad as everyone believed. My ancestor was truly a Knight Templar!"

Pride swelled inside him. After all these years, stories that were passed down from each generation to the next proved to be true. And now, Gideon had honored his father's dying wish. Today he would receive a treasure, one that was vast, indeed. If what he had been told was true.

Images came to mind. The *ton* would now welcome him back. He would purchase a multitude of estates. Yet the best to come was that he would marry Miss Sagewick and provide her with everything she could ever want.

Miss Sagewick placed a gentle hand on his arm. "So, your bloodline includes many men of adventure, it seems. How fortunate you are!" She walked to the other side of the tomb. "And look. There are holders of some sort."

Indeed, in each corner of the fence were iron cylinders with an opening just the right size for a stem. "Let's place a rose in each of them."

Once the roses were placed, they met in front of the low gate. Gideon had no idea what to expect. Certainly, the tomb would not begin to rumble, nor would his long dead relation rise from the grave.

And, of course, neither happened. Instead, a heavy oak door to their right opened, and a silver-haired man dressed in a long robe emerged. He was dressed in modern attire, but the cloak embroidered with red crosses was clearly as old as the temple itself.

"You've come to honor our fallen brother?" the man asked. "Tell me why."

With a reassuring nod from Catharina, Gideon said, "My name is Gideon, Earl of Hainsley. My father revealed a secret to me while on his deathbed." As he went on to tell the story, he began to smile. He had not been forced to take this adventure alone; Miss Sagewick had accompanied him the entire way, making the adventure all the more pleasant. "Therefore, sir, I am here to claim the treasure that is hidden here. The Holy Grail, perhaps? That is what the legend says, is it not?"

The man gave a single nod. "Indeed, the Grail does exist. But before you can see it, I must tell a story about a brave knight named Hainsley. Three hundred years ago, long after the Knights Templar were disbanded, we continued to protect the Church and the Crown in secret, for that was our sacred duty. One we were unwilling to abandon. Knowledge was passed from father to son of each generation, thus keeping the order alive, even today. For hundreds of years, the Knights did what they were meant to do without benefit of acknowledgment or commendation."

"But the power of the Grail is unparalleled, and thus also alluring. Two among our ranks turned to evil. They were willing to do anything to possess its power." He motioned to the grave. "Hainsley hid the Grail to keep it from falling into the hands of those willing to do whatever it took, even commit murder, in order to possess it."

Gideon's throat tightened as he glanced at the grave. "Are you saying that his death was not natural? Did those rogue knights kill him?"

The older man nodded. "They did. And his death was not slow. He suffered greatly, and still, Hainsley refused to speak."

Just the idea of such a thing appalled Gideon. "And his comrades, the knights who remained virtuous, were they able to retrieve the Grail from its hiding place and keep it safe?"

"They were, my lord."

Gideon's heart pounded in his chest. The Holy Grail, the very Grail from which Christ drank truly existed? The price one could receive in the sale of such an item would be more than any bank could hold!

"And is that why you honor him in this way? Because he protected it?"

"Yes," the man replied. "And it is why we've set aside certain clues for his worthy descendants, to lead them here to claim the reward."

A sudden surge of pride filled Gideon. He, not his ancestors, would claim the reward. Finally, he would have a means to restore his name.

"Excuse me, sir," Miss Sagewick said. "You mentioned other descendants. Can it be assumed that they, too, found their way here?"

"They did."

She frowned. "Then why did they not leave with it?"

The older man gave a sad shake of his head. "You'll soon learn why."

"Are you certain it is the one and only Holy Grail?" Gideon asked. He could pay off all his debts, secure his mother's estate in Cornwall, and purchase whatever Miss Sagewick's heart desired. Their future, and that of their descendants, would be set for eternity!

"The Grail is a powerful artifact, my lord," the man said. "For one to possess it, he must adhere to a single rule."

Gideon stood up straighter. "Whatever is required, I swear I will do."

The cloak rustled as the man took a step forward. "Very well, here is the single requirement. In exchange for adhering to the rule, whoever possesses the Grail will receive power and wealth that rivals any kingdom on this earth. But his dedication can only be to the safety of the Grail and nothing—or anyone—else. Therefore, the only requirement is that you must forsake any and all love for the remainder of your life." He clasped his hands behind his back. "I shall allow you time to consider your decision." Turning, he walked several steps away.

It was as if the air had been sucked out of the room. Gideon's head spun, and his temples ached. "This cannot be!" he shouted at the man's back. "How can a man forsake love?"

The man did not reply. In a single breath, Gideon had gone from the elation of having a way to see all his financial dreams realized to the truth of his financial ruin slamming him in the back.

"This is ridiculous," he fumed as he turned to Miss Sagewick. He lowered his voice, hoping the man would not overhear him. "There may be a way. If I send you away, just until I've secured the Grail, perhaps we can marry in secret. No one needs to know. Once I have the Grail in my possession, it will not matter. With the power it contains, I can do whatever I wish."

Miss Sagewick shook her head. "We cannot lie, my lord."

Gideon's ire sparked. "We have done nothing but lie since the inception of this quest. And we've cheated and stolen as well. We could become the wealthiest couple in England. In the entire world, for that matter!" Yet she did not appear to hear him, and he grabbed her by the arms. "I can buy you anything you want. We would rival even royalty. People will adore us. Does the idea of that not please you?"

A single tear rolled down her cheek as she shook her head. "No, my lord. *You* make me happy."

Gideon reached up to brush away the tear, but when his fingertip touched her skin, memories flashed in his mind. The first time they met and the lie he had told her. His distrust of her and his attempts to rid himself of her. All the while, she remained by his side, not once asking for anything for herself. They had worked together and now had found the treasure. Was that not what he had promised his father?

But how could he pass on such wealth? Surely, Miss Sagewick could understand why he would choose to dedicate his life to the Grail?

And now, more than ever, Gideon had an important decision to make. One that would decide the rest of his life. The only question was, would he choose correctly?

Chapter Thirty-Three

The promise had been untold wealth, yet the sacrifice it would take to have it made Catharina's heart break in two. For it meant that she and Lord Hainsley would be separated forever. His arguments made it clear what his decision would be, as did the longing in his eyes. Therefore, she braced herself for the heartache that soon would come.

"I understand what you must do," she said. "And I do not fault you for your decision. Giving up all that wealth would not be easy for anyone."

The words cut her as deeply as a sword to her breast, but she had to be brave enough to face the truth. Today, they would part ways. Wealth beyond imagination was not something with which she could compete. Nor was it something in which she had an interest. She might have stolen in the past, but the act had never been for the promise of riches.

Desperately blinking back tears, she tried to pull her hands from his, but he only gripped them tighter. She had to get away. Every moment in his presence would only make their parting that much more difficult. But she also wanted to savor every moment that she could.

Oh, but this was proving to be harder than she could have imagined! How could she live without him?

You can, she told herself. *Because you must.*

"Before I give you my decision," he said, "there is something you must know. I have lied to you."

Catharina could not keep herself from gaping. Lied? About what? But she did not ask the question but instead allowed him to explain.

"When we first met, I allowed you to believe I was a man of adventure. You were adamant that only such a gentleman could earn your admiration, so I told you what you wanted to hear. But the truth is, I lead a boring life, as you so aptly put it."

A sudden smile lit up his face, causing her heartbeat to quicken, just as it had every moment they were together these past weeks.

"But since that first meeting, my life has been anything but boring. It has been one long wonderful adventure, one of which I never thought myself capable. With a single word, I can have great wealth. With it, I can purchase anything in this world. Which leads to another truth I've kept from you. My estate is nearing financial ruin."

"I'm sorry," Catharina whispered. "I did not know."

His laugh lacked mirth. "And how could you? I was so fearful that you would leave me that I kept that fact a secret. Now I know better. You see, Miss Sagewick, I made a promise to my father on his deathbed. To seek out and find the treasure. Now I understand that I have done just that. You see, you are the most precious treasure in all the world. You have shown me what true wealth is, and it has nothing to do with gold. If a man loves a woman enough, he should be willing to give up anything for her. Miss Sagewick, the love I have for you cannot be bought, not even with the greatest treasure on Earth. Therefore, we shall walk out of here. Together. The richest couple in the world."

Catharina's heart soared at hearing his declaration of love. So much so that she wanted him to repeat it a hundred times more.

Yet she also had a confession to make before they could move forward. "You have no idea how much your words mean to me, my lord. But before I open my heart completely to you, you should know that I have not been completely honest with you either. I'm no master thief. The only thing I've stolen were the pearls belonging to Lady Langley, and I only took them as a way of ensuring that I would not be considered as a possible bride for her son."

She smiled and touched his cheek. "When I met you, I was willing to do anything to gain your admiration. Yet I learned that I did not need to stoop to thievery for that to happen. I've come to realize what is important in life, which is the love I have for you. And I have more love for you, my lord, than any woman has ever had for any man."

Lord Hainsley released her hands and took hold of her waist. "We've done some harrowing deeds. We've stolen a painting from the home of an enemy, removed documents from a church, and even took an artifact from right under the nose of a guardsman of the British Museum. Therefore, I no longer care if we are caught, even here in this temple."

Without warning, he pulled her close and pressed his lips to hers. The kiss sent an electrical current through her body, setting her insides on fire and threatening to burn her alive. She gripped his arms for fear of floating to the ceiling and did not release her hold even after the kiss ended.

"Have no doubt, Miss Sagewick, rich or poor, I will marry you."

Taking a moment to allow her heart to settle, Catharina whispered her delight. "I don't care what we have, as long as I have you."

"Then it is time we gave him our decision."

Walking together, they went to stand before the cloaked man.

"Have you come to a decision, my lord?"

Lord Hainsley looked at her, and she returned his smile. "I have, sir," he replied. "You may keep the Grail for the next Hainsley, for I have found the true treasure in my love for this lady."

Catharina could not imagine being happier than she was at this very moment. The earl had indeed sacrificed everything for her, a feat she would have never thought possible.

A sad countenance crossed the older man's face. "You should know that once you leave here, you are forbidden to return. Are you confident in your decision?"

He nodded. "I am. No wealth in this world can replace what I have already found. Good day to you."

The earl bowed, and they turned to leave, but the man raised his hand. "Wait!"

Catharina glanced at Lord Hainsley. What more could this man ask of him? He had already given up great riches for love.

"For more than a thousand years," the cloaked man continued, "the Grail has been protected. It can never be sold or given away as a reward."

The earl's brow knitted. "I'm confused, sir. Do the clues not lead to it?"

"Oh, they do, my lord. And your ancestors followed them, just as you did, arriving with the same hope, as you did. Knight Hainsley, and every knight before him, feared what men would do with the Grail once it was in their possession. Too many would use its power to rule over others. For that is what happens when a man has more wealth than he can manage. That is why we protect it at all costs."

When he smiled, he appeared years younger in a matter of seconds. "Your ancestor gave his life—and thus a vast fortune—to keep the Grail safe. That is why we have kept up his various estates and holdings, waiting for a worthy descendant to come along. One whose heart matched that of that great knight. One who valued the love of a woman more than gold. And now, that day has finally arrived. You, my lord, are the worthy recipient. Please, follow me."

Catharina was certain her look of wonderment matched that which Lord Hainsley wore. They followed the cloaked figure through the heavy wooden door from whence he came and into a dimly lit corridor lined with doors on either side. At the far end, the man stopped at a door that looked like every other one, put a heavy iron key into the lock, and turned it, a loud *click* echoing in the corridor.

"Your reward, my lord," he said, stepping aside.

Catharina followed Lord Hainsley through the open door and stopped dead in her tracks, her jaw hanging open. A table sat in the middle of the room. On it stood a gem-encrusted gold cross easily the size of a small child. Surrounding it glinted piles of gold coins, lavish pearls, diamonds, rubies, sapphires, emeralds, every kind of gem in existence.

The earl walked up to the table and picked up a document from a stack of many. "This is all mine?" He read the paper and his eyes widened. "This is a deed to a castle in Wales!"

The older man nodded. "One of three vast estates that have been cared for by us and is now required of you. The value of the jewelry will be enough to cover the cost of upkeep for generations to come. Or to invest in new businesses if you prefer."

As Lord Hainsley looked through the other documents, Catharina went to stand at his side. "These are not just deeds to estates, Miss Sagewick. This one is to a mine in Cornwall, and this is ownership papers for a shipping company out of Dover." He pulled out another paper. "This is for a cotton mill in Northumberland. The income from just these three businesses alone should be enough to cover the costs of upkeep for everything, including my mother's estate in Cornwall. I won't have to sell it." He laughed. "I could buy her ten more if I wanted to do so!"

Her heart beat with happiness for him. They had both been rewarded this day. He had a means to save what he nearly lost, and she had him.

Thirty minutes later, the contents from the room were loaded into a large trunk, which took three men to load into the carriage.

"Continue to walk the path of light," the cloaked man said. "For that is where the true wealth lies."

Lord Hainsley smiled down at Catharina. "Thank you, sir. I shall."

"Then goodbye, Lord Hainsley. Know that your ancestor rests better this day." And with that, the older man returned to the temple, closing the doors behind him.

As they joined Lena in the carriage, the earl settled onto the bench, grinning like a boy at his birthday party. "What a wonderful day, would you not say? Not only have I saved my estates, but I have also gained new ones. But more importantly, I've found you."

Catharina had never been happier, or so she had thought until Lord Hainsley turned to Lena and added, "I've asked Miss Sagewick to marry me. And she has agreed."

When they arrived back at Coventry House, Catharina and Lena followed the earl and several footmen to his bedchamber, although they waited outside the door.

"It will be safest here," he said, indicating to the footmen to place the trunk at the foot of the bed. After sending away the servants, Lord Hainsley removed a dozen or so documents. "I'll review these in greater detail after dinner this evening."

Catharina went to speak but suddenly felt someone behind her. Looking over her shoulder, she was surprised to find a young maid there, her eyes wide. It was the same maid who had been in the dining room last week.

"Do you need something?" Catharina demanded.

"No, miss. I… I didn't want to bother you by walking past, so I waited instead."

Catharina frowned. The girl made no sense. Why would walking past her be a bother? The corridor was wide enough for five men to walk through side by side. And the maid appeared far too nervous to have been there by coincidence.

"Is there a problem, Carrie?" the earl asked, joining them in the doorway to the room.

Catharina's frown deepened. He seemed awfully familiar with this girl. Why was that?

"Oh, yes, my lord," Carrie replied with a wide smile. "Was the parlor clean enough for your liking?"

"Indeed, it was. Thank you."

Beaming, the maid bobbed a curtsy and hurried away.

A thousand thoughts surged through Catharina's mind before Lord Hainsley said, "Poor girl used to work for Callingswell. He denigrated my father, and when she came to his defense, Callingswell threw her out without a reference. After showing such bravery, I had to hire her."

Catharina had her doubts about the maid. Something about her made her skin tingle. Why would a young girl be so adamant to defend the name of a lord she did not know?

Well, today had been the best day of Catharina's life. She did not want it to end with a line of questioning. Instead, she smiled at Lord Hainsley and said, "Seeing that we have a few hours before dinner, what do you think of us sharing a glass of wine in the drawing room to celebrate?"

Chapter Thirty-Four

In all his life, Gideon had never felt happier than he did this night. Not only had he confessed his love for Miss Sagewick, but she had also confessed her love for him. He would never forget their adventure, nor would he have to do so. For by marrying her, it would continue for the rest of their lives together.

It would be far different, of course, but it would be an adventure all the same. They could not go around stealing paintings and ancient artifacts now that they had the treasure, and sneaking into places under false names was out of the question. Yet they could enjoy other exciting experiences, ones that were much safer.

Lady Whitmore had given Miss Sagewick permission to remain at Coventry House for the remainder of the day and through dinner, which made his celebration all the more special. Midway through the afternoon, however, the excitement of the day had taken its toll on her, and she had gone upstairs to take a nap.

Her absence allowed Gideon time to pore over the documents he had taken from the trunk. And for the first time, he realized how wealthy of a man he truly had become. Not only did he now own the castle in Wales, but there was also a grand manor near Edinburgh in Scotland and a cliffside castle on the Isle of Wight.

Along with the Dover-based shipping company, the mine in Cornwall, and the Northumberland cotton mill, he owned more than a dozen buildings in London, all of which brought him a substantial rental income from the businesses and residences that resided in them. There was a hotel in Bath, a slew of inns along the major roads going in and out of London, and he owned a large stake in an Indian spice company. With this many sources of income, he would never want for anything ever again!

A document contained the name of a solicitor who had been managing the various holdings for the last twenty years. Gideon would write the man today to take control of his new fortune.

But there was one document he would keep aside. One he could not reveal to Miss Sagewick just yet. In due time, of course he would, but for now, he would keep it a secret.

Taking out a fresh piece of parchment, he penned a letter to his mother. He would not yet tell her about the treasure, but at least he would be able to ease her mind about the estate. She had been so worried upon her departure, and the thought of her suffering distressed him to no end.

After setting aside the letter to allow the ink to dry, he opened one of his ledgers and began a loose inventory of the items hidden in the trunk. Later, he would return to his rooms for a more exact count, but this would do for now. He decided to not sell the jewelry. It would bring him a fortune, certainly, but he would rather it remained in the family. Therefore, he would leave it to his heir.

Of course, Miss Sagewick could take any piece she liked to keep for herself. Just the thought of her wearing the sparkling sapphires around her neck and wrists and dangling from her lovely ears pleased him. And if she preferred to have the jeweler create several pieces with the rubies or the emeralds, she was welcome to do so. As far as he was concerned, the treasure was as much hers as it was his.

"Is this what I can expect to see once we are married, my lord? My husband poring over ledgers and ignoring me?"

He looked up to find Miss Sagewick standing in the doorway, Lena waiting patiently behind her. Freshly awakened, he thought her more beautiful than ever. Then again, each time he laid eyes on her, she was lovelier than the time before, so there was no reason for now to be any different.

"I warned you that I lead a boring life, Miss Sagewick," he said, rising from his desk. He motioned to the open ledger. "But how could you not think this exciting? Just think of the wonderful discussions we will have concerning the latest shipping manifests or the price of wool."

Miss Sagewick placed her hands on her hips. "If this is my new life, I may just have to take the gems from that trunk of yours and go off to have my own adventure."

This made them both laugh.

Collins entered to announce dinner, and Gideon glanced down at his clothes. He had not even changed since returning home!

"Don't worry, my lord," Miss Sagewick said, grinning that mischievous smile he had come to adore. "I'll excuse your lack of proper dress. This one time."

Gideon growled before turning to the butler. "Thank you, Collins. Oh, and do make sure you count the cutlery after Miss Sagewick leaves this evening. I would hate to learn too late that she has taken some of it home with her."

The butler, seemingly undaunted by this strange request, bowed and said, "Yes, my lord."

Miss Sagewick, however, was not as undaunted as Collins was by Gideon's words, for she gave his arm a playful slap. "If you think I would steal a fork, you are sorely mistaken." Gideon, feeling guilty for his quip, went to tell her that he believed no such thing, but she went on to say, "A teacup perhaps, but certainly not a fork."

With both of them laughing, Gideon offered Miss Sagewick his arm and walked her to the dining room, Lena trailing dutifully behind them. Footmen filled their glasses with red wine, as candlelight flickered from the candelabra on the table. Gideon took the place at the head of the table, and Miss Sagewick sat to his right, the chaperone beside her.

"The man we met today," Miss Sagewick said as a bowl of pea soup was set before her, "I was thinking that he was a very honest man, as were those before him. Any of them could have taken the treasure for themselves, but they did not."

Gideon nodded. "I considered that, too. It seems that the tales I've heard about the Knights Templar are true." He chuckled. "Wait until Mother hears our story."

"Our story," Miss Sagewick said with a dreamy sigh. "And what a story it is!"

Gideon smiled. One day, he would tell his children of their adventure. And the true treasure of love he had found along the way.

The conversation continued, eventually turning to the subject of marriage. By all accounts, Miss Sagewick's father seemed to be a decent man and would make no objection to them marrying.

"He will be here on Monday," Miss Sagewick said. "I look forward to—"

"Forgive me, my lord," Collins said, entering the room. "But you have a caller, and she seems rather distressed."

Gideon glanced at Miss Sagewick and set his napkin on the table. "Who?"

Before the butler could reply, Lady Madeline appeared. Her hair was disheveled, and tears stained her cheeks. Distressed, indeed!

Jumping from his chair, Gideon hurried to the lady's side. "What has happened?"

"Forgive me for interrupting your dinner, my lord, but I had no one else to turn to."

Gideon took her hand and led her to a chair. Once she was seated, he snapped his finger at a waiting footman, who hurried over to pour the lady a glass of wine.

"Please, tell us what has you so troubled," he said, sitting in the chair beside her. "We are here to help if we can."

He glanced at Miss Sagewick for her agreement but was surprised to find her wearing a frown of disapproval. Surely, she was not still jealous of Lady Madeline? Well, he would take care of that problem later. Right now, his main concern was for the woman beside him who was in desperate need of help.

"Lord Callingswell said something... something too foul for me to repeat. When I called him out as a liar, he... he slapped me!" She buried her face in her hands and began to sob.

Gideon slammed his fist in the palm of his hand. "What did he say?"

Lady Madeline shook her head. "I cannot say it. It is too vulgar, especially while in the company of another woman."

Before he could respond, Miss Sagewick rose from her seat, a footman hurrying over to remove the chair. "Please excuse me for a few moments. Lena?"

The two women left the room, and Gideon turned back to Lady Madeline. "We are alone now, so tell me what he said."

"He said... he said that he would exact his revenge by telling you..."

Her words trailed off, and Gideon encouraged her to continue.

"Please, go on."

She sighed heavily. "He said that he would reveal what he and Miss Sagewick did during one of her calls to his home."

Besides the party she had attended, Gideon was aware of at least one call. Had there been others? "What did he say happened?"

"He bragged that they had a... a tryst, my lord. That he had taken her to his bed."

Gideon's blood began to boil. He refused to believe such a terrible story. It was simply Lord Callingswell stirring up trouble again, he was sure of it. But to slap Lady Madeline merely for questioning his honesty was unacceptable!

"I appreciate you coming to me with this," he said. "Please, stay for dinner and rest. I'll have words with Callingswell soon enough."

Lady Madeline smiled. "You are kind. And brave."

Gideon's pride swelled. Of course, he was brave. He was the descendant of a Knight Templar, after all. Although, he could not say so aloud. The cloaked man had not ordered him to keep what he learned there a secret, but it was implied. Instead, they shared in small talk.

Glancing at the empty doorway, Gideon wondered what was keeping Miss Sagewick. Finally, thirty minutes later, she and Lena returned.

"Forgive me for my absence," Miss Sagewick said as a footman pulled out a chair for her. "Now, what are we discussing?"

"The weather as of late," Lady Madeline replied, now radiant rather than blotchy as she had been upon her arrival. "It has been much hotter than usual."

The conversation resumed, as did the meal. Once the last course was cleared, Gideon rose and offered Lady Madeline a drink in the drawing room, which she readily accepted. When they entered the room, the young maid Carrie was there, dusting.

"Oh, I'm so sorry, my lord!" the girl said, bobbing a quick curtsy. "I'm done in here."

Once she was gone, Lady Madeline sighed. "I should be going. I would like to speak to my father. But I appreciate your help, my lord. I truly do."

"Are you certain?" Gideon asked. "You're welcome to stay here if you would like. I'm sure Mrs. Potts can have a room ready for you, so you'll not have to travel so late."

A look of panic crossed her features, likely caused by the events of the day. Still, she declined his offer, so he walked her to the door.

"If you need anything," he said, helping her with her coat, "don't hesitate to ask."

"You have done so much for me already, my lord," she replied, smiling. "And it has been a pleasure, indeed."

Gideon thought the statement odd, but he shrugged it off as a nervous condition brought on by Lord Callingswell's mistreatment of her. When he returned to the drawing room, Miss Sagewick stood waiting for him, a smile on her lovely face.

"I do hope you're no longer jealous," he teased.

She shook her head. "Of course not. For she cannot steal you, or anything else, from me."

Relieved, Gideon sat just as Collins entered, carrying a tray with coffee. The day had been as exhilarating as it had been exhausting. Yet it had all been worth the effort. Perhaps he should have napped earlier, too.

All too soon, it was time for Miss Sagewick to leave. After seeing her to her carriage, he returned to the study to continue his work, all while wearing a smile.

Later, however, his smile fell when he entered his bedchambers. For the space at the foot of his bed was empty. The treasure was gone.

Chapter Thirty-Five

Alister had always been patient. Lord Hainsley was by no means a stupid man. Alister knew that if he bided his time, the earl would find that which Alister so desperately wanted. The treasure of the Knights Templar.

As far as Alister was concerned, nothing good came from being overeager. For weeks, he had waited for word that the treasure had been found. Not once had he lost hope. Lord Hainsley was by no means a stupid man, and Alister had not doubted that the man would eventually work out the many clues that led to that legendary treasure. The earl did all the work, and Alister reaped the benefits. It was a fine arrangement, indeed.

And now his patience had paid off. Alister could not help but feel smug as he sat in his carriage, the nondescript trunk at his feet and Lady Madeline across from him.

Earlier that afternoon, a servant boy had arrived at his home with a message from Carrie, the spy he had sent to Coventry House. In most cases, Alister would not have tolerated a maid ordering him about, but in this case, the benefits to allowing the slight outweighed his bruised pride. After all, if Carrie's news was what he expected, he had no time to waste on arrogance.

He had waited in the back garden of Lord Hainsley's humble estate until Carrie arrived.

"The treasure's in his bedroom, my lord," Carrie had informed him. "I caught Miss Sagewick talking to her chaperone just outside his door, and they mentioned jewels of all sorts. They're at dinner now, my lord. So, it's safe to send someone for the trunk. But it'll take more'n one man."

With a snap of his fingers, four of his most trusted men appeared from the shadows. They climbed a trellis to gain access to Lord Hainsley's bedchambers. Within moments, they had tied ropes to the handles on either side of the trunk and lowered it to the ground through that same window, the muscles on their arms bulging from the weight of its contents.

And now, Alister sat in his carriage, the trunk at his feet and Lady Madeline smiling across from him. Carrie had insisted on returning home, but Alister convinced her to remain at Coventry House so as not to arouse suspicion.

"Will you not open the trunk yet, my lord?" Lady Madeline asked. "I'm curious to see what it holds."

Were all women this ignorant? "Have you forgotten that I have guests back at my home?" he asked.

It had been his good fortune that several friends and business associates had called over for drinks. When he received the message about the treasure, he had asked them to stay while he saw to an important matter. At first, they were offended that he was willing to leave his guests unattended, but when he promised them a sight they had never seen before, they had agreed.

He smiled at Lady Madeline. The truth was, he was as tempted as she to see what the trunk held, but that would ruin his plans. "I want my guests to experience the excitement of opening the chest with me." What he wanted was to witness their envy. Every man had a boy inside him who dreamed of finding hidden treasure.

Soon, they arrived at his estate. The men carried the trunk to the parlor, where eight of Alister's peers waited, drinks in their hands.

"There you are," Lord Maxey snapped. He was a tall, thin man with a tuft of light hair on the top of his head and with cheeks so smooth, he rarely had to shave. "And what is that? Did you ask us to wait here so you could show us your grandmother's keepsakes?" His attempt at disinterest was marred only by the way he eyed the trunk like a Russian czar ready to sign in a new tax proclamation.

Unruffled by the round of laughter that followed, Alister tasked the servants to set the trunk on a table. "You will see soon enough, Maxey. And none of you will be laughing once you have seen what I've found."

Lord Gambrel frowned. "Well, come on with it. I've already missed dinner." Unlike Lord Maxey, he was a short, stout man in his middle years. He wore a coat ready to burst its buttons, it was so tight. Or rather, his stomach was so big. It was common knowledge that he enjoyed more than his fair share of sweet cakes.

Alister placed a hand on the trunk's lid and straightened his back. "Gentlemen, what you are about to witness is the unmasking of a treasure that was guarded by the Knights Templar for hundreds of years."

"The Knights Templar?" a gray-haired baron asked with a snort. "Everyone knows that nothing survived their disbanding."

Lord Teed threw his head back and laughed. "You've heard the rumors, Malson. The knights went into hiding. It's said they were given everlasting life in exchange for protecting a host of legendary items. Perhaps our illustrious host has one of them."

Alister grinned. They may mock him now, but they would be in awe of him in a matter of moments.

"I, for one, want to see what he's brought us," another gentleman said. Always a greedy one, he put forth a pudgy hand to touch the trunk, but Alister slapped it away.

"In good time, Frogge." Alister chastised him like a father to a son despite the fact the earl had to be as old as Alister's grandfather.

He waited several more minutes to build the tension. Once that trunk opened, he would be lauded as more than the great man he already was! Why, he might stand just below the King himself!

When he could not wait a moment longer, he waved a hand at a servant, who struck the lock on the trunk with an iron bar. Each time the metal peeled, Alister's ears rang, but the treasure was well worth the temporary pain.

When the lock fell open, the servant pulled it away and stepped back. Alister gripped the lock plate and smiled at his friends. "Behold, wealth unlike you have ever seen!"

With a grand gesture, he lifted the trunk's lid and took a step back, waiting for the outcries of admiration that were certain to come.

Admiration was not what he received, however.

"Good gracious, Callingswell," Lord Maxey said, reaching into the trunk to remove an item Alister had not expected to be there, "a boot?"

Lord Teed chuckled. "Are those women stockings? How much do you think they're worth, gentlemen?"

"Unless they are made of spun gold, I suspect not a great deal," replied Lord Gambrel with a loud guffaw.

Lord Maxey shook his head. "You've not seen my wife's stocking bill if you believe that!"

Alister dug through the contents of the trunk, rage pounding in his head. Chipped teacups, several cracked figurines, and all sorts of worthless items filled the space. Even an old dust rag had been thrown in for good measure. And buried beneath this collection of worthless odds and ends lay at least a dozen sizable stones one might easily stumble upon in an English garden or field.

"Now, gentlemen," Lord Dodson said with mock sympathy, "our friend did not lie. Just look here." He reached in and pulled out a shilling coin. "There must be at least a dozen more! But you must tell no one, for the Crown will be offended knowing their wealth has been rivaled."

The gentlemen roared with laughter, as Alister's face burned with embarrassment. Lord Hainsley had fooled him, and now he appeared the fool to his friends. No one was allowed to get the better of him!

And as the men filed from the room, their laughter following after them, Alister gritted his teeth. The treasure belonged to the Callingswell family. If it took a bout of fisticuffs—or even a duel—to get it back, then so be it.

Chapter Thirty-Six

Catharina had committed many dastardly deeds as of late, but there had been good reason behind each one. She had stolen the pearl necklace to get out of being forced to marry Lord Langley. The theft of the painting, the hidden note, and the mummified cat had been to help Lord Hainsley secure his future.

But that future no longer belonged to him alone, for it was now also hers. Thus, the reason why, upon the arrival of Lady Madeline at Coventry House the previous evening, Catharina chose to steal one last time.

It had taken her and Lena numerous trips to bring the treasure stuffed in burlap sacks from the kitchen to the carriage. Thankfully, the butler was not nearby, nor were any of the servants, or their efforts would have been for naught.

After the fifth trip, Lena suggested that Catharina continue while she filled the trunk with anything she could find, from stockings to an iron pot from the kitchen to several rocks from outside the back door. That would add appropriate weight to make up for what was removed. They just had to hope no one would break the lock before removing the trunk from the house.

As she sat in the drawing room of Ivywood Manor with Lena,

Catharina wondered if perhaps she was enjoying herself too much, trying on every piece of jewelry before her. Early in the afternoon, she would go to Lord Hainsley and explain what she had done.

Extending her hand, she smiled at the gold ring on her finger. "I don't believe I have ever seen a diamond so big," she said in admiration. "It alone must be worth a small fortune."

Lena nodded from the chair opposite Catharina. "I would say it must be among the largest in existence." She picked up a necklace. "Do you plan on keeping the ruby pendant?"

Catharina bit at her lip as she studied the tray in her lap. The large gold cross, a mountain of pearls, and other particular selections filled the tray. She would ask Lord Hainsley if she would have to save the ring for special occasions or would he allow her to wear it whenever she pleased.

Feeling a bit mischievous, she said, "I think I shall keep all of it." He would never agree to it, of course. Several pieces would have to be sold to pay off his debts and to make important purchases. But that did not mean she could not tease him beforehand.

Their laughter was muted by Lord Hainsley's booming voice. "As I thought! You bamboozled me! How dare you steal from me? I trusted you when you said you were no thief!"

Catharina was taken aback as the earl marched across the room. "Remove that ring at once!"

She swallowed hard. "My lord, you must understand."

"Understand what?" he demanded. "That you lied to me? That you stole what was rightfully mine? Everything has become as clear as crystal. Lady Madeline informed me of your liaison with Lord Callingswell. Though I still believe he is lying in that regard, I have to admit that I'm not shocked that you stole from him." He shook his head in disgust. "I may have been a fool before, but there is no doubt now. Not with the truth right in front of me!"

Catharina stood, her heart aching. "You think I would deliberately hurt you? After all we have been through together?"

"Enough!" Lord Hainsley snapped. "It no longer matters, Miss Sagewick. You stole from me. Whatever promises I made to you are forfeit. We are finished. Now, take off that ring this instant!"

She removed the ring and placed it among the other jewelry on the tray. "I—"

"No, I don't want to hear any more of your excuses. I will have the servants collect that trunk. And nothing had better be missing." He turned and snapped his fingers at the same servants who had removed the trunk from the Temple church. Two scurried over to shove gold coins and other valuable trinkets that had been piled on the table into the open white chest Catharina had brought from home. One man removed the tray from Catharina's lap—with stiff apologies—and settled it with the rest of the treasure. Then they lifted the chest onto their shoulders and headed for the door.

Lord Hainsley turned to follow the men from the room, but Catharina ran after him. "Please, my lord. I don't deny that I stole from you, but I did so with good cause."

He stopped at the open front door. "So you say."

"Please, I beg of you! Allow me to explain."

Lord Hainsley heaved a heavy sigh and turned to face her. "You have one minute. But make what you say convincing."

Catharina nodded. "You see, I solved another riddle. Well, not a riddle per se, but a mystery, nonetheless. Concerning Lady Madeline."

"A minute only lasts so long, Miss Sagewick."

Catharina growled under her breath. She would not be rushed! "Her sudden appearance seemed odd to me. As a woman, I can sense when another is appealing to a man's good heart. Then it dawned on me. Why would a lady call so late? And in her state of distress? There is only one reason that is reasonable. I'm almost certain she has been conspiring with Lord Callingswell in order to steal the treasure from you."

His laugh held no mirth. "'Almost certain' that Lady Madeline conspired with Lord Callingswell? Your explanation is not very compelling, Miss Sagewick. Where is your proof? Oh, yes, you sensed it. Well, answer me this. Why would Lady Madeline plot against me with a man who treats her no better than a harlot? Because she would not. She is far too intelligent. She has been a friend to me. Much more so than you. After all, who has *my* treasure, you or her?" He shoved his hat onto his head. "No, Miss Sagewick, you are the one who betrayed me. And now that I have returned to me what is mine, I want nothing more to do with you."

Heartbreak greater than anything Catharina had ever endured filled her soul, and she would have collapsed if Lena had not hurried to her side. With tears streaming down her face, she cried out after the man she had come to love more than life itself. "Father will be here tomorrow to meet you! Please, we've shared too much to give up now!"

But Lord Hainsley did not respond, nor did he acknowledge that he had even heard her. As the carriage pulled away, Catharina sobbed into Lena's shoulder, realizing how horrible things had gone.

"Oh, Lena, what shall I do?"

Lena patted Catharina's back. "Why don't you lie down and rest, miss."

As Catharina lay on her bed, Lena held her hand. "All will be well, miss. Lord Hainsley will realize he was wrong to accuse you and will then return to beg for your forgiveness."

Catharina wanted to believe that was so, but there was no denying that her adventures had come to an end. Once she had wept every last tear and exhaustion settled over her, Catharina fell into a restless sleep, only to be awakened by a gentle tap on the door.

"Catharina?" Lady Whitmore whispered into the room. "Lena told me what happened with Lord Hainsley."

Rubbing sleep from her eyes, Catharina sat up in bed. "Everything?"

The countess closed the door behind her and came to sit on the edge of the bed. "Indeed."

"Even about the painting and—"

"Everything. All I can ask is why?"

Catharina dropped her gaze. "For the same reason I stole the jewelry last night. Because I love him." For some time, she explained about the lies they had told each other and the adventure they had enjoyed. Once done, she said, "I hope you can forgive me for lying to you."

Lady Whitmore patted her hand. "Many young ladies have abandoned prudence for love, but this must be the oddest story I have ever heard." She shook her head. "Nevertheless, your father will arrive tomorrow to collect you, and he will not be pleased when Lord Hainsley is not here."

Catharina's mind raced. Her father had heard of their courtship, but they had planned to surprise him about the engagement. "He will want to marry me off to the first man who offers," she said, wiping tears from her cheeks. "How can a woman be married to a man she does not love?"

The countess stood and walked to the door. "I'm afraid there is nothing I can do about that, Catharina."

"But you and Lord Hainsley are friends," Catharina said, sliding from the bed. "Can you not intervene on my behalf?"

It became quiet, and Catharina began to worry. Lady Whitmore was her last hope. If she could not speak to Lord Hainsley, then all was truly lost.

"I can try," Lady Whitmore said. "But I cannot make any promises. Either way, you must pack for your journey home. I will send Lena to help you."

With a heavy heart, Catharina simply nodded. How could Lord Hainsley believe she would hurt him so terribly? All she had wanted to do was protect what was his. Yet he refused to listen.

"He must return for me," she said to the room. "He simply must!" The question was, how could she change his mind before her father's arrival.

The truth was, she could not.

Chapter Thirty-Seven

Turning the heavy gold cross in his hand, Gideon marveled at its weight. It would make a fine weapon if the need arose. Just as much as the silver candlestick beside it. Or the bronze chalice. Any number of items were heavy enough to cause a great deal of damage. But none were destined to such a terrible fate. He would ensure they were used for the beautiful objects they were.

Setting the cross on his desk beside the rest of the treasure, memories of yesterday materialized in his mind. Finding Miss Sagewick in possession of his treasure had been a terrible blow. But for her to accuse Lady Madeline of conspiring to do exactly what she herself had done was going too far.

If she had just admitted that temptation had gotten the better of her, he might have considered giving her a second chance, but to have her outright lying made him realize what a terrible mistake it had been trusting her in the first place. She was a thief, and, therefore, he should have known better.

He shook his head in wonderment. Indeed, she had lied. Most certainly she had tried to deflect the blame onto Lady Madeline. And yet, his love for her was as strong as it had been before he learned the truth. How could that be?

Because he, too, had lied to her. And why had he done so? To earn her trust. And her admiration.

He glanced at the letter from Lady Whitmore that had arrived this morning. Its message was simple. Gideon had made a grave error and should go to hear out Miss Sagewick. He had been tempted twice in the last hour to leave but managed to argue himself out of doing so.

Still, something about the entire situation—meaning the disappearance of the treasure to find it in her possession—did not sit well with him. Lady Madeline aside, Miss Sagewick had insisted that she had stolen everything to protect him. If that were true, would she not have simply taken the trunk as well? Why put it into the chest?

And how had she gotten it all out of the house without his knowledge?

"My lord?"

Gideon looked up at Collins and sighed. "Yes?"

The butler came to stand in front of the desk. "I wished to inform you that the young housemaid Carrie gave notice and left this morning."

Gideon raised his brows and sat back in his chair. This was a surprise. The girl had been so grateful to find a position and now she was gone? "Oh? Did she say why?"

"She did not give a precise reason, my lord," Collins replied. "But what she did say was quite unusual."

When Collins did not expound, Gideon said, "Well, go on. What did she say?"

"Oh, yes, my lord. I overheard her speaking to one of the other maids, saying that she had come into new wealth."

Sitting up in his chair, Gideon remembered the day Carrie arrived on his doorstep, desperate to find work. Was she not the very same maid who was in the drawing room when he spoke about the treasure? And again in the corridor outside his bedchamber after the trunk had been taken there?

Then there were the stories Lady Madeline had shared about Lord Callingswell. Her arrival the very evening the treasure had disappeared was suspect. And now the maid was gone?

Suddenly, everything seemed to line up perfectly. Too perfectly, in fact. He recalled Miss Sagewick confessing her love for him at the Temple church and all she had done for him up to that point. She would not harm him, for she had been helping him all along.

"I've been blinded by my own stubbornness," he said, pushing out his chair and standing. "Collins, have my horse saddled."

Gideon changed into his riding boots. The clock showed ten, the very hour Miss Sagewick was due to leave with her father from Ivywood Manor. If luck was on Gideon's side, the baron would either be running late, or the countess would have insisted that they remain for luncheon.

Donning his coat, Gideon hurried out the front door, only to come to a sudden stop upon seeing Lord Callingswell standing beside his carriage just beyond the iron garden fence.

"What are you doing here?" Gideon demanded.

Lord Callingswell took several long strides to come and stand nose to nose with Gideon. "The treasure," he growled, "I opened the trunk to find nothing but rubbish. Where is the real treasure, Hainsley?"

Gideon could not help but smile. He was right. Miss Sagewick had been telling the truth all along. She had stolen the treasure to keep it safe. He swore to himself that he would never again doubt her. He had a feeling she would remind him of that fact.

But the joy that thought gave him disappeared when he thought about what Lord Callingswell had done.

"You came into my home like a thief?" Gideon demanded, unbuttoning his coat.

"As you did mine," Callingswell said smugly. "Now, hand it over! Every last bit belongs to me."

Without thought of the consequences, Gideon drew back his arm and slammed his fist into the viscount's chin, sending him stumbling backward.

But Lord Callingswell was no milksop. "How dare you!" he screamed, spitting blood onto the carefully trimmed patch of grass beside the stone path. "You'll pay in more ways than you can imagine!" He raised his fists in the ready fighting position. "I've trained with some of the best fighters in the country, so take your best shot."

Gideon snorted. "I may not be formally trained, Callingswell, but I can hold my own," he said. Rather than readying his stance, he landed a second punch to the viscount's cheek.

Lord Callingswell moved his jaw back and forth. "You'll not catch me unawares again," Lord Callingswell growled.

The element of surprise was now gone, and soon, they were at each other like a pair of tomcats. Each man managed to connect to a body part of the other more times than not.

Lord Callingswell was indeed a skilled fighter, but Gideon had the advantage of honor. And indignation. Indignation at having the treasure he had worked so hard to find stolen. Of being called out by an enemy in front of his own home where everyone could see. Well, if this man believed he could be so uncivil, he had another think coming.

Leading with his shoulder, Gideon used all that rage, all the indignation, to barrel into Lord Callingswell's stomach, sending him crashing to the ground.

Placing a foot on the viscount's chest, Gideon towered over him. "Leave and never return, Callingswell, or so help me, you'll receive the same again."

Gideon removed his boot, and the viscount stood, dusting himself off before wiping blood from his nose. With a string of curses, he stumbled to his carriage, shouting at his driver to take him home.

As the carriage pulled away, a stable hand arrived with Gideon's horse. Gideon glanced at Collins, who stood on the portico, an intricately carved box in his hands.

"What is that?" Gideon asked as he approached.

The old butler grinned. "Why, your dueling pistols, my lord. I thought I should have them ready, just in case the need arose. One can never assume their fist will be enough when honor is at stake."

Gideon chuckled and slapped Collins on the shoulder. "I appreciate your preparedness, but I don't believe we shall be needing them this time. Now, I must go if I'm to catch Miss Sagewick before she leaves London."

"No offense, my lord, but you are in no state to call on a lady."

Gideon glanced down. The sleeve of his coat was torn, several buttons on his waistcoat were missing, and his breeches had green stains. "I have no time to change," he said, removing his coat and tossing it to the butler. "I'll return soon."

Mounting the steed, he heeled its sides, heading it toward Ivywood Manor, praying Miss Sagewick would still be there.

When he arrived at the Mayfair estate, the countess herself answered the door.

"Lord Hainsley," she said, her eyes wide, "you look—"

"I know, Lady Whitmore, but I don't care. Has Miss Sagewick left yet? Please tell me they are still here."

Lady Whitmore sighed. "I'm afraid they left an hour ago. Lord Sagewick was quite upset that you did not make an appearance. Catharina made excuses for you, of course, explaining that you had an important meeting or some other business matter, but her father did not seem to care."

Gideon lowered his head. "I made a mistake. She meant to help me, but I refused to see it. Now, I fear it's too late. If they have been gone for an hour, they will be well beyond the boundaries of London. I'll never catch up with them before nightfall."

"Not if you take the main roads," the countess said. "But for them to return home, they will be traveling through Bairdton. Remember, there are fields that can provide shortcuts between the outskirts of the town and that village."

Gideon nodded slowly. Yes, he could cut through diagonally and thus arrive ahead of them. "Thank you, Lady Whitmore. There is much to explain, but it will have to wait." He smiled. "I must go collect my fiancée."

"Do not just stand there," the countess said with a laugh. "Go!"

Returning to his horse, Gideon mounted and hurried through the busy streets of London. Riding gave him an advantage a carriage did not, and he managed to reach the green fields beyond town in no time. Once free of the crowds, he urged the stallion faster, the blades of grass whipping at his boots. But he did not care. He had spent a great deal of money on the horse, and its endurance was being tested. And like Gideon, the animal did not falter.

Soon, he came to a stop at a crossroads just outside of the tiny village of Bairdton. If his estimation was correct, the Sagewick's carriage would not have yet reached that point.

Wiping sweat from his brow, he settled into the saddle to wait. He did not deserve her forgiveness but would ask for it all the same. Even if it meant he had to beg.

Chapter Thirty-Eight

Catharina made every attempt to keep her father at Ivywood Manor to wait for Lord Hainsley, yet he refused. And nothing would make him change his mind once it was set.

"Earl or not, if he cannot be here when he says he will," her father had insisted, "then perhaps I should reconsider his request to court you."

And what arguments could she put forth? Lord Hainsley believed she was a thief, after all. Even if she was not. It was no wonder he had not come.

With a heavy heart, Catharina said farewell to Lady Whitmore. But saying goodbye to Lena was much more difficult. They had both come into her life under unconventional circumstances, and she counted them as friends.

Now, she was returning home and to an uncertain future. All she could wonder, however, was whether she would ever see Lord Hainsley again.

"Regardless, if this Hainsley fellow showed or not does not matter," her father said, interrupting her thoughts. "It's best that you leave London. Surely, you've heard about the rampage of thefts that have blanketed the Town? What's worse, there are women involved! I tell you, the madness that has infected this world makes me wonder if the Lord's return is nigh! Why, just last week—"

As her father continued on about the atrocities that were befalling the land, Catharina felt a twinge of sadness in her heart. She had always wanted a life of adventure, and for a short time, Lord Hainsley had provided just that. Now she had to resign herself to the mundane life other ladies of her station endured. At least she would have her memories to sustain her.

If all she was losing was the chance to experience more adventures, she would have been satisfied. Yet it was much more than that. She and Lord Hainsley had confessed their love for one another, and that she would miss more than any experience they could have shared together.

Then a thought came to mind. What if his confession had been a lie? What if she loved him but he had only used her supposed gift of thievery to get to the treasure and now had cast her aside? She had not truly considered that notion until this very moment. He knew the importance of meeting her father and the consequences if he did not show. The idea that his love for her was not true hurt worse than anything else she was enduring. Even the promise of marriage to someone else.

"Now what?" her father barked as the carriage began to slow and then came to a sudden stop. Her father stuck his head out the window. "Why are we stopping?"

"There's a highwayman blocking the road, my lord," the driver replied. "A rough looking one, at that."

Catharina peered out the window. Her heart clenched. A highwayman? Here? They were in the middle of the country, open green fields on either side of them. If this was a robbery, the brigand chose a terrible place to strike. Most attacked unsuspecting travelers as they traveled through wooded areas, that way they could make off with the goods and get lost in the forest.

And what now? she thought wryly. *Do you plan to become a lady highwaywoman?*

This was not the adventure she wanted! It was one thing to sneak a painting from a home—knowing full well it would be returned later—

and quite another to ambush decent, God-fearing people. Had her father done as she suggested and waited for Lord Hainsley, this highwayman would have attacked someone else. But he had insisted on being stubborn.

Men!

"What do we do?" she asked. "I have no money, but I suppose I can give up my jewels if need be."

"You'll do nothing of the sort," her father growled.

"Is this Lord Sagewick's vehicle?"

Catharina's eyes went wide. She would recognize that voice anywhere.

"Stay here, my dear. If some barbarian wishes to fight me, then so be it."

Had they been in the same situation with another brigand, Catharina would have readily remained inside the vehicle. Yet this was nothing like anything they had ever, nor ever would, endure, so she followed right after her father.

Her heart leapt with joy at seeing Lord Hainsley. Or some semblance of the earl. He was bereft of his coat, and his clothes were stained with dirt and what appeared to be grass. His hair was sticking out every which way, and a purple splotch surrounded one eye.

But she had never loved him more than she did at this moment.

"Who challenges me?" her father barked. "Tell me your name, man, so I know who I'm fighting."

He began unbuttoning his coat, but Catharina grabbed his arm. "No, Father. He is Lord Hainsley."

The earl took a step forward. "I must apologize for my appearance, but my morning has been less than ideal. Time slipped away from me, thus why I was unable to meet with you this morning. But I rode for more than an hour through fields and muck to ask for your daughter's hand in marriage."

Her father eyed him for several long moments. "Your rough appearance bothers me. Have you been drinking?"

"No, sir. As I said, I had an unexpected encounter with a man who wants my hide. But I can assure you, he did not fare any better. But know that he will no longer be a problem."

"I see," her father said, blowing out his breath through his nose. "I, too, had to settle many differences in my youth in very much the same way." He balled up his hand and stared at the fist he had made. "I used it so much that I became well regarded as a pugilist."

Catharina frowned. Her father never mentioned any stories about him fighting.

Her father dropped his hand to his side, and his lips thinned. "Still, in my reckless youth, I kept my appointments." After all they had been through, after all Catharina had endured, she refused to give up on Lord Hainsley now!

"Father."

He ignored her, clearly sizing up the earl.

"Father, please," she said, grabbing him by the arm. Finally, he turned in her direction. "How often have you said that you want a gentleman who can take care of me?"

"It is what your mother wanted, too," her father said.

Catharina smiled. "Then I ask you not to judge Lord Hainsley for his appearance. Nor his tardiness. He has proven that his honor is important enough to fight for. But he has also proven that he is willing to ride across the world for me. What more can a lady ask for?"

Her father sighed heavily and looked at Lord Hainsley. "Well, I suppose that is true. But how do I know that your bout of fisticuffs was not just an example of a drunken man who gets himself into trouble?"

"Because I am completely sober, for one," Lord Hainsley said, placing his hands on his thighs and standing taller. "And because the man I fought attacked me in front of my home. If I had allowed everyone to witness my defeat, what sort of man would I be? A weak one. And I assure you, I am far from weak. I could not have faced you if I had lost that fight, nor could I have faced your daughter. But it is because of my affection for her that I defended myself. And the state of my appearance and the swiftness of my horse shows how important your daughter is to me."

Her father looked him up and down. "I would say the state of your appearance says the opposite."

Lord Hainsley shook his head. "I disagree. Would you have

respected me more had I changed before going after the woman I love?"

"I suppose not," her father said, chuckling. "I suppose what you say is true." He glanced at Catharina and smiled. "If he is willing to go to such lengths to come after you, then it is only right that I accept your offer of marriage."

"Thank you, sir," Lord Hainsley said, pumping her father's hand like a thirsty man working a well. "You won't regret this decision." He looked at Catharina. "May I have a quick word with her before you go?"

Her father nodded. "I see no reason you should not." He stepped into the carriage and closed the door behind him.

Catharina thought her heart would burst, as the earl took her hands in his. "Miss Sagewick—"

"Catharina, please. We are engaged, after all."

His grin made her legs wobbly. "I was wrong about you, Catharina. I now understand why you took the treasure. You did not want it for yourself. You only wanted to help me. There is not enough wealth in the world to repay your ingenuity. But what we have goes well beyond the treasure itself. As much as you teased me about my stubbornness, I now see the truth in your words. I was a blind, pigheaded fool in so many ways, ways for which I am truly abashed." He took her hand, his eyes pleading. "Please, Catharina, can you ever forgive me for my distrust?"

Catharina, accustomed to the arrogant man he had been, was impressed by this display of humility. He had treated her unfairly, yes. Had accused her of a crime she had not committed. Yet she could see how truly contrite he was. After all, everyone deserved a second chance, did they not?

What she wanted to do was leap into his arms and have him thoroughly kiss her. But she also could not seem overeager. Otherwise, he would be under the impression that he could mistreat her whenever he chose and follow it with a sincere apology to return to her good graces. A way of life she was unwilling to accept.

Plus, such a public display of affection was not prudent with her father waiting in the carriage. Instead, she decided this was a good moment for a little banter.

Placing her hands on her hips, she let out a heavy sigh. She would forgive him, of course, but he would not be let off that easily.

"I was hoping..." He dropped his gaze. "You are the wisest, most precious woman I have ever met." He looked back up at her and grinned. "Or perhaps I'm a stubborn man and you recognize that we're equals."

This made them both laugh, and without regard for her father and his likely rebuke, she threw her arms around him. "Of course, I forgive you," she said.

"I love you, Catharina," he whispered in her ear. "That is all I can say."

"That is plenty for now," she replied. "We can speak more about this when you visit me. Which will be soon, I hope."

"Give me two weeks," he said, breaking their embrace. "Then we shall have the banns read and begin preparing for the wedding."

"And I eagerly anticipate that day, my lord." She smiled. "Gideon." Kissing his cheek, she added, "See you then."

Once inside the carriage, her father studied her for several moments. Catharina had already prepared herself for a firm reprimand, but she did not expect what followed.

"He makes you very happy. I can see that now."

Her cheeks heated. "He does. Very much so."

"So, how exactly did the two of you meet?"

Catharina smiled. "At a party he hosted. We learned rather quickly how very alike we are."

Chapter Thirty-Nine

Catharina, Lady Hainsley sat upon the white mare her husband had given her as a wedding gift. The ceremony had taken place the previous week, and for their honeymoon, Gideon had surprised her with a trip to Wales. It felt strange riding astride, but her divided riding habit made doing so easier. As did the fact that they had shared the saddle for this particular journey. Being in his arms always made everything easier.

She studied Gideon, who stood several paces in front of her, his hands on his hips as he stared at a small country church perched atop a high hill.

The sun hung low on the horizon, casting a warm glow on the dense forest surrounding the summit. It was a tranquil setting, made all the more beautiful by the presence of the man she had married. Their love grew every day, and more so since beginning their honeymoon. Why had no one told her how wonderful married life could be? Or perhaps it was she who had not listened.

The castle he had inherited from the Knights Templar was within a half-hour ride and was where they were currently staying. Soon, they would take up residence there full-time. There were many plans to make, many belongings to pack, and servants to hire. But that would all have to wait.

For now, sitting there upon her horse, watching her husband, Catharina thought nothing about the busy plans for their future. All she could do was smile. And she suspected hers matched that of her husband, who now faced her. Mischievous. "Are you nervous?" she asked.

He nodded. "I am."

"Yes, I was, initially. But I'm certain you'll handle it with aplomb."

Although her husband had shown her all the treasure, he had kept back one piece. But rather than give it to her directly, he had waited until now before revealing that fact. What she learned was that among the items in the Templar treasure, one more clue existed, one that would send them on a new adventure beginning on this very spot.

"That is easy for you to say, my love. You are a master thief. I, on the other hand, am but a humble gentleman."

Catharina laughed. "Humble gentleman?" she scoffed. "You must be the most arrogant man in all of England." She nibbled her bottom lip, knowing full well how much he enjoyed watching her do so. "I suppose I cannot fault you for that one shortcoming. After all, you are by far the handsomest gentleman in the entire country." She sighed. "But do not forget, I am not just a thief."

His smile made her legs grow weak. "No truer words have been spoken, for you are my lady thief. Now, my love, behold your man of adventure. I shall return momentarily."

And he was her man of adventure. And they were starting a new adventure, one that required an old wooden cross located inside the tiny church.

"Listen closely, my boring husband," she said, giving him a wink to soften her words. "Fetch me the artifact, and you shall earn a kiss as your reward."

"A kiss? And what if the clue leads to more treasure? May I retain what I find for myself?"

Laughing, Catharina ran her hand through his hair. "I shall give it some thought."

"When you first agreed to help me take the painting from Callingswell, you stated there were three terms," he said. "But you failed to reveal the last one. Will you do so now?"

Catharina grinned as she removed a cap from the saddlebag and placed it on his head. "That you would marry me."

"You knew from the beginning?" he asked, clearly stunned.

"Of course," she said with a giggle. "I'm a woman. We know everything. Now you have your disguise. So, off with you before I reconsider that kiss."

With a half bow, Gideon pulled open the heavy wooden door, peeked inside, and entered the building. Before the door closed, he glanced over his shoulder and shot her an impish grin.

The minutes ticked by, and Catharina began to worry. Dash it all! She knew she should have gone in his place. If her husband encountered a cleric while there, he would likely confess his intentions and walk out empty-handed. If the cleric even allowed him to leave.

"I have it!" Gideon shouted, causing her to laugh. He looked like a schoolboy as he held up a wooden cross the size of a large serving platter above his head in triumph. "It was quite easy, really. Perhaps a life of thievery is simpler than I first believed."

Catharina shook her head just as the door of the church opened again. A black-haired cleric stepped out, looking like a thundercloud.

"My lord," she called out, laughing while pointing. "You were saying?"

Upon seeing the clergyman, Gideon yelped and ran toward her, the cleric hurrying down the steps after him.

"Thief! That belongs to the church!"

"Don't worry, Reverend," Gideon called over his shoulder. "It will be returned to you very soon." He handed Catharina the cross and mounted the horse, settling in behind her. Wrapping his arms around her waist, he took the rein and said, "Now, my love, we are off!"

Catharina leaned back into his strong chest and sighed as the horse galloped away, the priest's voice fading behind them. They would not keep the cross, of course, but instead return it with a substantial donation to make up for the trouble.

For now, however, she simply enjoyed being in her husband's arms. He spoke of this new adventure, one that would be so much like their first—clever and daring. And as they rode off into the sunset, Catharina smiled. There would be one important difference this time—they would traverse this adventure with love as their greatest treasure.

Epilogue

Violet reread the letter she had just received. Another family was requesting her aid, or rather that of Lady Marigold's Matchmaking Service. What a pleasure it would be to help another young lady bound for spinsterhood find a husband.

What was more, this one just happened to be a very close friend of the newly wedded Lady Hainsley—Lady Olivia Burnsworth. Another headstrong woman, Violet looked forward to setting her on her path to true love.

Finishing her reply, Violet informed Lord Burnsworth that she would collect his daughter in one week's time. Once the letter was folded and addressed, she went in search of Lena, who she found at the bottom of the grand staircase, staring at a painting of Violet's son, Anthony.

"I think of him often," Violet said as she joined her friend. "Three years gone, and I still miss him."

Lena crossed her arms over her stomach. "I still cannot accept that he's dead," she whispered, a lone tear rolling down her cheek. "I expect to wake up one day and learn that it has all been a terrible dream." She turned to face Violet. Wearing a kind smile, she added, "How strange that we argued over a future mother-in-law who does not think much of me."

Violet nodded and wiped a tear from her own eye. Lena had come from a family of the gentry, and much to her shame, Violet had not believed her worthy enough to marry her son. Granted, according to custom, an earl should not have a wife from so far below his station. But after arguing for two full weeks, she had agreed for fear of losing her son.

Once Anthony returned from France, the happy couple would announce their engagement. Yet the ship he had boarded wrecked somewhere off the southern coast of England, and the entire crew and its passengers had perished. Including her Anthony.

It was after, with her heart engulfed in sadness, that the last person Violet expected to arrive at her home knocked on her door. It now seemed like yesterday that Lena stood in the doorway, saying, "I realize you do not like me much, and I am strong enough to admit that I have servants I favor more than you. But you have lost a son, and I have lost the love of my life, and therefore, we have a shared loss."

Violet had been confused. "What are you saying?"

"That if we are to grieve and wallow in sadness, let us do so together."

From that moment on, a bond began to form between them. Each day, they grew closer. Then one day, when they could no longer stand the pain, they devised a plan.

A matchmaking service for women entering spinsterhood. Lena would once again play the faithful companion and chaperone, a role she did not mind. She, too, was entering spinsterhood, for her heart belonged only to Anthony. And she had long since accepted the lonely life before her.

For Violet, it was the loss of her husband, Rudolph, that inspired her. When she was younger, she had played matchmaker to several of her friends, relishing in the game of bringing two souls together.

Sighing, Violet put her arm around Lena's shoulders. "We will be leaving soon to help another maiden. For now, would you be interested in a game of whist? While we play, perhaps you would like to share more about what you learned about this master thief who visited us."

Lena smiled. "I would like that. But you cannot get angry when I win."

Violet could not help but laugh as she looked once more at the portrait of her son. "Anthony used to say the very same thing. I guess you both were right."

The End

Thank you for reading *The Earl's Lady Thief*.

Dive into the next story of *Lady Marigold's Matchmaking Service*: The Lady Who Cried Wolf. A whimsical tale with hidden desires as Lady Olivia Burnsworth, the enchanting storyteller with dreams of the grand London stage, finds herself entangled in a web of fiction and love! When her father's matchmaking plans threaten to shatter her dreams, Olivia is swept away to the intriguing realm of Lady Marigold's Matchmaking service.

Read on for a sneak peak!

The Lady Who Cried Wolf

BOOK 2

Chapter One

England, July 1816

To flee or not to flee, that was the question that currently consumed Lady Olivia Burnsworth. She had spent countless hours debating whether it would be best to escape the horrible prison to which she was confined or to simply give in to the fate that had been placed before her.

Granted, her mattress was filled with the finest down, and she covered herself with the softest and warmest blankets. Her dresses were of the latest fashion and rarely remained in her wardrobe for more than a Season. She dined on the finest cuts of meat and consumed some of the most decadent of pastries. All were luxuries any daughter of an earl would possess.

Her present situation might have been one coveted by so many of lesser means than she. But it was not the present that frightened her, but rather what was to come. Her life should not be destined for whatever future her father chose for her, for he, like most men, thought of ladies as nothing more than trinkets. Pets to indulge their every whim. And for some of those women, they would never consider another life.

The trouble was that the drab, uneventful life of a gentlewoman, pampered and shielded with no other goal than to be admired by her peers just seemed so... dull. This life was hers, and she should be the one making the decisions on how it should be lived.

Over the past two years, her greatest wish had been to move to London, to perform in the Theatre Royal Drury Lane, and to marry the man she loved, the renowned actor Mr. Paul Harrison. The fact she and Mr. Harrison had yet to meet was of little consequence. After all, she had read enough about him in the newspapers to know that he was charming, handsome, and witty—everything she could ever want in a man.

Yet tickets were often hard to come by. Two years prior, she had been able to secure a pair for her and a companion, only to learn that Mr. Harrison had fallen ill and had to have someone step in for him for that week.

Last year, her father had gone to the theater the day they arrived in London and had been able to procure tickets for the first time in several years. Olivia was initially beside herself with excitement, only to learn that the tickets were for a play in which Mr. Harrison had not been cast. According to *The Morning Post*, he had accepted a role at a theater in Paris.

Yet Olivia would not take these signs that her destiny lay elsewhere. She was certain that she and Mr. Harrison were destined to be together. She was no fool. The daughter of an earl did not perform on a stage. Nor would she be allowed to marry an actor. Therefore, she was left with only one alternative—elopement.

Her plan, although simple, was brilliant. Once she and Mr. Harrison met, he would instantly become as smitten with her as she was with him. And before the sun rose the following morning, they would be well on their way to Scotland to get married.

Yet with each passing day, her dreams were slowly becoming nightmares. Her father was a constant irritation with his talk of finding her a husband. Granted, she was two and twenty, which put her closer to spinsterhood than debutante, but what was the harm in waiting to marry? Plenty of young women delayed marriage until the right man came along. And as she and Mr. Harrison's paths had not yet crossed, it only made sense for her to reject the line of suitors who called on her each week. At least they were fewer now than they had been in the past. To Olivia's relief.

"So, do I confine myself to this prison until Father finds me a husband?" Olivia asked her dear friend Lady Penelope Baxter. "Or do I make my escape to London?" She ended with her usual dramatic sigh.

She and Lady Penelope were of the same age, unmarried, and both daughters of earls. But that was where their similarities ended. Where Olivia was tall and willowy with tawny-brown hair and eyes the color of a winter sky, Lady Penelope was short and slim with corn-husk blonde hair and green eyes.

And neither wanted anything to do with the gentlemen their fathers paraded before them.

Lady Penelope shifted in the seat of the cream-colored wingback chair, shaking her head. "Glanton Manor is hardly a prison, Olivia. Your father fulfills every request you make and buys you whatever you want. And have you considered what you would have to contend with if you did run away? Have you any idea how difficult it would be to traverse the roads as a lady alone? Or the kinds of men you may encounter along the way? Why, the stories I've heard about the rogues and brigands make my blood run cold!" She shivered visibly to punctuate her point. "Will you still risk your life knowing this?"

The question was an easy one to answer. "Indeed, I would. My love for Mr. Harrison is too much to contain. Did you not read the latest article about him in *The Times*?" Although her friend nodded, Olivia picked up that very edition and opened it to the correct page, flicking it as she had seen her father do countless times. "I shall read it again for you."

Lady Penelope groaned, but Olivia ignored her. Her friend might claim to be less theatrical than Olivia, but Olivia knew better. They both enjoyed hearing the latest scandals and gossip.

"'One would find it impossible to measure the handsomeness of Mr. Harrison,'" she read aloud. "'Or the skills he commands on the stage. Nevertheless, when it comes to the world of the theater, there has never been a finer actor.'"

Olivia let out a contented sigh. Handsome and commanding, could a woman ask for anything more in a man? How many nights had she lain in bed, thinking of a life as an actress. She would perform alongside Mr. Harrison during the Season, playing the most prestigious parts and gaining great acclaim. Once the Season ended, they would retire to the coolness of their country estate, just as the rest of her peers did.

Of course, Olivia had never been formally trained in the art of acting. No self-respecting aristocrat would involve themselves with the theater beyond attending it. Her stepmother had laughed at the mere notion that Olivia had a gift for storytelling, daring to say that Olivia simply "embellished the truth."

Yet Olivia knew there was nothing further from the truth. Olivia did not lie. She told tales simply to bring happiness to those around her. And to gain their admiration, naturally.

Most of all, however, Olivia told her stories to mask the sorrow that was her daily struggle. When one escaped into a make-believe world, the pain eased. Who had time to consider sadness when lost in tales of being kidnapped by highwaymen? Or witnessing bouts of fisticuffs among the servants? Or any number of stories she had told over the years. And all were meant as rehearsals for her future life of performing on stage beside the magnificent Mr. Harrison.

"We have been good friends since childhood," Lady Penelope said as she placed a hand upon that of Olivia. "Therefore, I'll be as forthright as I can be. You and I both know that those articles are nothing more than glorified gossip columns. They are fabrications in order to sell more papers. Mr. Harrison is a known rogue, which is a truth they have yet to print. Don't throw away your life for such a man."

Olivia considered arguing but held her tongue. Despite her age, Lady Penelope was naive to the ways of the word. *The Times* was not the only paper to write about Mr. Harrison. Every one of them said that he was a true gentleman despite his lack of title. And everyone knew that newspapers were not allowed to lie. Everyone but Lady Penelope, that is.

The problem was that many women were enamored with Mr. Harrison, which created a great deal of jealousy. And jealousy made women speak untruths. After all, was he not quoted as saying that his love was for the stage and not a woman? Why would he become a rogue after making such a claim?

Well, Olivia would see that he loved both the stage and a woman. And that woman would be her.

The sound of several voices filtered into the parlor from the foyer, and Olivia rose to see who had called. Peeking through the cracked doorway, her eyes went wide upon seeing her father and three of his friends. Among them was the Earl of Fairbanks. One of her father's closest friends, he was at least sixty, as bald as a newborn pup, and every time he looked at her, her skin crawled.

She shivered. No, he did not merely look. He ogled.

Beside him stood a quiet man in his midforties. Lord Hayes had rounded shoulders that nearly touched his ears, making him appear as if he had no neck. If he ever looked her in the eye, Olivia did not remember it.

The third man was the worst of the three. Cecil, Baron Twomley was five and thirty, as tall as a tree and as thin as a broom handle. He had been a dinner guest twice in the past month and had clear intentions with Olivia. Whereas Lord Fairbanks ogled her, Lord Twomley looked at her as if she were a statue of a Greek goddess.

Olivia could have appreciated being compared to a Greek goddess —if the baron was not as tiresome as a stone. It had been her overhearing her father and stepmother's discussion about finding her a husband that had sparked the urgency to escape. They must have chosen Lord Twomley as that man.

Some problems in life had simple solutions if one only searched hard enough. Once she and Mr. Harrison ran away to Scotland to be married, her father would no longer have any say in her future. After all, she was old enough to choose for herself.

"He's ghastly," Lady Penelope whispered. "Could you be mistaking your father's wishes? What if he was invited to discuss some business venture that has nothing to do with marriage?"

"No," Olivia replied, watching as her stepmother spoke to the gentlemen. "I feel it in my bones, Penelope. Just look at him! Have you ever seen such a corny-faced man? If he has so many pockmarks now, what had he looked like as a younger man? And how can he stand upright? Even the slightest breeze would have him flitting about in the wind. Now do you understand why my leaving is so important?"

Lady Penelope nodded. "Perhaps wandering the countryside with a highwayman would be a better life than one with the likes of him."

Marrying Lord Twomley would mean no chance of being on the stage. No being a part of bringing to life the greatest works of all time. Instead, her life would be exactly what she did not want—boring. And seeing him now only flamed the need to run away.

Returning to their seats, they contemplated how Olivia would make her escape. Her parents planned to remain at their country estate for at least two more months, which was far too long to wait. If she were not careful, her father would see the banns read and have her married by then.

"I've a marvelous idea!" Olivia said, sitting up straighter in her chair. "I'll stay with you for the weekend. Or at least that is what I will tell my parents. I'm sure one of the servants would be willing to sell me one of their dresses, and then I'll buy passage on a coach to London."

Lady Penelope shook her head, her cheeks turning red. "I'm sorry, but Father has made it clear that you are not welcome to stay with us for the foreseeable future. Not after the story you told the last time you were there."

Olivia sighed. The previous month, Lord Baxter had hosted a party, to which she had been invited. But Olivia had found the entire gathering less than engaging. Therefore, she told a tale to a group of guests as a way to liven things up. Granted, the story included games of chance where the women were the stakes, which might seem distasteful to some. However, she suspected that Lord Baxter's disapproval stemmed from her including a vicar as the host of the entire event.

The door opened fully, and her stepmother entered the room, with her pale-blonde tresses piled atop her head and pinned them with ruby hairpins. Lady Leekdom had raised Olivia since she was five. They were as close as any mother and daughter could be, but Olivia knew full well how frustrated her stepmother had become with her. Which was as frustrated as her father was.

"Olivia," her stepmother said, "your father requests that you come and greet his guests."

Olivia stood, rage coursing through her. "You mean that he would like me to parade myself in front of the baron like a hussy at *Place de Roi*."

Lady Penelope covered her giggle with a cough, but Olivia's stepmother gasped at the mention of the well-known London brothel. "Behave yourself, Olivia," she snapped. "You know very well that your father wants nothing of the sort. But you are expected to make a good impression on Lord Twomley. He wishes to invite you to luncheon next week, and you are to accept."

The rage turned to fury. "Does that mean he'll be asking for my hand in marriage soon? I overheard Father saying as much."

Her stepmother narrowed her eyes at Olivia. Close they might be, but she was still her stepmother. "Have you been spying again?"

"No. I just happened to overhear, is all." The truth was that she *had* been listening at the keyhole to his study for twenty minutes, but that did not matter. What did was that her life was not her own, and that was simply not fair! "I've already told you. I shall marry Mr. Harrison."

As usual, her stepmother would have none of it. "You will forgo that silly notion right this instant! Daughters of marquesses do not marry men from untitled families. It simply isn't done. And you've not so much as met this man, nor will you ever. Now, come. We mustn't keep Lord Twomley waiting a moment longer."

"May I have just one more minute?" Olivia asked. "Lady Penelope was just leaving, and I would like to show her at least some semblance of courtesy and see her to the door."

Her stepmother lifted a finger. "One minute," she said and then left the room.

"Oh, Olivia!" Lady Penelope said, hurrying to her. "It's true! You are destined to marry the baron. Oh, my dear friend, I'm so sorry. Your dreams of life in the theater will end this very day."

Olivia turned away and began to pace. "No, today my dreams begin. I'll make certain that Lord Twomley never speaks my name again, let alone asks for my hand in marriage."

Lady Penelope's jaw dropped a little more with each word Olivia shared of her plan. "But if word were to get out, your name will be ruined forever!" she said once Olivia finished.

"That is my hope," Olivia said. "Do you not see? This is the only way I can be free." She gave her friend a hug. "If you would like to listen, follow me. But wait until the count of five. I don't want Father to see you. He'll not be pleased as it is, but if he learned that one more person knows what I've done, he might just send me away!"

With that, she exited the parlor and made her way to the drawing room on the other side of the grand staircase. Her stepmother waited at the door.

"Please, do your best to impress him, Olivia," her stepmother whispered before leading Olivia into the room.

The gentlemen fell silent and rose upon their entrance, and Olivia felt the eyes of everyone upon her. Well, she aspired to be on the stage. Now was as good a time as any to practice her skills. But that did not mean she had to enjoy how the old earl licked his lips as if he had just been served a juicy leg of lamb. Even from this distance, she caught a whiff of stale tobacco wafting from his clothing.

"Gentlemen, you remember my daughter, Olivia?" her father said, beaming as he gripped the lapels of his blue morning coat. His hair was the same tawny color as Olivia's, and she had also inherited his gray eyes.

Lord Twomley bowed over her hand. "How could I forget the lady above all ladies whose reputation is as spotless as the newly fallen snow." His nasal tone turned Olivia's stomach. Never had she known a greater prig in her life! If her father thought she would marry this man, he was sorely mistaken.

Olivia sighed inwardly. She loved her father and stepmother so very much, which made what she had to do all the ghastlier. But her father had given her no choice. He had no one to blame but himself for her next action.

"Good afternoon," Olivia said, curtsying low. "I was reading from one of the great poets when my stepmother came for me. Would you like me to recite one of them for you?"

Her father went to interject, but Lord Twomley spoke first. "I, for one, am intrigued to hear your lovely recital, Lady Olivia. I'm sure we all would love to listen. Am I correct in saying so, gentlemen?"

After the others agreed, Olivia asked the men to return to their seats as she walked to the cold fireplace. The poem she chose for this moment was one she had written herself. One of which she was quite proud.

A woman's duty is to honor her man,
To help him wherever and whenever she can.
Though when struggles come, and he cannot pay the rent,
She will sell kisses for just one pence.
The cheek or the lips, there is no shame,
For all kisses are the same.
And as I stand here before you fine gentlemen,
I shall tell you my wish.
I'm in need of a new dress,
So, which among you has a pence for a kiss?

The only sound in the entire room came from her stepmother's gasp, but Olivia ignored it. "A friend of mine, a woman who works at *Place de Roi*, shared that poem with me."

Despite her bravado, her heart thudded in her chest. *Place de Roi* was not mentioned among polite society, given that the "services" offered there went well beyond simple kisses. Or so Olivia had heard. Oh, but would she be getting an earful once these gentlemen left! But it had to be done. Mr. Harrison could not marry her if she was already married to someone else.

"She will be arriving within the hour to meet you," she continued, surprised that her voice rang clear, given how tight her throat felt. "I do hope your purses are full!"

As if emerging from a trance, her father leapt from his seat. "Olivia!" he roared. "How dare you!"

Lord Hayes rose from his seat, his head now so low between his shoulders he could be peering from his chest. And he was as red as the velvet drapes on the windows. "I... I have a... I've scheduled a... I must go. Good evening to you all." He made a semblance of a bow before hurrying from the room.

The old earl shook his head and laughed, his eyes twinkling. "I knew she was a spitfire, Burnsworth, but she's more so than I ever imagined."

Lord Twomley reared his head back in disgust. “Our arrangement is forfeit, Burnsworth! I’ve changed my mind. There will be no marriage agreement with the likes of her.”

Olivia could not stop herself from smiling in victory. But her triumph was short-lived when her father grabbed her by the arm and pulled her out of the room. When they passed Lady Penelope, who waited by the front door, her friend flashed her a quick, yet sympathetic, smile.

When they reached the parlor, her stepmother following close behind, her father slammed shut the door and turned his rage on Olivia. “How dare you embarrass me in front of my friends! What has come over you?”

Olivia had never seen her father this angry before and found herself frightened of him for the first time in her life.

Thankfully, her stepmother stepped in. “You have guests waiting in the drawing room, Howard,” she said. “I’ll speak to Olivia.”

He harrumphed at her, shot a glare at Olivia that should have left her with a wound the size of a melon, and left the room.

“What you have done today was very hurtful, Olivia,” her stepmother said. “To your father and to me. I cannot believe I must say this to a woman of your age, but go to your room and we’ll discuss this later.”

With a nod, Olivia did as her stepmother commanded. Lady Penelope was already gone as Olivia walked up the grand staircase. Her friend would want to know everything, and for once, she would not have to embellish her story. After all, the truth was terrible enough. She had not meant to hurt her parents, but she could not think of any other way to secure her future.

Olivia sighed heavily. Once they had time to calm down, her parents would see that what she had done was worth the cost, and all would be forgotten. She was sure of it.

Also by Jennifer Monroe

Lady Marigold's Matchmaking Service

#1 The Earl's Lady Thief

#2 The Lady Who Cried Wolf

#3 How the Duke was Won

Sisterhood of Secrets

#1 Duke of Madness

#2 Baron of Rake Street

#3 Marquess of Magic

#4 Earl of Deception

#5 Knight of Destiny

#6 Captain of Second Chances

Prequel: Gentleman of Christmas Past

Secrets of Scarlett Hall

Victoria Parker Regency Mysteries

Regency Hearts

Defiant Brides

About Jennifer Monroe

USA Today bestselling author Jennifer Monroe writes clean Regency romances you can't resist. Her stories are filled with first loves and second chances, dashing dukes, and strong heroines. Each turn of the page promises an adventure in love and many late nights of reading.

With over twenty books published, her nine-part series, The Secrets of Scarlett Hall, which tells the stories of the Lambert Children, remain a favorite with her readers.

Connect with Jennifer:

www.jennifermonroeromance.com

facebook.com/JenniferMonroeAuthor
instagram.com/authorjennifermonroe
bookbub.com/authors/jennifer-monroe
amazon.com/Jennifer-Monroe/e/B07F1MRXDN

Made in the USA
Middletown, DE
24 February 2024